EVIL HOURS

ALSO BY RAYMOND BENSON

FICTION

Face Blind

James Bond 007 Novels
The Man With the Red Tattoo
Never Dream of Dying
DoubleShot
High Time to Kill
The Facts of Death
Zero Minus Ten
Die Another Day
   (based on the screenplay by Neal Purvis & Robert Wade)
The World is Not Enough
(based on the screenplay by Neal Purvis & Robert Wade
and Bruce Feirstein)
Tomorrow Never Dies
(based on the screenplay by Bruce Feirstein)

NON-FICTION

The Pocket Essentials Guide to Jethro Tull
The James Bond Bedside Companion

www.raymondbenson.com

EVIL HOURS

A Novel

by

Raymond Benson

For Randi

JANUARY 1999
SHANNON

"My mother was murdered when I was six years old."

It was a statement she had long ago grown accustomed to making, although it was information she didn't readily divulge. She inevitably had to reveal the fact when someone mentioned their own mother and asked Shannon about hers, as Frieda Williams had just done. Shannon could have simply said, "My mother *died* when I was six years old," but she never hid the truth that her mother had met a tragic, violent end.

"Really?" Frieda asked. "You poor thing! What happened?"

Shannon Reece handed her two cold beers from the refrigerator. "Here's one for you and one for Sam." She then took one for herself and another for her own husband. The men were in the living room watching the Super Bowl. The kids were playing in Billy's room.

The Reeces had just become friendly with the Williamses. They had met at church. The Reeces didn't have a lot of friends, and the Williamses were new in town. Shannon and her husband thought it would be nice to invite the couple over. It turned out that Sam Williams was as much a football fan as Carl, and Frieda enjoyed daytime soaps and women's magazines with the same fervor as Shannon.

"Let's go back in the living room," Shannon said.

"Wait, no, Shannon, tell me," Frieda said. "Unless... well, I'm sorry, I mean I didn't want to upset you or nothin'. If it's painful to talk about..."

"No, it's okay," Shannon said. "Like I said, it happened when I was six, so I don't remember much about it. All I know is what I've been able to find out from reading the newspapers at the library. God knows my dad won't talk about it."

Frieda Williams was staring at her friend with incredulity.

Shannon said, "Frieda, it's not that big a deal."

"Well, I think so! Did they catch who did it?"

"Sort of. He went to prison, but he wasn't convicted for the murder of my mom."

"Why not?"

"It's a long story. Come on, let's go back in."

1

Frieda followed Shannon into the living room with newfound respect.

"It's about time," Carl Reece said. "Bring me beer, woman!" he said with a Tarzan imitation.

He swung her down onto his lap. Frieda and Sam laughed.

"Carl! We have guests!" Shannon said, pretending to be embarrassed. In actuality, she enjoyed the attention.

He let her up after taking the beer from her hand.

Carl and Shannon Reece made an attractive couple. She had black hair, blue-eyes, and was thirty-two years old. Even after two children, she had stayed slim and shapely. Her morning run around Woodchuck Park did her a world of good. Carl was thirty-five, just as fit, and was tall and handsome. He had brown hair and brown eyes and looked like a movie star. They had two adorable children, Billy, age six, and Cathy, age four.

Carl was an accountant who worked downtown next to the tallest building in Limite, Texas. It was sixteen stories high, and the rest of the city was as flat as the ground upon which it sat.

Shannon was a housewife who worked part-time as a secretary at an oil field supply company on the highway between Limite and Mitchell. They had lived in Limite all their lives, and they had had their fair share of scrutiny over her mother's legacy. The neighbors avoided them. Billy and Cathy had trouble getting playmates to come over. Shannon herself had few friends as a child. It seemed that as soon as other girls' mothers learned who Shannon was, the girls were no longer allowed to play with her. This affliction followed her into adulthood. Carl was aware of the problem but married her anyway. At least he had sets of friends that the Reeces saw every now and then. Every Sunday they went to church, the only place where they found some acceptance.

Shannon had learned to handle the questions and stares long ago. What she didn't like to be reminded of was her dissatisfaction with the historical conclusion to her mother's case.

Frieda and Sam Williams were a little older, having just moved to Limite four months ago from El Paso. Frieda sat by her husband and handed him a beer. "So who's winning?"

"Nobody," Sam said. "It's half-time, anyway."

Shannon slipped off Carl's lap and moved to the table where she had set some chips and salsa. "I'm gettin' hungry, is anyone else ready for dinner?" She popped a chip into her mouth.

"Sure," Carl said, "how about ya'll?"

Sam shrugged. "Whatever..."

"You don't need to go to any trouble," Frieda said.

"Don't be silly," Shannon said. "I'll be right back. Carl, can you help me with somethin' in the kitchen?"

Carl sighed and rose from his easy chair. As soon as he followed Shannon out of the living room, Frieda whispered to her husband, "Sam, Shannon tells me her mother was murdered!"

"I knew that," Sam said.

"You did? Why didn't you tell me?"

He shrugged. "It's old news. Everyone at church knows about it."

"Well I didn't! What's it all about?"

"Don't you remember that guy Gary Harrison?"

"No."

"It happened, hell, nearly twenty-five years ago. Nineteen-seventy-three or seventy-four or somethin'. I remember it from the El Paso newspapers. It was big news back then. They called him the 'Oil Field Killer,' or somethin' like that. I'm surprised she'd talk about it. Haven't you noticed that they have one of those... what do you call it?... you know, those bad things that hangs over someone and follows them around?"

"A black cloud?"

"No... a stigma, that's it. They kinda have a stigma attached to 'em. Haven't you noticed that they always sit by themselves at church?"

"Never thought about it."

"Well, don't mention it. It's probably an uncomfortable subject for 'em."

Carl came back in the room and resumed his spot in front of the television. "The boys seem to be playin' nicely," he said.

"Sonny makes friends pretty easily," Frieda said.

Then Carl caught Sam and Frieda off guard by asking, "So you didn't know about Shannon's mother?"

After a moment's pause, Frieda said, "Well, no. She just told me in the kitchen. I'm sorry if I..."

"No no, don't worry about it," Carl said. "She's used to it. We're all used to it. Her brother and sister are used to it. I think the only person that ain't used to it is her dad. I don't think he ever got over it, even though he's now in his fourth marriage, if you know what I mean." Carl mimed taking a drink out of an invisible bottle.

"What happened?" Frieda asked.

"Her mom-- Mary Parker was her name-- was abducted from a nightclub on the north side of town one night in January 1973. They found her body over a month later out in an oil field."

"How awful!"

"She was really just one of several women the guy was suspected of killing. I think he might have been West Texas' first known serial killer."

"Shannon said he's in prison now."

"He was, but he was murdered by some other inmates not long after he was sent to the pen," Carl said. "They never could convict him of Shannon's mom's murder."

"Not enough evidence?" Sam asked.

"No, in fact he confessed to the murder, but some idiot judge in Austin threw out the confession."

"How come?" Frieda asked.

"There was some question as to whether the confession was coerced by the Lucas County Sheriff's Department here in Limite. It's a long story. Shannon's okay about it, but I think the one thing that bugs her is that justice wasn't served-- even though they know the guy did it."

Shannon entered the room on this last bit. "I tried to get the D.A. to reopen the case when I was a teenager. I couldn't understand why Gary Harrison wasn't tried for mom's murder. He gave me some B.S about not enough evidence without the confession and all that. Besides, the guy was dead. So I tried hirin' a private detective but I couldn't afford it. I wanted to find out more about what really happened. I finally gave up. There was nothing anyone could do."

Billy and Sonny ran into the room shooting imaginary pistols at each other and making a tremendous racket.

"Boys! Boys!" Shannon shouted. "Take it to your room or outside."

"It's cold outside," Billy said.

"Then put on your jacket."

"Let's go back in my room," Billy said to Sonny.

"Where's your sister?" Shannon asked.

"In her room." They ran out shouting war cries.

The football game resumed, so nothing more was said that night about Shannon's fascinating past.

* * *

After the Williamses had gone home and the kids were in bed, Shannon stood in the bathroom and washed her face. She often wondered why she and her husband stayed in Limite, although life wasn't too bad. They lived in a small brick house on the north edge of town, not far from where her parents had been living when she was six years old. Her father, Larry Parker, still lived on that side of town with his young, fourth wife. The back of the house faced a vacant lot that expanded into wilderness, which, in Limite, was the desert. Shannon liked to sit at her kitchen table and gaze out the glass doors into their unfenced back yard and beyond to the horizon. It could be mesmerizing at times.

Limite, Texas was a bustling blue-collar city of about 80,000 people. Its beginnings could be traced to the extension of the Texas and Pacific Railroad across the south plains area. Legend had it that the Mexican workers who helped build the railroad named the town, as it had been a boundary of sorts set by the railway owners. For several years, the line ended at the site-- the railroad had reached its "limit." Indeed, many Texans and Spanish-speaking residents pronounced Limite properly-- "LEE-mi-tay." Others ignorantly pronounced it "Li-MEE-tay." There were those around the state that pronounced the word in English, "Limit," but the majority of people, and the residents themselves, called it "Li-MEET."

There were less than a thousand people in the county until 1926, when the discovery of petroleum changed everything. By 1930, 3,000 people had moved into Lucas County, and this figure tripled by 1940. The oil companies laid claim to the fields around the town by 1950, and Limite experienced a boom of sorts. Smaller satellite towns sprouted up-- Preston, twenty miles northeast, Mitchell, forty-five miles west, and Sandhill, thirty miles southwest. An airport was in place outside Limite by 1960.

The flat, endless plains of West Texas were now cluttered with pumpjacks and other remnants of the productive oil decades between 1950 and 1980. The distinct odor of petroleum still permeated the air, especially in the summer months. The oil industry continued to possessed an iron hold on the area's commerce and the town was culturally tied to it. The bars and honky-tonks on the outer edges of the city were mostly filled with roughnecks from the fields, still dressed in greasy overalls or blue jeans. The town had its fair share of cowboys, too, as some ranching business existed outside city limits. Sometimes cowboys and roughnecks didn't mix well.

Limite was always a little wilder and rougher than its more white-collar neighbor, Preston. An old saying went-- "Preston was a great place to raise your kids. Limite was a great place to raise hell." The nightspots on both sides of the tracks had always been trouble, as altercations inevitably broke out every other night. As the only sizable town between El Paso and Dallas, Limite was a major stop for drug smugglers. It was also a choice jump-off point for illegal aliens. In the eighties, Limite developed a teenage gang problem, influenced by the far-reaching tentacles of the gangs in Los Angeles.

Shannon might have left Limite long ago if it hadn't been for what she thought was the natural beauty of 180 degree sunsets. Because the land was so flat, the spectacular orange and red streaks would spread across the sky to the eastern horizon. When there were clouds overhead (which wasn't often), the effect was breathtaking.

The desert had its beauty, even when the landscape was dotted with oil derricks and the ever-rocking pumpjacks. When she was in a contemplative mood, Shannon loved to drive out on "the loop"-- a state highway that surrounded the entire county. The oil fields, full of mesquite and tumbleweeds, held a certain mystique for Shannon. After all, her mother's body had been found lying in the open by a couple of ranchers. She had lain there for over a month before being discovered a quarter of a mile east of a graded county road, seven miles northwest of Limite.

Mary Parker's body was still clothed in what she had been wearing when she disappeared, although the pants were open and pulled down around her hips. Her blouse and bra had been removed and were lying under her head.

A nylon stocking had been used to strangle her. It was still tied around her neck when the body was found. Not only that, a metal bolt had been placed inside the knot so that it could be used as a tourniquet. This meant that her mother did not die quickly. Gary Harrison had intentionally kept her alive long enough to do whatever it was he wanted to do with her, then probably enjoyed killing her slowly-- twisting the bolt, then releasing it, twisting the bolt, then releasing it...

Shannon pushed the image away, finished in the bathroom, and undressed. She put on a pink, silky nightgown and got into bed beside Carl, who was already on his side, breathing heavily. Shannon turned out the light on the nightstand and stared at the dark ceiling.

She resigned herself to another night of insomnia. It was something that happened every two weeks or so. Her mind raced, covering dozens of topics in seconds. Inevitably, she ended up obsessing about her mother.

January was the anniversary month of her mother's disappearance. It had happened on January 2, 1973. Shannon used to make a pilgrimage out to the site where the Moonlight nightclub used to be. She stopped doing that after her second child was born. Still, she wondered what had really happened that night.

Her uncle Fred had been babysitting her and her siblings at the time. Uncle Fred, her mother's brother, had told her a lot of what had gone on, but Shannon always felt that he held some things back. It was no secret that Mary Parker had been rather wild and hard to control. Everyone in the family always said that Shannon was the spitting image of her mother. She had Mary's coal-black hair and blue eyes, as well as a pale complexion that had to be protected from the West Texas sun. Some even called her "little Mary." The only difference was that Shannon didn't have her mother's restless disposition.

"Your mama never could sit still," her Uncle Fred had told her in a thick West Texas accent. "She was a *wild* thang, and she *loved* men."

Mary Parker had dropped out of high school and never attempted to further her education. Shannon thought her mother may have been "wild" because she'd been rebelling against her conservative parents. Ed Barnes, Shannon's grandfather, had always been a controversial figure in the family. He changed jobs often and invested in one hairbrained scheme after another. He had a close business partner who got into some legal trouble. The man's name was Chuck Davenport. He was in and out of court with various lawsuits, arrested for embezzlement, and ultimately spent some time in prison. In court he had accused Ed Barnes of complicity. Uncle Fred used to say that contributed to the heart attack that killed her grandfather a few years later. Shannon had always wondered if Davenport's accusations were true.

Her mother had married too young and had not experienced enough life before settling down. It didn't help that a town like Limite was incredibly dull. At the time of the murder, Limite had only three indoor movie theaters, three drive-in theaters, a miniature golf course, and a stadium where everything from rodeos to rock concerts was held. But even those were few and far-between. High school football was perhaps the biggest attraction in Limite. The Limite Lynxes were legendary in the state for winning the championship several times. Just about everyone in the town was football-crazy, and it was all they cared about. When football season was over, however, the only thing for young people to do back then was cruise the streets.

The house lights outside seeped through the curtains of the bedroom window and cast a dim glow on the framed photo of Mary Parker sitting atop the dresser. Mary's eyes were looking directly at Shannon. Sometimes when Shannon gazed at the picture, she thought she could remember her mother's voice. It was so long ago, though--she was never sure if the memory was real or only imagined. One thing she knew was true was that her mother used to make up affectionate baby-names for her.

"Hi Shannon-wannon... how's my little Shanna-banana?... I love you, Shannon-girl..." her mother would say.

Another vivid memory was chasing tumbleweeds with her mother. They wouldn't actually *chase* them, but they'd see one blowing in the wind and follow it with their eyes, fingers pointing, until they couldn't see it anymore. Sometimes, if Shannon saw a tumbleweed from the window, she would shout for her mother to come and look. Then they would both run outside to see where it went. Shannon used to believe that tumbleweeds were little messengers that came through town, said hello, and then went on to their next destination.

Aside from fleeting images, Shannon didn't remember much about her mother at all. The painful truth was that her mother hadn't been home most of the time.

She had been too busy being a wild thing.

* * *

The phone rang early the next morning after Carl had gone to work. Billy was off at kindergarten, and little Cathy was transfixed in front of the television.

"Hello?"

"Hi Shannon." It was her younger sister, Jackie. Shannon winced. She loved her sister, but she could be a pain. Their relationship was often strained. Jackie, or Jacquelin, was divorced and had a five-year-old boy. She was always hitting up Shannon for babysitting whenever Jackie wanted to go and do something "fun." Shannon was very vocal in her opinion that she thought Jackie hung out with the wrong kind of crowd. Jackie liked to go to bars, see a lot of rough-looking men, ride motorcycles, and drink more than she should. Sometimes she acted as if she were still seventeen and single. Perhaps she had more of their mother in her than did Shannon or her brother, Jeff.

"What's up, Jackie?"

"I was wonderin' if you could watch Tyler for me for a couple of hours this morning."

Shannon sighed. She could have bet money on it.

"What are you doin'?"

"I've got a job interview!"

This got Shannon's attention. Jackie had been looking for a daytime job for months. She currently worked as a barmaid at a raunchy dive on the north side of town. "Oh? Where?"

"Fredna's Beauty Parlor. They need a hairdresser to work weekends."

Oh, great, Shannon thought. That meant that Tyler would be spending the weekends at their place. But if it helped Jackie get back on her feet...

"That's wonderful, Jackie. Can you still remember how to cut hair?"

"Of course, silly. It's like ridin' a bike. Once you learn, you never forget."

"All right, bring Tyler over. I might have to take him with me to do grocery shopping."

"Oh, he'll love that. Besides, he likes his cousin."

That was true. It would give Cathy someone to play with for a while.

Jackie arrived twenty minutes later. She was twenty-seven and looked more like their father than their mother. Her hair was lighter, almost sandy brown, and her eyes were brown like her dad's. Shannon thought she could be pretty if she tried to be, but she dressed like "trailer trash." She wore five pierced earrings on each earlobe, had a tattoo of a rose above her right breast (which she enjoyed displaying by wearing low-cut tops), and wore black clothes that were too tight. Her makeup couldn't disguise the fact that there were dark circles under her eyes and she looked terrible. They once had a fight when Shannon told Jackie that dressing the way she did made her look like a slut.

"You have time for a cup of coffee?" Shannon asked. "You look like you were up all night."

"I was. Sure, I'll have some," Jackie said, depositing Tyler on the floor by Cathy in front of the television. "I have thirty minutes or so."

Shannon poured two cups and sat down at the kitchen table. "Have you heard from Jeff?"

"I never talk to anybody. He's busy makin' money, I guess."

Their brother was twenty-nine and had never married. He lived in Austin, which was far enough away to be considered exotic. Jeffrey Parker left Limite as soon as he finished high school and he rarely came back.

Of all the members of the family, Jeff was the most intolerant of Limite's lack of culturally and intellectually stimulating facets. He had gone off to the University of Texas, studied computer programming, and now had a high-paying job in the state capital.

"I wish he'd come home to visit," Shannon said. "I miss him."

"Why? He'd just complain about how awful Limite is and then leave after three days."

"I know, and he's probably right. I don't know why I never left either."

"Where would you have gone?" Jackie asked, sipping the coffee.

"I have no idea."

"See what I mean?"

There was a typical moment of silence between the sisters.

Jackie had dropped out of Limite Junior College after two years to marry Zach Thompson, someone Shannon thought was a real loser. That was where it had started. Jackie never had good taste in men. At the end of three years of spousal abuse, Tyler was born; but Jackie had seen the light. Zach was kicked out of the house and Jackie changed her name back to Parker. Until the real Mr. Right came along, her son was going to be known as Tyler Parker. In the meantime, Jackie found every possible excuse to leave him with relatives or babysitters so that she could go out and party like a bad girl. It wasn't fair to Tyler. Shannon felt a kind of empathy with the little boy. She had been just a bit older than he when her own mother... disappeared.

"You still seein' what's-his-name?" Shannon asked.

"Travis? Sure. We're thinkin' of runnin' off together."

"What?"

"I'm *kidding*," Jackie said. She pulled out a cigarette from a pack in her purse.

"Jackie, you know you can't smoke in here," Shannon said.

"Oh, yeah, right," she replied, stuffing it back in. Shannon knew her sister would now look at her watch and say it's time to go just so she could smoke a cigarette.

"I should get goin'," Jackie said, looking at her watch.

"What does Travis *do*, anyway?" Shannon asked.

"He's in some kind of business thing, I don't know. He always seems to have enough money."

"It's probably illegal."

"Oh, it is not."

"Well, he looks like a crook. He's so much older than you are. You really find him attractive?"

"Hey!" Jackie said, offended. "He's not a crook, and yes, I find him attractive."

Shannon shook her head. "You always went for the bad boys."

"I guess so," Jackie said. "Kinda like momma, huh?"

There was another long pause before Jackie asked, "Have you been thinkin' about mom lately?"

Shannon put down her cup. "I was about to ask you the same thing. That's really weird."

Jackie laughed slightly. "I've been thinkin' about her a lot lately. I guess it's that time of year, y'know?"

Shannon nodded. "We were talking about her last night. Some friends from church were over and the subject came up."

"Listen," Jackie said. "I was talkin' to a friend of mine at the mall the other day. She's married to a lawyer. She said her husband knows a guy that's a detective, and that he was familiar with the Gary Harrison case. He told her there was a lot to it that wasn't public knowledge."

"We knew that."

"Yeah, but she seemed to think he knows a lot more. You want talk to him?"

"Do you?"

Jackie shook her head. "I'm not as obsessed about it as you are."

Shannon shrugged. "What good would it do?"

"Exactly."

But then Shannon said, "I don't know. It's just that... I still want to know what really happened. I mean, I know she was kidnapped and strangled to death, and Gary Harrison left her body out in the oil fields and all that. He probably killed a bunch of women that way, including Kelly White and Grace Daniel. But there were always so many questions about it all. It *really* bothers me sometimes."

"Didn't you try to find out a bunch of stuff when you were in high school?"

"I spent nearly a year of my life tryin' to piece together what really happened. I spent weekends at the library collecting newspaper articles. I must have spent all my free time at the court house buggin' the D.A.'s office and then tryin' to get information out of the sheriff and the police department. They were always so tight-lipped. No one wanted to talk to me. That old Sheriff Barton was a mean guy. He told me not to stick my nose into it or I'd just get hurt."

"Well, he was probably lookin' after you. He didn't want you to learn things that would really upset you. You know, you might have seen pictures of mom's body or somethin'."

"Oh, I've seen pictures of mom's body. They published them in the damn newspaper, for Christ's sake."

"You know what I mean. Color pictures of her on the autopsy table and stuff."

"Oh, please. I think he just didn't want me findin' out the truth."

"Well, what do you think the truth is? Don't you believe Gary Harrison killed her?"

"Yes, I do, but there's more to it than that. You know the story. He confessed to killing Kelly White and then later he confessed to killing mom and Grace Daniel. But those confessions were thrown out of court and he wasn't convicted for those."

"Wasn't there another one he confessed to?"

"There were two. That older woman, Barbara Lewis, and the barmaid, Tina Lee Peters. But he was never even indicted for those. I'm not sure why."

"Right, I remember now."

Shannon shook her head. "There're more weird things about that guy and those murders than anyone could possibly straighten out. It just really gets to me that he was sent to the pen for life after pleading guilty for Kelly White's murder, and not for mom's. They were saying he had committed as many as forty-three killings in Texas, New Mexico, and Oklahoma. You know, I wanted to hire a private detective back then, but I couldn't afford it."

"Well, here's your chance," Jackie said. "I got the guy's number if you want it. Can you afford it now?"

Shannon nodded. "Actually, I've been saving money for a rainy day. Seein' as how it never rains in Limite, I can use it for something else, right?"

"Whatever." Jackie looked at her watch again. "I gotta go. I'll be back after lunch, okay?"

"Sure. Are you okay? You look kinda pale."

"Nah, I'm fine. Just worked until two, then partied till dawn..."

Shannon walked Jackie to the door. As her sister walked outside toward her car, Shannon said, "Hey, call me with the name and number of that lawyer's friend, will you? I think I do wanna talk to him."

"Okay."

Shannon watched Jackie get in the car and drive away. She worried about her little sister. There was definitely something wrong. She was drinking too much and was probably doing drugs. That Travis Huffman she was seeing was no good. He was a drifter in his forties, and it seemed that all he liked to do was shoot pool at bars and drink a lot. Once he yelled at Jackie in front of them and called her a "bitch." Jackie didn't protest. She silently took the abuse and later smiled sheepishly at her sister.

Shannon went back inside and sat on the couch in front of the TV. The two kids were sitting like zombies in front of it, fascinated by Big Bird and the gang. Shannon missed the days when the children *wanted* to take naps. Besides, it wouldn't be long before Billy was home from kindergarten and then the daily afternoon soap marathon began.

11

Shannon could lose herself in other people's troubles. She didn't have to work but two days a week, so she saw enough of the shows to keep up with the storylines.

Restless, she stood and moved to the bedroom to gather the laundry. Shannon stooped to pick up a discarded blouse by the dresser and, upon rising, accidentally bumped a half-opened drawer hard. Her mother's portrait fell off the top and hit the drawer with a "crack."

"Oww," she said, rubbing her back. There would be an ugly bruise there by nightfall. She picked up the frame, sat down on the bed, and held her mother's face in her hands. The glass was cracked. Shannon ran her finger over the line and inadvertently cut it.

"Damn!" A drop of blood spread over the glass. Shannon put her finger in her mouth but continued to stare at the picture. Her mother's piercing eyes gazed back, beckoning her… to do what?

She attempted to wipe the blood off the broken glass with her finger but only managed to smear it across her mother's face. Doing so inexplicably caused a chill to creep up her spine.

"Oh, mama," she sighed. "What happened to you? Why do you keep haunting me? Won't you ever leave me alone?"

For twenty years her mother's ghost had interfered with Shannon's happiness. The many questions about Mary Parker's death had distressed her far too long.

Shannon made up her mind that it was time to finally do something about it.

An hour later, Billy came home on the bus with a puzzled look on his face.

"How was school today, Billy?" Shannon asked him.

"Mommy?" he asked.

"Uh huh?"

"What's a whore?"

Shannon was taken aback. "What?""What's a whore? I think that's what he said…"

"What who said?""This kid at school. One of the big kids."

"What did he say?"

"He said my grandma was a whore. What is that?"

HOMEWORK

What happened to Billy at school was the last straw. The next day, Jackie Parker got the phone number from her friend and passed it on to Shannon.

"He's a private investigator of some kind," she said. "Myrna said he used to be with the FBI."

"How come he's not anymore?" Shannon asked. She was standing in the kitchen, holding the receiver to her ear and watching Cathy eat a bowl of Sugar Frosted Flakes. Billy would be coming home on the kindergarten bus any minute and she needed to decide what to make for dinner that night.

"He's an old man, I guess. He's retired."

"So what's his connection to the case?"

"All I know is that he worked on it. He was an investigator."

"Jackie, I've talked with so many investigators that supposedly worked on the case and none of them know doodly-squat."

"Well, look, you've got the number," Jackie said. "Do whatever you want with it. I gotta go."

"All right. Thanks. What happened at the beauty shop?"

"Oh, forget it. I make more money at the bar. I'm a night person, what can I say?"

"Well, are you sure you're safe there? Aren't there a lot of rough types that go there?"

Jackie snorted. "You kill me, Shannon. I can handle myself. I'm a big girl."

"So was mom."

"Oh, Jesus," Jackie moaned, "don't give me that shit. You really live in your own little world, you know that? I gotta go. I'll talk to you later."

The receiver went dead. Shannon hung up the phone and stewed for a few seconds. Jackie didn't used to be so mean. What was *with* her lately?

She looked at the pad of paper where she had scribbled the name-- STAN McHAM-- along with a local phone number. She tore the sheet off the pad, folded it once, and stuck it on the refrigerator with a magnet that looked like a jalapeño pepper. Shannon then sat at the table beside her daughter and opened a tattered manila file folder that she had dug out of her filing cabinet in the garage the night before. It was something she hadn't looked at in years.

The folder was full of newspaper clippings and other odds and ends pertaining to the murder. Shannon unfolded the clippings one by one, refreshing her memory with the sordid contents. The most striking one was from the *Limite Observer*, dated February 8, 1973. The headline screamed, "MARY PARKER'S BODY FOUND." Underneath the title was a large black and white photo of lawmen standing beside the corpse, which was lying on the ground amidst mesquite brush and tumbleweeds. Thankfully, the photo wasn't very clear, and the angle from which the picture had been shot didn't reveal a whole lot. Still, its impact was powerful.

Other clippings referred to Mrs. Parker's disappearance, other victims, and finally the arrest of Gary Harrison in January, 1974, for the murder of Kelly White.

The doorbell interrupted her. She looked out the window and saw her father's 1990 Ford pickup in the driveway. She quickly hid the folder under the counter. What was he doing? He was supposed to be at work.

Larry Parker was dressed for the job-- blue jeans, boots, a plaid shirt, and baseball cap with the words "Dallas Cowboys" on it. He was medium-height, extremely thin, and his weather-beaten face, framed by grey hair, revealed a tired man.

"Hi dad," Shannon said when she opened the door. "Why aren't you at work?"

"I wanna talk to you."

"Well, come in."

Parker stepped inside after wiping his boots on the "Welcome" mat in front of the door. He ran a forklift at an oil field tools and supplies warehouse. Over the years he had held a number of jobs. When he was married to Shannon's mother he was a bail bondsman. That had been the job he had enjoyed the most, but "overwhelming circumstances" had forced him to resign the position after his wife disappeared in 1973. He never got over it. Shannon figured that he was probably the number one suspect in her mother's disappearance. She knew from reading mysteries that it's standard operating procedure to take a hard look at the spouse in such cases. Larry Parker became a bitter, cantankerous man who never spoke much about his past. When Shannon asked him about her mother, he would only say that "she was a good woman." He never revealed his true feelings about the murder. He buried his pain with booze and television. Whereas some people gained weight when they drank too much, Larry Parker seemed to wither away. He was virtually skin and bones.

He had re-married not long after his first wife's murder. The marriage didn't last three years. Shannon barely remembered living with her first step-mom. Her father married again a year later-- to none other than his second wife's younger cousin! She was fifteen years younger than Larry. As a stepmother, Nadine left a lot to be desired. She treated Shannon and her siblings as second-rate citizens, while she doted on her own children with Larry-- two girls and a boy. The burden of supporting a family of eight took its toll on Shannon's father and he grew more and more withdrawn and sullen. When Shannon was sixteen years old, that marriage fell apart, too. He exchanged vows with his fourth wife a year after Shannon herself got married. Caroline was twenty-five years younger than Larry Parker, and Shannon didn't think much of her either. It seemed that her father just wanted a young, attractive woman around the house and didn't care what she had inside her head. Caroline was one of the dumbest women Shannon had ever known. Caroline thought that the NAACP was an organization that prevented cruelty to animals. Shannon thought her father had at least shown restraint in not having any children with Caroline.

He followed Shannon into the kitchen.

"Want some coffee?" she asked.

"Nah." He stood there with his hands in his pockets, not sure of what to do. He had never been good at talking about anything other than work or football.

"So what did you want to talk about?"

"I saw Jackie last night."

"And?"

"She looks bad. Can't you talk some sense into that girl?"

"Dad, I've tried," Shannon sighed. "She does what she wants."

"Have you met that boyfriend of hers?"

"Yeah, I think he's no good. He really controls her. I wouldn't doubt it if he's into drugs or something."

Her dad frowned. He seemed to be searching for the words to say.

"You didn't come over here to talk about Jackie, did you?" Shannon asked.

"Jackie told me you were gonna look into your mother's case again," he replied.

"I don't know about that," Shannon said. "I haven't decided."

"I don't think you should."

"Why not? You never told me anything about it."

"There wasn't anything to tell."

"Come on, dad, when are you gonna stop burying it? Don't you think it would do you good after all these years to talk about it?"

"There ain't nothin' to talk about," he said.

"Dad, there's *tons* to talk about! Don't you realize that my mother was murdered and I have no idea why? I know there's more to Gary Harrison than what was in the papers. Aren't you outraged that he wasn't convicted of her murder? You were *never* vocal about that."

"There was nothin' I could do about it. The law's the law. You should know that, too."

"So what did you come over here to tell me?"

"Let it go, Shannon," he said. "Don't go diggin' in the dirt, 'cause you may not like what you find."

"Well, what will I find? You never say anything, so what am I supposed to do?" Shannon found herself becoming exasperated with him, which was a common occurrence in her relationship with her dad.

"Fine, forget I ever said anything." He turned to go.

"Wait a minute..."

"I gotta get to work."

"Dad! Stop it!"

He halted and stood at the front door, looking out. Shannon could only imagine the kind of pain he had gone through. He was a broken, sad man, and it showed.

"Dad," she began.

"What?"

She didn't know what to say to him. "Nothing. Better go on to work. Don't worry about me."

He walked out the door without looking back. Before he got into the truck, though, he turned and said, "Just be careful, Shannon. Don't step on any toes."

After he had gone, Shannon wondered what the hell he meant by that. Whose toes could she possibly step on? The case was twenty-five years old and the suspect was dead.

She went back into the house and sat at the table. Cathy had crawled out of her chair and was now playing with a doll on the kitchen floor.

Shannon loved her father, but she was constantly frustrated by him. He came over to "talk" and didn't say twenty words. Mr. Personality. Caroline *had* to be dumb, or else she would never put up with a man like that.

She continued to turn the clippings over in the folder in front of her and finally came to one that featured a photo of Gary Harrison, grinning mischievously at the camera. He was a tall, light-haired man with sinister eyes. It showed him at his arraignment in Limite, apparently laughing at the photographer's reaction to something. The caption said that Harrison had jumped at the camera man, frightening him.

Despite the man's evil aura, he was handsome in an overtly confident way.

What's your story, you bastard? she thought to herself. Did you really kill my mother, and, if so, why?

* * *

The Lucas County Coliseum was an ugly but functional monstrosity that was the home of the annual Limite Rodeo. The only other attraction that drew a larger crowd every year was the Petroleum Show, which was a commercial celebration of the industry that put Limite on the map.

Shannon and Carl Reece tried taking their kids to the rodeo the previous year and it was a disaster. Cathy cried the entire time and Billy threw a tantrum when he couldn't get a second cotton candy. Nevertheless, the Reeces threw caution to the wind and tried it again this year. They bundled the little ones up, for the temperature was a nippy 41 degrees Fahrenheit. Winter was never too bad in West Texas but it wasn't uncommon for a freeze to come through and ice up the streets. Limite citizens never knew what to do when that happened. Motorists tended to drive too fast and not take into account the hazards of slick surfaces.

It was warm and cozy inside the coliseum and it appeared that the kids would have a better time this year. The noise and the crowd kept their attention and they especially loved the cowboy clowns. Billy and Cathy both got cotton candy and this kept them quiet-- and sticky-- for quite a while.

At one point during the show, the announcer entered the ring in the center of the field and spoke into his microphone.

"Ladies and gentlemen, tonight is very special for those of us livin' in Lucas County. Not only is it the openin' night of the Sixty-Eighth Annual Lucas County Rodeo, but it's also the birthday of someone we decided to pay a special tribute to. He's a man that really needs no introduction, but I'm gonna give one anyway."

The audience snickered a bit.

"He came to Limite in 1952, hailin' from Mississippi. An ex-World War II paratrooper, this giant of a man made a name for himself in the sheriff's office as a deputy for five years, then was successfully elected to Sheriff in 1956. He remained in that position for twenty-four years, a record that has so far been unsurpassed. He probably would still *be* Sheriff if he hadn't stepped down on his own accord, citin' his wishes to do other things. As we all know, his woodcarvings are famous throughout the southwest. Who woulda thought that Buck Barton was such an *artiste* with a knife?"

Some of the crowd laughed.

The man continued, "Throughout his tenure as Sheriff, there were some who said he was tough, hard, and mean as a bull. I happen to know that he was the most honest and fair man I ever met in my life. Let's give a warm 'Happy Birthday' to former Sheriff Buck Barton!"

The crowd went wild as the tall old man stepped into the ring. The band started up the strains of "Happy Birthday to You," and the audience sang along with a deafening roar.

B. D. Barton was a bear of a man at six feet, three inches. In his prime he was heavy, but he had gained a lot of weight over the years and was now around 290 pounds. His gut hung over his belt like a sandbag. He had brown eyes and white hair that he had worn in a crew cut ever since he came to Limite. A neat but thick white mustache covered his upper lip. He was dressed, as always, in cowboy boots, blue jeans, a western shirt, and a large white cowboy hat. Now pushing eighty, "Buck," as he was called by everyone who knew him, walked a little slower and moved more cautiously. There had been reports that his health had not been good. He had been in the hospital a few years ago for a double bypass operation. Nevertheless, he appeared just as tall and mighty as the legend that preceded him. He smiled and waved to the crowd.

Shannon watched and listened with interest. It was Barton who had been in office when her mother was killed. He had arrested Gary Harrison and got him to confess to the murder of Kelly White. But she had also heard all sorts of rumors about the man over the years that he was not as clean as the people of Limite liked to think he was.

The announcer went on. "Buck, it is my pleasure to present you with the Heritage of Limite Award. As you know, only six other people have been so honored, the last bein' Mayor John Sweeney, fourteen years ago. It's an award that the Chamber of Commerce gives only to the very best who have served our great city and county."

With that, the announcer handed Barton a gold statuette of a horned toad, a replica of Limite's "historical landmark"-- a giant statue of a horned toad that sat in a downtown square. Because the rough-backed, spikey lizard was in abundance in the fields of West Texas, the "horny toad," as it was called by the locals, was something of a mascot.

Buck Barton took the microphone and said in a raspy voice, "Thank you all. I'm not gonna tell you how old I am, but let's just say I don't chew tobacco anymore."

The audience laughed, for one of Barton's trademarks when he was sheriff was that he was never seen without a mouthful of Redman.

Shannon thought he sounded frail and just a bit senile.

"You know, my kids used to hunt these horny toads out in the pastures," he said. "They'd bring one home in a shoe box or bottle or somethin'... and I'd tell 'em that the critter wouldn't eat as long as they kept him in captivity. And if they got him mad enough, he'd spit blood out of his eyes at 'em. They never would believe me, and sure enough, either the darned thing would just sit in its prison starin' at its captors until it died of starvation... or it would scare the hell out of 'em by spittin' at 'em. Once that happened, they'd let him go. Well, in a way, Limiteans are like horny toads. You can't keep 'em penned up. They're tough and they're stubborn. That's why we here in Limite never give up. We'll spit at anyone who tries to take away our liberty. I spent thirty years of my life protecting this county from the likes of every kind of low-life you can imagine. But you know what? They were nothin' but bugs. Little creepy-crawly bugs. And you know what else? Horny toads like to *eat* bugs!"

The audience cheered.

Shannon didn't know what the hell he was talking about. The old man didn't make a bit of sense but the crowd loved it.

"My children thank you, my wife Naomi thanks you, and I thank you."

There was more applause as Barton left the ring, holding the bizarre golden trophy.

Shannon had tried to talk to Barton back when she was investigating her mother's murder. She visited his little shop in a strip mall on the east side of town where he sold woodcarvings. He didn't want to help her. The man seemed put off by the very notion that she wanted to know the details of her mother's death.

"Whatcha wanna know all that for?" he asked her. "It's gruesome and it'll scare the hell out of you."

She remembered that he had stood behind his desk and towered over her. The huge man's appearance, with his short white hair and thick mustache on a weather-beaten face, had struck her as *odd*, but not frightening. It was the mustache that seemed out-of-place, as if it didn't belong with the rest of the picture.

"Young lady," he had said. "You just go home and forget about your mama. I think you're better off not knowin' the details. You'll sleep better at night. We caught the guy who did it and he's dead now. He'll never bother anyone again. Don't you worry. Now run along home, little girl."

Buck Barton would have intimidated most kids her age but what he said made her so angry that she struck back.

"Fine, Mr. Barton," she had said. "I happen to be in high school. I can overlook you calling me a little girl, but don't you ever tell me to forget my mama. She brought me into this world. Her picture still sits on my dresser. She'll always be my mother."

Barton had registered surprise at her reaction. "My, my, you got a lot of spunk. Just like your mama had, you know that? Now run along, I've got a carving to finish here."

Shannon had turned on her heels and stormed out of the shop. It didn't register on her until later that Buck Barton couldn't have said what he did if he hadn't known her mother personally.

* * *

It was after ten o'clock when the Reeces got home from the rodeo. They had to carry the kids into the house and put them in bed.

While Carl was in the bathroom, Shannon picked up the phone and dialed Jeff's number in Austin. She got his answering machine.

"Hi, this is Jeff Parker," the voice said. "I'm not here right now, so leave a message."

At the beep, Shannon said, "Jeff, it's Shannon. Give me a call when you can, will you? Thanks. Hope you're okay. Bye."

After hanging up, she saw the piece of paper on the fridge with Stan McHam's name on it. She fingered it but decided it was too late to call him. Besides, she didn't know if she was really *ready* to call him.

Shannon went into the bedroom and found her husband in bed watching television. She sat on the edge of the bed and said, "I've been thinking a lot about my mom."

"I know," Carl said.

"You gotta admit that there are a lot of funny things about that case."

"Uh huh."

"Jackie gave me the name of someone who knows something. A detective. I might give him a call."

Carl shrugged. His attention was on the news.

Shannon was waiting for some kind of approval. When she didn't get it, she sighed and stood up, ready to get undressed.

"Why didn't Jackie call him herself?" he asked.

"You know Jackie. She always gives me the responsible stuff to do."

"Ain't that the truth..." Carl didn't care much for Jackie.

"I'm worried about her lately," Shannon said. "I may *look* more like my mother but Jackie definitely acts more like her. I'm really afraid she's gonna get herself in trouble. She hangs out with the wrong crowd."

"Just like your mom did."

"Yeah," she said. "I've thought of that. That could be why I'm suddenly so obsessed with all this again. I can't help but think that the change we've seen in Jackie over the last couple of years is hereditary. She's gettin' reckless and it's like she doesn't care anymore. She's a disaster waitin' to happen."

Carl nodded in agreement.

"Anyway, I've just got to learn more about my mother, Carl. Especially after what happened to Billy at school. It's always bothered me, and seeing Jackie self destruct like this only makes me more anxious about it. I think I will call that detective. You know I saved up some money to pay for it? I was just waiting for the right time."

"What happened with the school?"

"Oh, I talked with the principal," she said. "She said she'd speak to the boy's parents. Apparently it was a third-grader."

After a pause, he said, "Honey, you can do what you feel you need to do, you know that. I'm behind you all the way."

She smiled and removed her blouse.

Carl's eyes shifted from the television to his wife. He enjoyed watching her remove her clothes.

"Honey?" he asked.

"Hmm?" She was slipping into her nightgown.

"I think there's part of that rodeo we didn't see tonight."

"What's that?"

He grabbed her hand and pulled her down onto the bed beside him.

"You didn't see the White Stallion do the Bucking Bronco Act."

She laughed as he shut off the television and moved on top of her. They kissed deeply and then she whispered, "How did I ever end up with such a good guy?"

"Luck of the draw, I guess," he said. He slipped out of his t-shirt and boxers, then slowly and passionately made love to his wife. Shannon, who had needed this kind of release for days, surrendered to him and thanked God that she had been so lucky.

* * *

Shannon saw her husband off to work, made sure Billy got on the bus to kindergarten, set Cathy up with the television, then sat down to re-familiarize herself with the clippings. She went through the stories chronologically and made notes on a pad of paper. Shannon had always been meticulous and organized.

An hour later, she had written on her notepad--

TIMELINE
OCTOBER 13, 1970
VICTIM 1 - GRACE DANIEL
Grace Julia Wade Daniel; 27 years old; divorcee with 6 year old daughter; carhop waitress at Shelly's Drive-Inn; blonde hair, green eyes; had left daughter at home in care of boyfriend; had been doing laundry at Fresh N' Dry Laundrymat on Lucas County Road; last seen between 11:00 p.m. and midnight on Saturday, October 10, 1970; never came home; her 1966 car left in parking lot with keys in ignition; had left pile of clothes; was wearing brown shorts and brown and white striped blouse.

OCTOBER 27, 1970
VICTIM 2 - BARBARA LEWIS
Mrs. Barbara Jane Lewis; 43 years old; found shot to death in her apartment at Cowboy Courts Motel (west Limite); was owner and manager of motel; had been shot once in head; hands tied in front of her body with television cable; empty cashbox found in room; robbery listed as motive for attack.
* Very different M.O. from Grace Daniel.

DECEMBER 8, 1970
GRACE DANIEL's body found in oil field northwest of Limite; three ranchers hunting jackrabbits came across mummified body; covered in tumbleweeds; had been strangled with nylon stocking still wrapped around her neck; electrical cord also found at site, probably used

to tie her hands; skeleton still wearing clothes she had on when she disappeared, except they had been torn open; panties removed and found stuffed inside open shorts; sexual assault?-- impossible to tell because of advanced decomposition of body.

FEBRUARY 18, 1971
VICTIMS 3 & 4?- RICHIE AND LAURA SALDAÑA
RICARDO "RICHIE" SALDAÑA; body found in room at Limite Motor Inn, on highway between Limite and Preston; a Limite policeman!; 31 years old; shot twice; his wife LAURA was missing; 28 years old; manager of motel claimed that Saldaña had registered at front desk with his wife the night before.

FEBRUARY 19, 1971
LAURA SALDAÑA's body found off road near Limite trash dump south of town; partially clothed; had been strangled with nylon stocking; hands bound in front of her with electrical cord.
*Was Laura Saldaña abducted from motel room after her husband was shot? What were they doing in motel?? They had a house in Limite!

FEBRUARY 26, 1971
SALDAÑA MURDER drug related; police investigation reported Richie Saldaña was involved in criminal activities on south side of town; killer came to murder Saldaña; it just happened that his wife was in room; what happened to her was situational ("a secondary crime that was not assailant's intention"); police and sheriff's office were still hunting for killer.
* If it wasn't Gary Harrison, the killer was never caught!

JUNE 14, 1971
ESCAPED VICTIM?-- UNKNOWN
UNIDENTIFIED WOMAN; 23 years old; escaped being abducted from Fever Club parking lot on northwest side of town; she reported that a "tall, blond-haired man" had attempted to force her into his car at knifepoint; screamed as loud as she could, attracting attention of club's doorman; assailant fled, got into "red car"; no one could identify make/model.
* Very similar to what happened to mom. Where is this woman now? Was this case ever followed up?
* Gary Harrison was a tall blond-haired man.

JULY 9, 1972
VICTIM 5 - TINA LEE PETERS
Tina Lee Foster Peters; barmaid; found nude and dead in her Limite apartment; 22 years old; pretty blonde worked at Tempest Club in south Limite; separated from husband, Jack Peters, who was living in Abilene; was found by apartment manager after being told that she had not been seen in several days; body was on bed, dead at least 4 days; stabbed several times; estimated time of death possibly July 5 or July 6; billfold missing.
* Different M.O. again.

SEPTEMBER 9, 1972
VICTIM 6 - SUSAN POWELL
Susan Morris Powell; housewife; disappeared from her home in Limite; husband came home late from work and found lights on, sewing machine plugged in, wife's shoes under table; blue-eyed brunette; 29 years old; no children; had been wearing beige double knit dress; half-smoked cigarette in ash tray; purse and billfold left behind; lawmen found her clothing scattered along highway between Limite and Mitchell (distance 45 miles); dress slashed to pieces.
* Similar to Grace Daniel abduction-- forced to leave quickly!

JANUARY 5, 1973
VICTIM 7 - MARY PARKER
Mary Jo Barnes Parker; 28 years old; reported missing by bail bondsman husband when he came home morning of January 3 after business trip; she came home from her job as cashier at Donny's Cafeteria around 10:00 p.m. night before (Jan. 2); children were in care of her brother, Fred; she went out to grocery store; never came home; was wearing navy pants and beige corduroy coat; next day car discovered parked in front of Moonlight Nightclub on north side of Limite; keys still in ignition.

Writing that entry forced Shannon to stop and take a break.

* * *

Shannon felt one of her infamous panic attacks threatening to ruin her day. She had always considered herself the strongest one in the family but she was prone to terrible anxiety at times. Her doctor had said that the attacks were probably due to subconscious feelings about her mother's disappearance when she was very young. Before she let the current one get any worse, she went into the bathroom and found the Klonopin that the doctor had prescribed for her. She swallowed one tablet with water, then paced around the living room. A feeling of dread had crept up on her and she had the inexplicable urge to scream.

She jumped with fright when the phone rang. She grabbed the receiver and nearly shouted, "Hello?"

"Shannon?" It was her brother Jeff.

"Oh, Jeff, hi."

"Are you all right?"

"I'm fine, I was just startled by the phone. How are you?"

"I'm good. What's goin' on?"

She sighed heavily. "Oh, I don't know. I guess I just wanted to hear your voice. We all miss you."

"Awwww. Why don't you bring the kids down to Austin for a weekend?"

Unlike the relationship she had with Jackie, Shannon and Jeff really *were* "like brother and sister."

"It's too long of a drive, and we can't afford flyin'," she said. "Why don't you come home for a visit?"

"I can't. I'm really busy at work," he said. "Besides, I can't stand Limite. I'd go stir crazy after a few hours."

"That's what Jackie said you'd say."

"How is Jackie?"

"Oh, pretty much the same." She had discussed this subject with her brother before. "She just gets weirder and weirder. She's really livin' like white trash, Jeff. I swear her boyfriend must be an ex-con. If he isn't, then he should play one on TV."

Jeff laughed.

"No, really, I guess I'm worried about her."

"I'm sure she'll be all right," he said. "She's a big girl."

"Listen, Jeff... you know the second was the anniversary of mom's death?"

There was a hesitant silence at the other end.

"Yeah?"

"Well, you know, I just have a hard time with the weeks building up to it around Christmas-time, and then the whole month of January is like, you know, crappy."

"Shannon, you *never* use poo-poo words!" Jeff teased her.

That made her laugh. "Oh, stop. Come on, I'm serious. You know it's always bothered me more than you or Jackie."

"Yeah."

"You remember when I was in high school and I spent a lot of time trying to find out what really happened?"

"Yeah." Jeff didn't sound happy with this subject.

"Well, I'm gonna look into it again. Something's really botherin' me about it and I can't explain it. The subject came up the other night when some friends from church were over. Afterwards, I got to thinkin' about it. Ever since that night, I've been obsessed with findin' out more."

"Shannon..."

"Now wait, Jeff," she said. "Don't you want to know what really happened? You can't tell me you're satisfied with the way things went down?"

"Shannon, Gary Harrison is dead."

"But he wasn't convicted of killing mom."

"Does it really matter? He got convicted. Period. Whether it was for Kelly White or for mom, at least they got him. Now he's dead."

"But Jeff, do you think he really did it?"

"Of course I do! Jesus, Shannon, we've had this discussion a million times."

"All right, all right," she said, exasperated. "I think he did, too, but there are an awful lot of weird things about the case. You know that Sheriff Barton? You got to admit there were some shady things about Harrison's arrest and confessions and all. First he implicated his wife, then he took it back..."

"I know..."

"Don't you think there's more to the story?"

"There's always more to a story than what's reported, Shannon. And they'll never tell us, we're only the victim's family! Forget it, Shannon. You'll just make yourself crazy. I've learned to live with it."

"Have you?"

Jeff was silent.

She had him. She knew her brother better than anyone. Jeff Parker had never learned to live with it. It's why he had withdrawn from the rest of the family and moved away.

"Look, Shannon, you're my big sister, and you can do whatever you want," he finally said.

"Will you help me?"

"How can I? I'm here and you're there!"

"Well, just give me moral support."

"Fine."

"Jackie found the name of an investigator that worked on the case that I never spoke to. He's some kind of ex-FBI guy."

"Fine."

"I think I'm gonna call him. I have some money saved up that I can use to pay him."

"Fine."

"Well, do you want to be in the loop or not?"

She heard him sigh. In some ways, he was just like her, but he was mostly like his father.

"Sure, keep me informed."

"I know you want to know just as much as me."

"Okay, okay. Look, I gotta go."

25

"Okay. I love you."

"I love you, too. Just be careful."

"I will." She hung up the phone and felt a lot better.

The tranquilizer had calmed her down and she was able to go back to the table. She picked up the pen and looked at the next few clippings in the pile and continued her timeline.

JANUARY 7, 1973

MARY PARKER investigation continued-- she had apparently not gone to grocery store, as she had told Uncle Fred; instead drove to Fever nightclub (it's just down the road from Moonlight Club!); Mary was supposed to have met a man there-- a fellow employee at Donny's Cafeteria; was seen entering Fever Club; had asked bartender if he had seen one of her girlfriends; Mary waited for man she was supposed to meet; didn't stay long; left Fever around 10:30 p.m.; must have gone straight to Moonlight from Fever; no one that worked at Moonlight remembered seeing her come in but car was parked in convenient spot near front door.

* Who was mom going to meet at Fever from Donny's Cafeteria?

* Which girlfriend did mom ask for at club?

FEBRUARY 8, 1973

MARY PARKER's body found by ranchers on horseback; only a few miles from where Grace Daniel was found; body still clothed in what she was wearing; pants were open and pulled down; blouse and bra removed and lying under her head; she was lying on top of beige coat, which had been spread out on ground; nylon stocking tied around her neck; no evidence of sexual assault.

*Can't remember where I heard about bolt stuck in knot of stocking...

* Sexual assault?-- if bra and blouse removed, it sounds like sex assault to me!

FEBRUARY 11, 1973

TINA PETERS billfold found by owners of vacant house in Mitchell, TX; 7 months since Mrs. Peters' murder in Limite; Mitchell lawmen had no idea how billfold got there.

MAY 28, 1973

SUSAN POWELL's body found by oilfield worker near well on oil lease off highway close to Mitchell; bones scattered over radius of twenty-five yards; upper right arm missing; lawmen speculated that animals were responsible for spreading remains; cause of death could not be

determined; kitchen knife found near body; case given to Mitchell authorities because body was found closer to Mitchell.
* Connection between Limite and Mitchell? Peters billfold was found in Mitchell!

JUNE 13, 1973
VICTIM 8 - KELLY WHITE
Kelly Ann Crowell White; 30 years old; on June 10 she disappeared from office of Wynn's Mobile Village on highway between Limite and Mitchell; happened in broad daylight between 11:30 and 12:00 a.m.; she worked as assistant manager of trailer park inhabited mostly by oil field workers and their families; on outskirts of town but entrance faced busy highway; divorcee lived in trailer park with twin 5-year-old daughters; blonde hair; blue eyes; last seen by saleswoman around 11:00 a.m.; postman stopped by office around noon to deliver mail; he found door wide open but no one there; on his way out of trailer park, he saw manager Sam Wynn; he reported what he had seen; Wynn was surprised that she wasn't there and went to office; 1969 Volkswagen was still parked by her own trailer; Wynn said she wouldn't leave without checking out with him first; purse was in desk drawer; it contained small amount of money; cash kept in office was undisturbed; she was wearing white sleeveless dress, white gold watch, gold ring with diamond setting.

JANUARY 13, 1974
KELLY WHITE's body found 5:30 a.m. underneath old mattress in a "wash" (a gully) in a vacant lot/trash dump in south Limite; seven months and three days after her disappearance; GARY HARRISON told Sheriff Barton where body was located while in hospital in Cortez, TX; skeleton still wearing white button-down dress; electrical cords were tied around neck, arms, ankles; no weapon found at site; death believed to have been caused by strangulation.
* Where is Cortez, TX??
* How did Harrison become a suspect?

Shannon decided to stop there. Her son was already home from kindergarten, and Carl would be getting off work shortly.
There were still so many questions.
What about the Saldañas and Susan Powell? Harrison was never charged with their slayings. The Susan Powell case was strikingly similar to her mother's, Grace Daniel's, and Kelly White's. All of these women, including Laura Saldaña, had been abducted and later their bodies were found strangled out in the oil fields. Shannon had read enough mystery stories to know that a killer's methods might differ between slayings but

that there would be enough similarities to link them together. It was pretty obvious to Shannon that whoever *did* kill her mother also killed Grace Daniel, Laura Saldaña, Susan Powell, and Kelly White.

Shannon closed the file folder and took a deep breath. There had to be more to the story than what was reported in the papers.

It was time to call the detective.

STAN

The voice was slightly gruff but had the familiar West Texas twang to it that seemed to be accentuated with local lawmen and television newscasters.

"McHam Incorporated."

Shannon cleared her throat. "Uhm, hi. My name is Shannon Reece. Is Stan McHam there?"

"Speakin'."

Another voice, a woman's, came on the line. "McHam Incorporated."

"I got it, Merle," McHam said.

"Oh, sorry," the woman said, and hung up.

"I apologize for that," McHam said. "You still there, ma'am?"

"Yes. Uhm, your name was given to me by... well, actually it was given to me by my sister, and she got it from a friend of hers..." Shannon was flustered. She thought she sounded like an idiot. "Actually I don't know her friend's name, sorry."

"That's all right, ma'am, what can I do for you?"

"She said you were familiar with the Gary Harrison case."

"Yeah, that's right. I remember George Frost asking me about it. Is he the one?"

"Probably. He's a lawyer?"

"Yep. He said a friend of his wife's was the daughter of one of the victims."

"Uh huh, that was my sister, Jackie. Well, it's me, too." She laughed nervously.

"What can I do for you?"

"Well, she said that you knew a lot about the case and I was wonderin' if I could talk to you about it. I mean, I've spent a lot of time tryin' to find out what really happened back then because, you know, there are a lot of unanswered questions..."

"Uh huh..."

"...and I'd just like to... well, see what you know."

"I'd be happy to talk to you. You wanna come by my office?"

"Uhm, sure. I have a child at home, I need to find a babysitter. What time are we talkin' about?"

"You name it, I'm pretty free today," McHam chuckled.

"Okay, let me make a call to my sister and I'll call you right back."

Shannon hung up and dialed Jackie. Jackie reluctantly agreed to watch Cathy while Shannon went to see McHam.

"I might have to take her and Tyler with me to buy shoes."

"Oh, Cathy loves to look at shoes."

"Well, Tyler hates it. Come on, bring her over."

Shannon hung up and called McHam back. He gave her directions to his office, which was near the newly-remodeled West Texas Mall on the northeast side of town. She got Cathy ready, took her out and buckled her in the child seat, then drove over to Jackie's house. She frowned when she saw the black Mustang in the driveway.

When she rang the doorbell, a male voice hollered, "It's open!" She opened the door and a blast of tobacco smoke hit her in the face. Shannon almost turned around and took Cathy away, but she didn't.

Travis Huffman was slouched on the sofa, watching television. He had a beer in one hand and a cigarette in the other. He looked as if he hadn't taken a bath in a week.

Travis was in his mid-forties, not quite twenty years Jackie's senior. He was a small man, perhaps five feet, five inches, but he made up for it with broad shoulders and large biceps. Apparently, he worked out with weights a few years ago but had given it up. Now the muscle had turned flabby. He had slicked-back black hair, a five o'clock shadow, and was wearing black, tight-fitting pants. He was shirtless, and had a monstrously hairy chest. Now Shannon knew where Jackie had been getting her fashion ideas.

"Hey there, Shannon," he said, his speech slurring slightly.

"Hi, Travis. Where's Jackie?"

"I'm back here!" she called from Tyler's bedroom. "Come on back."

Shannon took Cathy with her and found Jackie wiping up a spilled soda from the carpet.

"Damn it, I should never let Tyler bring soda out of the kitchen," she was muttering.

"What the hell is he doing here?" Shannon asked.

"Huh?"

"Your boyfriend. What's he doing here? He's smoking up the place and looks like a pig."

"Are you saying you don't want me to watch Cathy?" Jackie stood up and faced her with her hands on her hips. Her speech was slurring slightly, too.

"What's wrong with you?" Shannon asked. She squinted, looking into her sister's eyes.

"What do you mean?"

"You're drunk. Or something."

"No, I'm not. Look, don't worry. When will you be back to get her?"

"An hour or two. Don't go anywhere with her, all right?"

"I said I might have to go shoe shopping."

"I don't think you should drive," Shannon said.

"I won't. Travis will."

"Oh, that's comforting!"

"Would you get off your high horse? Don't *worry* about it!" Jackie always got belligerent when she was intoxicated.

Shannon glanced at her watch. If she was going, she had to move.

"Jackie, I'm holding you responsible--"

"I can't believe you don't trust your own sister--"

"It's not that, it's just that--"

"Is somethin' wrong in here?" Travis had ambled to the doorway. He sniffed and wiped his nose on his bare arm.

"I was just leaving," Shannon said. "Come on, Cathy." She took her daughter's arm and then pushed past him.

"Don't leave on my account," he said, flirtatiously.

"Where are you goin'?" Jackie asked. "I thought you wanted me to watch Cathy."

"Never mind," Shannon said, angrily.

"Well *excuse me*!" Jackie said, spitefully. "What, am I not good enough to be your babysitter?" She followed Shannon and Cathy out of the house.

Shannon turned and confronted her sister face to face. In a low, controlled voice, she said, "Jackie, I don't want to leave Cathy here with him. I don't want her here with you when you're stoned or drunk or whatever's wrong with you."

"Oh, fuck you, Shannon, you don't know what the hell you're talkin' about," Jackie said, her words slurring more than before.

Outraged, Shannon spun around and walked away. She put Cathy in the car, got in the driver's seat, and backed out into the street. She looked in the rear-view mirror and saw that Jackie was giving her the finger.

What was *with* that girl? she asked herself. Sometimes Jackie could be the sweetest kid sister and other times she was a complete bitch. Shannon attempted to get hold of herself and not let the encounter upset her. It did anyway.

What was she going to do with Cathy now? Thinking quickly, she headed downtown toward Limite's tallest building.

Ten minutes later, she parked at a meter in front of the H & R Block office where Carl worked. She got Cathy out of the car, telling her that she was going to spend some time with daddy. She went inside and asked the receptionist for Carl Reece.

Carl appeared with a confused look on his face.

"Hi, what's up?" he asked.

"I need a favor," Shannon said. "Can you watch Cathy for a couple of hours?"

"What?"

"Can she sit and play in your office for a while? I have an appointment with the detective and I don't have any place to leave her."

"Did you try Jackie?"

"Yeah," Shannon said, rolling her eyes. "That's a long story. Please, Carl?"

This had happened a couple of times in the past and he wasn't happy about it. "Well," he said, "I have a lot of work to do and I got clients comin' in."

"Can't she sit in the corner of your office with some crayons and paper? You still have some of her toys here, don't you?"

"Damn." He frowned, thinking through the day's schedule in his head. "All right, if you have to, you have to. But we can't make a habit of this."

"I know. Thanks, honey. I'll be back after lunch, okay?"

Cathy shouted, "Oh boy!" At least she thought that hanging out with daddy was fun. "Can we go to McDonald's for lunch, daddy?"

Carl scratched her head. "Maybe so, sweetheart." He looked at Shannon and said with plenty of sarcasm, "*I* wanted to eat at McDonald's for lunch today, too!"

Shannon smiled at him, kissed him on the cheek, and said, "See you later." She bent down, gave her daughter a hug, and left the building. Finally, she was on her way. She left downtown and headed east.

Limite had changed little in thirty years except in the more affluent east side of town, where a university had sprung up nearly twenty-five years earlier. There had been a real estate boom on the east side around that time but the developers had been a bit too optimistic. Students didn't flock to the new school, and the apartment buildings and condos stood empty for many years. Limite went through a bad depression in the eighties after the oil industry faltered in West Texas and many thought that the university might close. Luckily, the economy picked up in the nineties and more money came in from the state to help build up the school. As a result, much of Limite's established downtown retail businesses moved to the east side of town into or near the mall.

Streets were extremely wide in Limite. Shannon hadn't traveled much, but she had always been amazed by how small the roads were in other towns. Perhaps it had something to do with how flat Limite was. Everything was just so... horizontal. It was also extremely bright, even on a grey winter day. Sunglasses were a necessity in West Texas. The sun seemed to bounce off the sidewalks and roads directly into drivers' eyes.

She drove her 1992 Ford Tempo along 54th Street, one of the larger east-west thoroughfares in the town. The poor old car was on its last legs and she was hoping Carl would get the raise he had been promised so they could afford a new one. She had been tempted to spend her nest egg on a new car but she decided to wait and see what this private detective was going to charge her to look into her mother's case.

She passed a few of the newer strip malls and soon came to the large West Texas Mall on her left. Stan McHam's office was in a small adobe building in a lot across the street from the mall. The glass door bore the words "McHam Incorporated-- Private Investigations." Inside was a small reception desk, behind which sat a mousy, elderly woman with white hair. She was chewing gum and reading a Danielle Steele paperback.

The woman looked up and asked, "Can I help you, honey?"

"I'm here to see Mr. McHam."

"And who should I say is callin'?"

"Shannon Reece."

The woman picked up the phone and started to punch a number when the gruff voice boomed from the open door behind the desk.

"Come on back!"

The woman blinked, then put the phone down and smiled. "Mr. McHam will see you now. Just go on in."

Shannon went through the door and found a man in his late fifties sitting at a large desk and staring at a computer screen. He was a bit overweight, had white hair, glasses, and was dressed in a suit that appeared to be a size too small.

"Hi there, I'm--" Shannon started to say, but McHam interrupted her by holding up the index finger of his left hand. He was concentrating on the screen and moving the mouse furiously with his right.

"Come on, baby," he muttered. "You can do it...! You can... do... it! Ha ha!" he shouted triumphantly.

Shannon moved across the room so that she could see the monitor. Stan McHam was in the middle of playing an arcade computer game. He had just blown the head off of some kind of monster.

"Sorry," he said. "It's how I take out my frustrations." Groaning, he stood up and shook her hand. "Stan McHam. Sit down, sit down. Can I get ya a cup of coffee?"

"No, thanks," she said, taking a seat in front of the desk.

"I'm gonna get some. Be right back." Instead of leaving the room, he limped to the door and said, "Merle, can you get me my usual?" Shannon could now see that there was something wrong with the man's hip and that it seemed to "roll" as he walked. If she wasn't mistaken, one leg was shorter than the other. "Sure I can't get you somethin'?" he asked again.

"Maybe some water?" Shannon asked.

"And some H2-O for the young lady," McHam ordered. He limped back to the desk and sat down.

"So you're Mary Parker's daughter, eh?" he said.

"Yes, sir."

"You look just like her. If I hadn't known better, I woulda said she had just walked into my office."

"That's what everyone that knew her says. Did you know her?"

"No. But I seen pictures."

"Do you know my father?"

"I met him once, back when he was a bail bondsman. That was a long time ago, I guess."

"Yes."

"How is he?"

Shannon shrugged. "He's okay."

Merle brought in a cup of coffee and a glass of ice water. "Here you go, dear," she said to Shannon. "Can I get you anything else?"

"No, thanks."

"Thanks, mom, er, Merle," McHam said. When Merle left the room, McHam grinned and said, "Merle's my mom."

"That's nice." Shannon felt very shy.

"Okay," McHam said. "Gary Harrison. What a mean, uneducated, cunnin' little son of a bitch, if you'll pardon my French. He was a piece of work, I tell you."

"You knew him?"

"I met him in jail. I better explain. I was with the FBI in the late sixties and early seventies. I was stationed here in West Texas, one of two agents out here in the field, and when I say 'field,' I do mean 'field!' When the abductions and murders were happenin', the FBI wasn't called in to help but we were advised to conduct our own little investigation, you see. The Lucas County Sheriff's Department was doing most of the work and the Limite Police Department was handling the city cases, and frankly, they didn't want us interfering. But because some of these cases had similarities to other cases around the state and in other states, we had an unofficial directive from headquarters to take a look at the situation. Well, after Harrison got arrested in 1974, every lawman this side of the Mississippi wanted to talk to him. I got the privilege of meetin' the scumbag and askin' him some questions. I did a lot of work on the Kelly White case, because it was that one that really got the FBI's attention. Well, no, I take that back. It was your mother's case that got their attention, so when Kelly White got abducted, I was on it from the beginning. So, I guess you could say that's the case I know the most about."

"You're not still with the FBI?"

"Nope," McHam shook his head. "In early 1975, I got shot. I was investigatin' some of the Dixie Mafia doings on the south side and got into a fire fight. I had to have my right hip replaced. Forced me into 'early retirement,' as they say. I'm damned lucky to be alive, though. I became a private investigator."

"Dixie Mafia?"

"Well, that's what we call the organized crime in the southern states. It's a term that's used broadly, but basically they're the ones that control gambling, narcotics, prostitution, and all that stuff. Corrupt officials, loan sharking, you name it. They're not so powerful these days, at least not in Limite, but back then they had a big hand in the criminal activities in these parts. Gary Harrison was associated with the Dixie Mafia."

Shannon was surprised. "I never heard that before."

"That was my pet case when I was with the FBI. I was tryin' to crack open the Dixie Mafia. I think they knew it, too, which is why they tried to kill me."

"They did?"

"Yep. That bullet was no accident. They wanted to put me right out of business. And would you believe that after nearly twenty-five years, I finally have a line on who might have pulled the trigger! But anyway, that's enough about me. What can I do for you? How can I help you?"

"Well," Shannon said, "it's like I said on the phone. I've read up on all the murder cases and as you know, Gary Harrison wasn't convicted of my mother's murder, even though he confessed to it."

"Confessed twice, as a matter of fact. He made one confession implicating his wife, then made another one exoneratin' her."

"Right. But then the confessions were thrown out and the indictments were dropped."

"Yeah, that stupid judge in Austin didn't know his ass from a pumpjack."

"Well, it just seems that there's a whole lot more to the story than what the papers printed. I mean, you know, like you said, his wife was accused of helpin' him commit my mother's murder, and then he said she didn't. Then there was that pre-trial hearing where it came out that Sheriff Barton supposedly paid some kind of reward money to Janice Harrison in exchange for a confession. Everything sounds so... fishy, you know what I mean?"

McHam nodded. "I sure *do* know what you mean. It's all *very* fishy, and I thought so at the time. Now, I know Buck Barton. He's a good man. He was a good sheriff. Probably the best sheriff this town's ever had. But between you and me and my mom out in the other room, I'm not so sure he was the most honest man in West Texas. Some of his best friends were crooks, and some of them went to prison!"

"Did you know my grandfather?" Shannon asked.

"Ed Barnes? Yes, ma'am, I did. He passed away not too long ago, am I right?"

"Yes, sir. Four years ago."

"Sorry to hear that."

35

"I didn't know him well," Shannon said. "They moved away when his partner, Chuck Davenport, went to jail. I was eight at the time and I never saw him much after that."

"Oh yeah, Davenport. I certainly remember that guy. He went to the pen for embezzlement, didn't he?"

"Yes, sir."

"Well, like I said, Buck Barton had a lot of shady friends. Did you know that Chuck Davenport and Buck Barton were friends?"

"No, I didn't."

"They were. Them and Lucky Farrow and Guy Simms-- you know who they are?"

"I think I've heard of them."

"Lucky Farrow started the 'Lucky's liquor store chain."

"Oh yeah."

"Guy Simms had the biggest pawnshop in downtown Limite. Well, they're both dead now. But they were supposedly pretty crooked. They were pals with Davenport. I can only assume that they also knew your grandfather."

"What's this got to do with my mom?"

"I don't know, I'm just sayin', you know, I happen to know that Gary Harrison was mixed up in that stuff. I was agreein' with you that there are a lot of fishy things about the case. But look, let's get our goals in mind here. What exactly do you want to know? What are you hopin' to find out?"

Shannon sighed. "I don't even know. I guess I just want to know what really happened to my mom and if Gary Harrison was solely responsible for it. I'm pretty resigned that he'll never answer for her murder 'cause he's dead, but I'd just like to know that it was him and only him-- or not. And if not, then I'd like to know who else was responsible."

McHam nodded. "Well, that's always been a question in a lot of people's minds. We'll have to do some diggin'. I know a few people that might be able to help. I've kept some stuff on the Harrison case."

"I don't have a lot of money. What's this going to cost?"

McHam waved her away. "I usually charge two hundred dollars a day, plus expenses, but seein' as this is something different and interestin', how about we just say five hundred bucks a week? I've got some other cases that pay the bills."

"Really? Five hundred dollars a week?"

"Right. Is that too much?"

"No, no." She was expecting it to cost a lot more. She had roughly $3,000 saved up for the expense. "Okay, it's a deal." Hopefully it wouldn't take more than a couple of weeks.

"You're sure?"

"Yeah."

"Fine. I'll have mom... er, Merle... draw up a Contract of Services. In the meantime, let's go get some lunch at the Taco Casa and I'll tell you what I know. I have a couple of theories, neither of which I can prove."

Shannon smiled. "All right."

* * *

It wouldn't have been Shannon's choice for lunch, but there was something about the busy fast-food atmosphere of Taco Casa and Stan McHam's enthusiasm about the case that made the excursion exciting.

They sat at a table next to the window that faced the mall across the street. Stan wolfed down three tacos and a bean burrito in no time before Shannon barely started on her taco salad.

"I think the best place to start," Stan said with a mouthful of food, "is for me to tell you everything I learned about the case when I first got on it."

"I'm listening," she said.

"You see, I knew Gary Harrison was a suspect even before the sheriff and police did. Not of your mother's murder, or of Grace Daniel's-- but of Tina Lee Peters, the barmaid, do you know who she is?"

"Yes, I'm familiar with all the ones he might have killed."

"And also a case out at a motel..."

"The manager?"

"Barbara Lewis. You see, there are a couple of theories. I believe those two killings were mob hits. Barbara Lewis was pimping out of her motel, and Tina Lee Peters was runnin' her own little private hoochy-koochy business out of her apartment. The mob didn't like that so they had 'em bumped off. I think they hired Gary Harrison to do it."

"He confessed to both of them."

"Yeah, I know. His story was that he knew Barbara Lewis had a lot of cash on her and the motive was strictly robbery. Well, how did he know the cash was there? He knew her, of course. He also knew Tina Lee Peters. They frequented the same nightspots."

"One of the articles in the paper said Harrison's wife worked for Barbara Lewis at one time."

"That's correct. And do you know what kind of work Mrs. Harrison did?"

Shannon's eyes widened. "Was she a *prostitute*?"

"Yep," McHam said. "That's how Gary Harrison knew the layout of the motel room and everything."

"He knew his wife did that?"

"Sure. Janice Harrison was the bread winner of the family."

"Oh my god," Shannon said. This was weirder than she had expected.

"Gary Harrison was a white trash, street smart, psychopathic thug. But for some reason, he had a lot of charisma. He was a good-lookin' guy, I guess. Women liked him. Well, some did. He liked to control 'em, though. He controlled his wife. He pimped her out himself. Before comin' to Limite, they moved all over the place. He'd take whatever oddjobs he could find-- roughneck, dishwasher, whatever... and she'd work out of the nearest Dixie Mafia-run motel or hotel. They have a couple of kids... grown now."

Shannon listened with fascination.

"You know the old Washington Hotel downtown?" he asked.

"Didn't it become the Lodge of the Western Plains?"

"That's the one." He laughed. "Funny that it's an old-folks retirement home now. Anyway, Janice Harrison worked out of there when it was the Washington Hotel. That was one of the hot spots for the Dixie Mafia. They ran gambling and prostitution out of there on one entire floor. Well, not too many people know this, but Lucky Farrow owned the Washington Hotel."

"Really?"

"He got out when it was sold and it became the Lodge of the Western Plains. But before that he controlled what went on. The hotel was the upscale place of business. For the lower classes, they had to go to the Flats in south Limite."

"The Flats?"

"Yeah, you don't know about the Flats?"

"No."

"It was a block or so of illegal gambling parlors, bars, and brothels across the tracks. It was run by blacks, of course, but the mob had its hands all over it. Hell, a lot of the blacks were *in* the mob. Janice worked down there, too. So did Harrison, at a small booze joint."

"Geez..."

"The police and sheriff's office knew all about the Flats. It was a sort of unofficially designated zone for that stuff. The police figured that it was better to have a designated spot-- that way they could keep an eye on it. So they mostly turned a blind eye, unless there was trouble. Which there often was. They were always down there breakin' up fights or pickin' up dead bodies or somethin'. I tell you, more white teenagers got rolled in the Flats in those days. They'd get the crazy idea that they could go across the tracks and get laid with cheap black hookers. They'd end up gettin' their heads bashed in with a bottle and left lyin' in the street somewhere. It was a dangerous place to be. That's where I got shot."

"I remember guys in high school bragging about riding around across the tracks as if it was some kind of big deal," Shannon said.

"Oh, all the wilder kids that lived in middle to upper class white neighborhoods went cruisin' through colored town at some time or another. It's like a rite of passage or somethin'."

Shannon had always winced when someone used the term "colored town." She had grown up with that epithet, or its worse, less polite alternative name. Like nearly every small town in West Texas and, in general, the south, segregation had been a part of life since the town's origins. The poverty-stricken, mostly African-American side of town was south of the railroad tracks, and it consisted of shanties, dilapidated old buildings, and vacant lots. In the early seventies there was an all-black high school there but it was closed later that decade and the kids were bused to the two "white" high schools in Limite.

"What was the other theory?" she asked.

"Pardon?"

"You said that was one theory, about Gary Harrison working for this Dixie Mafia. What's the other one?"

"Well, the other one is the one that is public. That he was a crazy sex offender and murderer and was probably West Texas' first known serial killer. That was all before a guy at the FBI had even coined the term 'serial killer'. At the time, the newspapers all called him the 'Oil Field Killer.'"

"That's the theory everyone believes."

"Right."

"What do you believe?"

McHam shrugged. "Like I said, I know for a fact that Harrison was involved in all that mob stuff, and so was his wife. Whether or not the killings were mob-related or not, I haven't been able to prove."

Shannon shook her head. "Wait, you think my mom's murder was a mob hit?"

"I didn't say that. I meant that the mob used Harrison to do some of their killing for them. The Barbara Lewis and Tina Lee Peters killings were not like the others. Very different M.O. You can tell a lot about the perpetrator by studying the crime and how it was committed. Some would say those two were done by someone completely different from whoever killed your mother."

"But you don't think so?"

"No. I think Harrison did all of them. You know about the Saldañas?"

"Yeah. You think he killed them, too?"

"Richie Saldaña was mixed up with stuff goin' on in the Flats. I think he knew Gary Harrison, too. Word on the street was that Saldaña stole a shitload of money from the Washington Hotel. Pardon my French. If you ask my opinion, I think Harrison's murder in prison was mafia connected."

Shannon didn't know what to think. "Tell me more about Harrison."

"Sure. Let's take a drive, though. I want to show you some places on the south side. We'll ride in my four by four. Go ahead and finish your lunch."

"I'm done." She had barely touched it. She had lost her appetite a while ago.

They got into his red Ranger and drove southwest to the opposite end of Limite, near downtown. It was the part of town that hadn't changed in thirty years. For all intents and purposes, downtown Limite was a ghost town. All the major retail business had moved to the more affluent east side. The two movie theaters that were busy in the sixties and seventies had closed down after being converted into Spanish-language cinemas. The only things left downtown were the few banks, law offices, a hospital, the public library, the court house, and of course, Carl's office.

They went across Division Street, which was also the highway that connected Limite to Preston to the east and Sandhill to the west. The railroad tracks separated the rest of Limite from "colored town."

It was certainly a different world from the rest of the city. Shannon always felt uneasy when she was south of the tracks. The poverty was very depressing and she still found it hard to believe that people still lived that way in the late nineteen-nineties. Racial prejudice was still a blight in these parts.

McHam spoke as he drove. "Gary Harrison came from a small town near San Antonio. His mother was most likely a prostitute. He never knew his daddy. When I interviewed him in jail, he told me he hated his mama-- but he always went to see her when he wasn't in trouble. Supposedly she entertained men on the table in front of her kids. He was an abused kid, like most killers. When he was a juvenile, I know he spent some time as an out-patient in a mental illness clinic in New Mexico.

"Gary Harrison was very nocturnal. He liked to sleep in the day and come out at night. When he was givin' statements and stuff to the sheriff and others, it was always in the middle of the night. He'd call up Sheriff Barton at 3:00 a.m. and say that he wanted to talk. Barton and his men would go down to the county jail and sit with him for hours until he finally said something. When I interviewed him, it was after midnight. He was a cunning guy. He was uneducated, but he was smart.

"Like most bad kids, Harrison had his fair share of trouble with the law when he was growin' up. His first known arrest was when he was fourteen. It was somewhere in Texas. He was popped for forgery and sentenced to two years in a juvenile facility, but he only served about nine months. When he was eighteen he got arrested in Houston for city vagrancy, but didn't serve any time. There were other minor offenses-- drunk and disorderly, petty theft, that kind of thing. By 1960, I think, he was married to Janice. It was 1963, I believe, that he was arrested in Oklahoma for forgery and selling mortgaged property in Texas. He was brought back to Texas, and in 1965 I'm pretty sure he was sent to Huntsville on the forgery charge for four years. The Harrisons' kids had been born by then."

"What's selling mortgaged property?"

"That's when you obtain furniture or a car or something that's got a mortgage on it, and then you sell it illegally. It's a felony offense in Texas."

The Ranger pulled along a street that contained a wide vacant lot. They were next to an intersection that McHam indicated with a sweep of his hand.

"Right here is where the Flats was, on the four corners of this intersection," McHam pointed out. "It's all torn down now. Wait, there's one building over there that's still standing. On this side of the street was a burn barrel, where they would all stand around and keep warm in the winter or roast marshmallows in the summer. On that corner was the Elks Lodge, the black chapter, that is. Across the street on that corner were a bunch of little bars. One of them was called Freddie's Paradise, and it was run by this funny black guy named "Ankles." He had the biggest ankles anyone had ever seen, I guess 'cause they were swollen or somethin'. Whenever he was workin' too hard he'd always say, 'My ankles hurts, my ankles hurts.' Anyway, Freddie's Paradise was a big gambling joint. Across the street on that corner were the flop houses. Sometimes you could drive by there and see a woman standin' there topless in the doorway, beckoning fools to come inside. They weren't always black, either. Lots of white prostitutes worked outta there. And right over here," -- He pulled the Ranger a little further up to the corner-- "was where Pal's was. It was a small nightclub where Gary Harrison worked for a time, especially during the Kelly White case. After he abducted her, he brought her to Pal's and locked her in a storage room for a day."

"God..."

"Anyway, let's go back to the office, now that you have some geographical reference to what I'm talkin' about."

Shannon was glad to leave the area. It gave her the creeps. They drove back north of the tracks and headed towards the mall.

"So how long was Gary Harrison in jail in the sixties?" she asked.

"I think he served two years for that charge and got out in sixty-seven. That same year he was charged with rape up in Wichita Falls. It was alleged that he had raped and tortured his brother's ex-wife, if you can believe that, after tying up her new husband and makin' him watch! There was a trial, and he was acquitted. But because he had violated his parole, he got sent back to the pen for another four years."

"Then what happened?"

"He got out. In less than a year. That's the trouble with a lot of petty criminals. They get slapped on the hand and then let go. The good guys can't get it in their heads that these assholes are just gonna get out and do somethin' else. Pardon my French."

"It's okay."

"Well, sure enough, Harrison was out about four months and committed another rape. This one was in Oklahoma, but again, there wasn't enough evidence to convict him. The case was dismissed, but we're pretty sure he did it. So, you see, he was already showin' signs of deviant sexual behavior. Janice Harrison was makin' a living as a whore. They had small kids. Classic case of white trash. Sad, really. They came to Limite in 1969. Janice went to work at the Washington Hotel for some time, and she also went to work for Barbara Lewis for a while. Gary got a job as a roughneck out in the oil fields."

"How do you know all this?"

"I'm an investigator, Shannon," McHam said. "It's my job. I knew all that back when we were all lookin' for Kelly White's body. Come on, let's go inside the office and I'll tell you about that. You got time?"

She looked at her watch. Carl could stand to keep Cathy a while longer. "Sure."

He parked the Ranger in front of his office and they got out. Shannon followed him inside, totally engrossed in his stories. Merle was still at her desk, reading a paperback.

"No calls," she muttered.

"Thanks, Merle," Stan said.

They went into McHam's office and sat down. He popped a pill and took a swig out of a jug of water.

"Pain pill," he explained. "Damn hip acts up on me after I sit in a car for a while. Okay. Kelly White. I'll tell you what I know about the Kelly White case."

JUNE - JULY 1973
KELLY

Summer had hit full force in West Texas. Locals called it a "dry heat" because there was little or no humidity. Unlike the muggy Texas coastal areas, Limite in the summer was just plain hot. This was the desert. New Mexico was less than an hour away. It wasn't uncommon for temperatures to reach 100° Fahrenheit or more. The sun was always painfully bright if a dust storm wasn't brewing, and it seemed to be hotter out in the oil fields.

Wynn's Mobile Village was a community of twenty-two trailer homes on the Mitchell highway, about seven miles northwest of town. Roughnecks, laborers, and other oil field personnel lived there, along with a few elderly retirees. It was a large property, so the homes were spread out and private.

It was just after 11:00 a.m. on June 10. Kelly Ann White was about to eat an early lunch at her desk as she worked on balancing the books. Her boss, Sam Wynn, wanted all the rent checks ready to deposit by the end of the day. He also wanted the "second" ledger in order for his inspection tomorrow.

As she made an entry in the book, Kelly thought that it was a damn good thing that Sam had brought her in on the rent scam he had dreamed up. She and her boss skimmed a little off the top of each rent check and split the money between them. The owners of the trailer park lived in Arizona and never suspected a thing. As long as she helped Sam cover it up, he allowed her to participate in this "bonus plan." It didn't feel like she was doing anything illegal, although she knew that it was. If she hadn't been on the take in this fashion, her pay wouldn't be enough to support her and her two little girls. Besides, she couldn't wait to move out of that awful trailer home and rent a real house. Her daughters needed a yard to play in and neighborhood kids for friends. Lord knew her ex-husband wasn't much help. He was off in another town working his ass off, barely surviving himself. It was important to Kelly to land on her feet soon, so she was only too happy to help Sam out with his little scheme.

The second ledger she took care of supported the rent scam that they had concocted. It had done so well that between them they had pulled in an extra two or three thousand dollars a month.

43

She glanced at her watch. It was nearly 11:30. The radio was blaring George Harrison's *Give Me Love (Give Me Peace on Earth)*. Kelly got up from the desk, leaving her shoes underneath, and walked barefoot to the bathroom. She was wearing a sleeveless, white, button-down dress that was airy and cool in the hot weather. Thank God the office had air conditioning, she thought. Her last job had been at a well service contractor and they had to depend on infrequent, blessed breezes to blow through the open windows. This also allowed all sorts of desert critters to come flying inside-- something Kelly couldn't tolerate.

Kelly was all alone in the office, as was usually the case. Sam Wynn never stuck around. He did most of his work out on the golf course that was five miles down the highway. She could contact him at any time by radio, if he was in his car. Every once in a while one of the men who lived alone in the park would come and visit her, which she enjoyed. Even though they were often sweaty and dirty from the rigs, Kelly savored the attention. Sometimes it could get pretty lonely sitting in the office all by herself. There had been a small reprieve a few minutes ago. Mrs. Luper, a saleswoman from a firm that sold playground equipment, had just been in the office. They had sat and had a cup of coffee together, but Kelly had to turn her away. Sam handled all new purchases and Kelly was powerless to help her out.

After using the toilet, Kelly washed her hands and looked at herself in the mirror. Framed by short blonde hair, her face was very pretty. She batted her blue eyes at the mirror, thinking that she would surely land a man soon. She had gone on a couple of dates in the past month, but like most of the roughneck types in Limite, the men were dull and stupid. Kelly liked to read and talk about other things besides football and the oil fields. She liked movies. There was a new James Garner comedy, *Support Your Local Sheriff*, playing at the drive-in. Maybe it was just the crowd she ran around with. She needed a change.

She heard the music segue into the Edgar Winter Group's *Frankenstein* as Kelly went back into the main office. A man was standing in the open doorway. She recognized him as Gary Harrison, a creepy guy that had rented a trailer home for two weeks but his check had bounced. When he had insulted Sam, the manager had evicted him.

"Hi, Kelly," he said, flashing his wicked grin. Gary Harrison had flirted with her a lot when he was staying on the property. She had to admit he had what she called a "charm-smile," and at first he seemed nice enough. But then, after she had refused his advances a couple of times, he had started to get pushy. One of the other roughnecks had told her that Harrison was a "real nut" and that all he talked about was "torturing his in-laws."

"What do you want, Gary?" she asked.

"I came by for my deposit," he said. "You told me you'd have it for me this week."

"It's not ready yet," she said. "We have your new address, don't we? We'll mail it to you."

"No, I want it now." There was something about his voice that suddenly made Kelly nervous. He was acting strangely. His eyes were darting around, and he kept looking back out the open door.

"Well, I don't have it now, you'll just have to come back tomorrow."

Suddenly, with the speed of a tiger, Gary Harrison leaped several feet across the room and grabbed hold of Kelly's waist. A knife flashed and pressed against her throat. Her first thought was that she was going to die.

"Don't scream," he whispered. "Don't say a word. Don't try anything. Just come with me. Now."

She had no choice. Frightened as hell, she allowed him to lead her out of the office and around the back to the parking lot. There was absolutely no one in sight. He shoved her into the passenger's seat of a 1964 red Chevrolet, then went around to the driver's side and got in.

"Where are you taking me?" she asked with a whimper.

"Shut up," he said. He started the car and pulled out onto the busy highway and headed for Limite.

As they drove, Kelly's heart was pounding. She remembered that several women had been abducted from the Limite area in the past year or so. They had just found the body of that one woman near Mitchell a couple of weeks ago.

My God, she thought. Was Gary Harrison the killer? Was she next?

Kelly closed her eyes and silently prayed.

* * *

Sheriff Buck Barton bit down on a greasy hamburger from Pitts Bar-B-Q that one of the deputies had brought to him. It was nearly quitting time, but that didn't mean he could go home. Barton often stayed at the office past suppertime. There were always a million things still left to do.

Captain Ernie Jones stuck his head in the door and said, "Buck, I think we might have another abduction."

Barton nearly choked. "You gotta be shittin' me," he said, but with the food in his mouth it came out as, "You gwaddabe shat an me."

Jones continued. "Nope. We just gotta call from a Sam Wynn out at Wynn's Mobile Village on Mitchell highway. His secretary disappeared from the office this afternoon. No one knows where she is."

Barton swallowed his food and said, "Well, did somebody check the goddamn ladies' room?" He wiped the bar-b-que sauce off of his bushy mustache.

"Yes, sir. It looks pretty suspicious. Her car is still parked at her home there and she left her purse at her desk. She didn't leave with her shoes on, neither."

Uh oh, the sheriff thought. That sounded too familiar.

"All right, let's go," he said. He scooped up the rest of his meal and took it with him.

They got to the trailer park a half-hour later, found Sam Wynn, and obtained the whole story. Wynn told them that the postman found the office empty around noon. Wynn came back to look for Kelly and couldn't find her anywhere. He had thought it "mighty strange" that she had left her purse and shoes under the desk. Wynn confirmed that Mrs. White often took her shoes off when she worked, but she would never have left the building without them on. A ledger, open bank statement, and two stacks of rent checks were on the desk. She must have been balancing the books when she was interrupted.

Captain Jones took down the statement and did a sketch of the building and its parking lot, while Sheriff Barton obtained a list of the trailer park residents from Wynn.

Over the next five days, the sheriff's department continued its investigation into Kelly White's disappearance. She had not shown up anywhere and Barton feared that she may have met the same fate as other women who had been abducted in the area. Her small daughters had been sent to their father and no clues were found in their modest home.

Beginning the following day, deputies interviewed the residents, one by one, and several times one name kept coming up-- Gary Harrison. Apparently he had lived on the property for two weeks in May of 1973, but Wynn had evicted him.

"Harrison talked a lot about sex," said a man who lived at the trailer park and knew Harrison from oil field work. "I remember him sayin' that he thought Kelly White was good-looking."

Another neighbor described Harrison as a "nut" who seemed preoccupied with the other missing women cases in the Limite area.

More roughnecks who knew Harrison were found. A man named John Stone said he had befriended Gary Harrison by getting him the job at a well service firm. He had known Harrison from other oil field jobs and had received a phone call from Harrison in early May. Harrison had claimed that his wife Janice had run off and left their children with him in a small town near Abilene. Harrison was broke and had no way to feed them. Stone said if Harrison could find his way back to Limite, then maybe he could get him a job. Supposedly, some black woman brought Harrison and the kids back to Limite.

When deputies came back and told Barton what they had heard, he frowned. That name Gary Harrison had come up before. It was entirely possible that Harrison might be responsible.

"Well, hell, Ernie, I guess you'd better hunt him down. Find out where he's working now and all that," Barton said. This wasn't good.

After Jones was out of the room, Barton made a call to his friend Guy Simms.

* * *

Deputies learned that Gary Harrison was currently employed as an assistant manager at a small nightclub called Pal's, located in the Flats in south Limite. On the 12th, Sheriff Barton sent Captain Jones out to interview the manager, Greg Walker.

Walker hadn't seen Harrison since the 10th, the day Kelly White disappeared. Walker had gone to the club late that afternoon to check on the progress of some fix-up work that was being performed. Harrison had met him at the door and said that he had told the plumbers and painters to come back the next day.

"He seemed awfully excited about something," Walker said. "He was all flushed and seemed like he was in a big hurry to close the place up." When Walker asked him why he was sweating so much, Harrison had blamed it on the hot weather.

"I told him I had to go to Preston that night on some business and I didn't look forward to driving my Bonneville because it didn't have air conditioning," Walker said. "Gary offered to let me use his Chevy for the evening, because it did. I thought that was mighty nice of him, so I said 'okay.' Gary's car is a real dump-- in fact, he keeps all his clothes in it. But it has A-C, so that was okay. We agreed to swap cars again later that night. So he gave me the keys to his car and I gave him the keys to mine. I went on to Preston and didn't get back until around eleven o'clock that night. I went to the club and found Gary there waitin' for me. We swapped cars again and he ain't shown up for work since."

That was enough for the sheriff's department to widen the investigation. Deputies tried to find anyone who might have been in or near Pal's on the afternoon in question. Surprisingly, by the 13th, they found several witnesses who were willing to talk.

One black man named Tommy said that he had seen Gary Harrison driving a blue Bonneville south on Mississippi Avenue, away from the Flats and toward the petro-chemical plant that was on the south outskirts of Limite. That was around 7:00 p.m.

A regular Pal's patron who gave his name as "Waffles" said he had been at the club that afternoon. He related that two plumbers working there had heard a woman screaming for help from a storage room inside the building, but they left when Gary Harrison told them to go. Waffles had heard this story in a roundabout way and didn't know the identity of the plumbers.

Deputies took a look around the club and found the storage room in question. It was a small six foot by six foot closet. Inside was a white sheet, which Walker said had not been in there before. They also found strands of tape that looked as if they might have been used to bind someone's mouth, arms, and hands. A blonde hair was evident on one piece of tape. The officers then took a look at Walker's blue Bonneville. Inside were two red tablecloths similar to those used inside the club, and Walker again said they had not been in the car earlier.

While the deputies were examining the car, the phone inside the club rang and Walker went to answer it.

"Greg, this is Greg Junior," the voice said on the other end. Walker immediately recognized it as Gary Harrison.

"Greg Junior? What the hell?" Walker said.

"Listen, Greg, are there any police lookin' for me?" Harrison asked, nervously.

"Uh, as a matter of fact, they're here lookin' around the place now. Where are you?"

"Shit, don't tell 'em I called, all right? I'll call you back later."

When Captain Jones entered the club, Walker told him what had just happened.

"If he calls again," Jones said, "you try to find out where he is. Act like you're on his side, you know what I mean? Don't tell him you're talkin' to us."

Walker agreed. He didn't like the idea of employing a woman-snatcher.

On the 14th, Walker called Captain Jones at the sheriff's office and told him that Harrison had phoned him twice that morning. He said that Harrison claimed he was calling from Abilene and that he was running because his "in-laws were trying to get his children." He had apparently been looking for his wife for a few weeks, because she had run off with the kids. Unfortunately, Walker had no idea where Harrison was going from there.

When a Texas Ranger stationed in Pecos, Texas, heard that the Lucas County Sheriff's Office was looking for another missing woman, he called Buck Barton with a tip. He had heard from a Department of Safety intelligence agent that a "real nut" lived in Limite and that the sheriff's office might want to talk to him about the West Texas women murders. The nut's name was Gary Harrison. Apparently a woman friend of Harrison had told this agent that Gary was some kind of "sadist." The only way he could get his kicks was to beat a woman during sexual intercourse and often used strangulation during the sex act. He would tighten a nylon hose around a woman's neck during sex until she was on the verge of passing out. Fetishists claimed that this heightened sexual pleasure and orgasm. It wasn't something that was commonly seen in West Texas, but Sheriff Barton knew that there were weirdos that were into that kind of thing.

More witnesses were found and questioned about the afternoon of the 10th. One black kid named "Peanuts" hung around Pal's a lot looking for oddjobs. He stated that he saw Gary Harrison come out of the storage room looking "wild, like he was real nervous." He was carrying a long, brown-handled knife. Peanuts remembered that the manager's blue Bonneville was parked with its rear up against the front door of the club and the trunk was open.

It wasn't long before the two plumbers who had been working at Pal's that day were located. They were interviewed at length and told a most interesting story.

The two men had been working on leaky pipes in the bar, when they indeed heard a woman screaming in the back. Suddenly, she came running into the club. They described her as a blonde-haired woman who was partly bound. She was crying for help and begged them to call the police. But Gary Harrison was right on her heels and pulled her away. He shoved her back into the small room then told the plumbers that the woman was his wife.

"She's always getting out of hand," Harrison told them. "We get into these fights all the time and sometimes I just have to teach her who's boss. I'll stop this noise when I get her home."

After that, Harrison sent them away and told them to come back the next day, implying that they should forget about what they saw or they might lose the plumbing job.

On June 15, Buck Barton issued a statewide pickup for Gary Harrison. He was officially a suspect, wanted for questioning in the Kelly White disappearance.

* * *

Sometimes the system worked quickly. That very afternoon, Sheriff Barton got a phone call from Sheriff Joe Evans in Posse, Texas. Posse was a small town about fifty miles south of Dallas.

"I understand you're looking for a character named Gary Harrison?" Evans asked.

"Yes, sir, I am," Barton replied.

"Well, he just left our jail cell about an hour ago. I only just now saw your request to hold him, or he'd still be here."

"Why was he there?"

"His wife's in jail here. He had us arrest her for child desertion. Janice Harrison is her name. We picked her up a week ago. We also learned she was working as a prostitute out of one of the motels here. We have yet to charge her with that."

"She's still there?"

"Yes, sir, she is."

"Is Gary Harrison comin' back?"

"Probably so. I think he's gonna drop the charges. But she just told me something interesting."

"What's that?"

"She said he told her that he had bought some furniture in Lucas County and had sold it while it was still under mortgage."

"Well now, that's good news for us," Barton said. "That gives me the authority to issue a warrant for his arrest. You pick him up and hold him on the charge of disposal of mortgaged property. My captain and I will be there tomorrow."

He hung up and called for Ernie. "Ernie, tell Mike Patton we're goin' to Posse tomorrow."

"Posse? What for?"

"They're holdin' Gary Harrison there, or they will be by the time we get there."

Early the next day, on June 16, Buck Barton and Ernie Jones were on the road, heading east toward Dallas. They arrived in Posse around noon to find Sheriff Evans waiting for them.

"You're not gonna believe this," he told them. "We picked Gary Harrison up last night. He wasn't in the cell an hour when we found he'd slashed his wrists. We had to take him to the hospital!"

"Shit!" Barton said. "Is he gonna live?"

"Oh yeah, he didn't hurt himself too bad. Superficial wounds. They're gonna discharge him today. We have his Chevy out back if you want to take a look at that before goin' over to the hospital."

"Is his wife still here?"

"Yes, sir, after we arrested her husband, we held on to her, too."

"We'll want to talk to her," Barton said. "Come on, Ernie, let's go look at that car."

They went outside where the temperature had reached 105° F. Barton wiped his brow with a handkerchief, then stuck a wad of Redman tobacco in his mouth.

Harrison's red Chevy was parked in back next to the sheriff's own pickup. Greg Walker hadn't exaggerated-- the car was a dump. It was full of clothes and trash, as if Harrison had been living in it for weeks. It smelled of dirty laundry and sweat.

They spent an hour going through the stuff and came up with two red tablecloths from Pal's.

"These are just like the ones we found in Greg Walker's car," Ernie observed.

"Hey, look at this," Barton said. He had his hands on a couple of Polaroid photos. They featured an attractive woman wearing a red wig, black hose, black garter belt, and high heels. She was posed provocatively on a bed in a non-descript bedroom. Someone had scribbled "For

Couples Only" on the back of the photos. Barton showed the pictures to Sheriff Evans.

"You know this woman?"

"I sure do," Evans said with a grin. "That's Janice Harrison! 'Cept she's wearin' a red wig in the picture."

Barton nodded. "Yeah, she looks familiar to me too. Let's go talk to her."

Janice Harrison sat glumly in her cell. There was no red wig and no black garter belt. Instead she was wearing simple county jail coveralls-- and a black eyepatch. She was about thirty-two years old, had sandy blonde hair, one green eye, and was surprisingly glamorous despite the eyepatch and her surroundings.

"Janice, this is Sheriff Barton from Limite," Evans said.

She looked up at the sheriff with the one sultry eye and said, "Everyone knows Sheriff Barton from Limite." Her voice was deep, husky, and quite sensuous. Sheriff Evans opened the cell and led her into a room where she could talk with Barton and Jones.

"Mrs. Harrison," he said, "we want to talk to Gary about Kelly White. Do you know who she is?"

"No."

"She's a woman from Limite that went missing last week. We think Gary knows somethin' about it."

"He ain't said nothin' to me." Janice spoke slowly, with a tantalizing drawl. Barton had to admit that she was a sexy woman, even though she had "white trash floozy" written all over her.

"Why did he come here?" Ernie asked her.

"He had me arrested for child desertion, which is a crock of shit," she said. Even the way she swore was sexy. Crude, but sexy. "I left 'em with my parents. They were fine. Gary just didn't want me runnin' away from him."

"Mrs. Harrison, were you workin' out of a motel?"

"I don't know what you mean," she said.

"Were you, you know, workin' street business?"

"I ain't sayin' nothin' without a lawyer," she said defiantly. "I know my fuckin' rights."

She said it without malice. There was a smile on her face, as if she was playing with the sheriff, provocatively challenging him.

Barton was having none of it. "Come on, Ernie, let's go to the hospital." Before they left, Barton turned to her and asked, "What happened to your eye, Mrs. Harrison?"

"I lost it a couple of months ago. It was an accident." Again, she said it casually, as if it wasn't a big deal. "I was gonna get a glass eye, but Gary said the patch was sexy. What do you think, sheriff?"

Barton didn't answer her. Instead, he and Jones left the cell and submitted the official paperwork to Sheriff Evans that allowed them to take Harrison back to Limite. They then went to the hospital to pick him up and found the suspect in good spirits. His wrists were in bandages and he seemed happy to see the sheriff.

"Well if it ain't Sheriff Buck Barton himself!" Harrison said. "I suppose you're here to make me give back that furniture I stole. Well, I done sold it."

"Gary Harrison," Barton said, "we have the authority to bring you back to Limite under arrest for disposal of mortgage property."

"Well, you can get it back."

"Too late for that, Gary. Come on, get out of that bed. The doctor says you can go. Get dressed. We'll wait here."

"Do I get to see my wife before we leave?"

"I don't think so."

Within an hour they had him packed up and ready to go. They threw him in the back of the squad car and began the six hour drive back to Limite.

"Say, Gary," Barton said, looking back at their passenger. "I understand you knew a woman named Kelly White."

Harrison looked at Barton suspiciously. "Yeah, why?"

"Well, you know she's missing."

"I think I heard that. It's been in the papers, ain't it?"

Barton nodded. They drove a while longer in silence. Then he turned back to Harrison and asked, "You wouldn't have any idea where she might be, would you?"

"No."

"When was the last time you saw her?"

"She works at the mobile home where I lived for a little while last month."

"Did you ever date her?"

"I'm married," Harrison said, defensively.

"Did you ever try to date her?"

"Fuck you, I ain't answerin' your questions," he said.

"Fine," Barton said.

They drove the rest of the way in silence. Barton knew that it wasn't going to be easy getting him to answer anything.

When they got to Limite that night, Gary Harrison was placed in the Lucas County Jail and charged with Disposal of Mortgaged Property. Deputy Chief Mike Patton came in with a third charge that had come in from Preston.

"Assault With Intent to Murder?" Barton asked. "Gary, what's this all about?"

"Oh, that," Harrison said, dismissing it with a wave of his hand. "That's bullshit. There was this guy in Preston, a musician, that used to be a friend of mine. He owed me some money and I tried to get it out of him. I had a gun with me but I didn't think it was loaded. I accidentally shot him. He didn't die, he was just wounded, you know? It was a fuckin' accident."

"Right," Barton said. "Well, it looks like you've got two serious charges against you, Gary. Now, are you sure you can't remember anything about Kelly White? Where did you take her?"

"I don't *know* what happened to Kelly White!"

Barton was a patient man. He took his time with interrogations, and Ernie Jones was always impressed with the man's technique.

"We'll let you think on it a while," Barton said. "But you should probably know that some witnesses saw you with her at Pal's on the afternoon that she disappeared. It seems you had her tied up in the closet, isn't that right?"

"All right, listen, that wasn't Kelly White," Harrison said. "That was my wife. I was mad at her for workin' as a whore. I wanted to teach her a lesson."

"So you tied her up and put her in a closet?"

Harrison nodded, as if that was the most natural thing in the world to do.

"Hold on a minute," Barton said. He went out of the jail area and picked up the phone on this desk. He called Sheriff Evans in Posse.

"Sheriff, what day did you say you picked up Janice Harrison?" Barton asked.

"The eighth."

"Thank you."

Barton hung up, walked back into the jail area, and confronted Harrison again through the bars. "Gary, I know you're lying. Your wife was in jail in Posse on the day that Kelly White disappeared. So who was it that you had in the closet at Pal's?"

"I ain't sayin' nothin' else."

"You know we can get a court order for a polygraph test," Barton threatened.

"Bring it on, sheriff," Harrison said, defiantly. "I ain't got nothin' to hide."

Barton shrugged and got up to leave the room. As an afterthought, he turned back to the suspect. "Gary? How did your wife lose her eye?"

Harrison chuckled with a beastly sound that sent a chill up Jones' back.

"Oh, that. Stupid bitch poked herself with an ice pick. Bled all over the place. It was somethin'."

Barton suspected he was lying but didn't say anything.

The next day, the sheriff made arrangements with authorities in Dallas to perform a polygraph on Harrison. They had the best lie detector facilities in the state there and he wanted an impartial examiner to perform the work. Meanwhile, Harrison was held without bond, pending a hearing after the polygraph test.

The search for Kelly White's body continued daily. Officers combed the oil fields all around Limite. The sheriff knew he had to find that body before the D.A. could possibly make a case against Harrison.

* * *

On June 20, Sheriff Barton and Captain Jones took Gary Harrison to Dallas for the polygraph test. There were new revelations but the results were inconclusive. They did not, however, absolve Harrison of guilty knowledge in the Kelly White case.

Harrison said the last time he saw Kelly White was when he went back to the trailer park on June 1 in an attempt to pick up his deposit. The woman that was in the closet at Pal's was not his wife after all, but rather a prostitute who had run away from her pimp in Los Angeles.

"He's a friend of mine," Harrison said. "He called and asked for me to hold her there until he came and picked her up. I didn't hurt her and I didn't tie her up. I just handed her over to my friend later that day."

"What were you doing earlier in the day?" the tester asked.

"I slept late at the motel where I was staying, then I went to the club in the afternoon."

"What did you do while Mr. Walker was in Prescott?"

"Nothin'. Stayed at the club. We exchanged cars that night and I slept in the car."

"What did you do the next day, on Friday?"

"I went to San Antonio with a couple of friends of mine. Colored couple, husband and wife. I went to visit my sister and gave them a lift. You can verify that." He gave their names and addresses in Limite.

"Did you know Grace Daniel?"

"No."

"Would you say you have any sexual problems?"

"No."

"Do you drink much?"

"I used to. I quit after my prison term, except for one or two beers every now and then."

"Did you know Tina Lee Peters?"

"Never heard of her."

"Ever been to the Moonlight club?"

"Sure. Lots of times."

"How about the Fever club?"

"Everyone goes there."

"Did you know Mary Parker?"

"No."

"Ever been to Mitchell?"

"Yes."

"Did you know Susan Powell?"

"No."

"Ever been to the Fresh N' Dry Laundrymat on Lucas County Road?"

"Yeah, my wife used to do our laundry there. We lived a couple of blocks from there for a while."

"When did you live there?"

"Nineteen-sixty-nine to nineteen-seventy-two."

"Did you know Barbara Lewis?"

"No."

"Ever been to a county road northwest of the city, near the John Finch Ranch-- it's between the Loop and Mitchell Highway?"

"I know the John Finch Ranch. I don't know nothin' about a county road."

"Did you know Richie Saldaña or his wife Laura?"

"No."

The tests went on for several hours. At the end, the tester told the sheriff that Harrison was a difficult subject because of the life he had led. His sense of logic was irrational and he showed reaction to a question on one chart and no reaction to the same question on another test.

"His polygraphs are what I'd call 'typical nut' charts," the tester proclaimed, throwing up his hands.

Disappointed, Buck Barton and Ernie Jones returned their prisoner to Limite.

* * *

"We gotta find the goddamned body!" Sheriff Barton shouted to his men.

The entire department had assembled for a meeting on the morning of June 23. Gary Harrison was still in the county jail, waiting on a bail hearing.

"We got the city police looking and the FBI are sniffing around too. I don't like it when people think we're not doin' our job. Now, I'm convinced we can convict this guy on circumstantial evidence but we really need that body. I'm settin' up three shifts of search teams. You're gonna go over every inch of Limite and all the territory in the county. I want you to comb every field, every oil rig, every vacant lot, and every pile of cow dung that's in sight. I've got a helicopter on special loan from Dallas to help us for a day, and believe me, that ain't cheap. Now get out there and find her. I know she's gotta be there somewhere."

Barton dismissed the men and went back to his desk. He had to return a call from D.A. Rusty Franklin.

"Rusty? Buck Barton."

"Mornin', sheriff," the new D.A. said. He was a young man, but he was sharp and the sheriff thought he had balls. He would make a good D.A. for Limite.

"What can I do you for?"

"The hearing for the writ of habeas corpus is set for June 29. You think you can find the body before then?"

"I sure as hell hope so! If we don't, then that hearing is all we got."

"What about his wife?"

"She was released from Posse this morning and Captain Jones went to pick her up. We're gonna question her here."

"Any other witnesses?"

"Yeah, we got a guy that was the Harrisons' neighbor when they lived in west Limite. He's comin' in today. And we've got a couple of other guys who know him."

"Okay, keep me informed. Talk to ya later, Buck. Gotta find that body!"

The neighbor didn't have much to say. As far as he knew, the Harrisons were a "nice couple" and that Gary Harrison would have done "anything for his kids." Harrison bought his kids everything they wanted (when he had money), and supposedly expressed a great love for his family. Once he held a party for all of the neighborhood kids in the yard of his home. As for Janice, the neighbor admitted that she was a "good-looking woman" but he never saw her much.

"They always had a lot of company, though," the neighbor said. "There would be people comin' and goin' at all hours of the night. They threw a lot of parties, I guess."

Sheriff Barton could imagine what kind of parties they were throwing.

One of Gary Harrison's "friends," Jimmy Garrigan, a roughneck with a few drunk and disorderly charges against him, made a statement that the couple held sex orgies in their home and often invited some of the other roughnecks to participate. If they could bring other females with them to play along, fine, and if not, that was fine, too. According to Garrigan, Gary Harrison made his wife dress up in a red wig, black garter belt, black hose, high heels, and then he would tie her feet "spread-eagled" to the bed with nylon hose. Garrigan said that Janice Harrison "enjoyed" rough treatment and that she "got off on pain and humiliation." Both Gary and Janice were heavy into "bondage," a term that wasn't used much in Limite.

"Gary would like to watch his wife make it with other men, too," Garrigan said. "He had poked a hole in their bedroom closet so he could hide in there and watch his wife and other men. He did the same thing in the living room, so he could move from the living room to the bedroom without being seen. Janice knew he was watching but the men didn't."

Another so-called "friend" of Harrison, Shorty Shirer, confirmed all of this. He admitted he was one of the men that had sex with Mrs. Harrison. Shirer said that Gary would often bring home teenage boys for Janice to enjoy, while he watched from the closet. He would charge the boys money, which they were only too willing to pay. Afterwards, Harrison would re-enact the sex acts with his wife.

"I know for a fact that he liked to use a nylon hose around Janice's neck in a sex strangle act," Shirer said. "He'd slowly strangle her until she was near the point of passing out and then he'd release it. I guess it made her come harder or something. He'd make us do that to her, too."

A habitual criminal named Jordy Mack Blanton, another friend of the Harrisons, claimed that they asked him to make "sex movies" with Janice. Gary believed they could make a lot of money selling amateur pornographic films on 8mm. Blanton agreed and made several reels of sex acts with Janice while Gary served as camera-man.

Blanton also claimed that Gary and Janice belonged to several "wife-swapping clubs" and would often attend parties in which sex partners were traded. "In fact," he added, "I know they were friends with a few Limite cops and their wives. There was a wife-swapping thing going on over at the police department for a while."

When Janice Harrison got to Limite, Captain Jones brought her into an interrogation room. She asked to see her husband first, which Barton granted. He ordered the jailer to give the couple some privacy and waited a half-hour. Afterwards, she came out with tears in her eye.

Barton brought her some coffee and tissues and sat her down in the interrogation room again. At times, Buck Barton could be grandfatherly and kind, and this was the persona he displayed when questioning Janice. Ernie Jones sat in on the questioning, taking notes.

"Now, Janice, it's important that you tell me the truth about things. It'll make everything go a lot smoother for yourself and for Gary, too," he told her.

She nodded. She had waived her right to have an attorney present.

"Now, it's true you've been workin' as a prostitute, isn't it?" Barton asked her.

She sniffed and nodded again.

"Did Gary pimp you out?"

"Yes," she said. "For the last three years, off and on. I worked out of the Washington Hotel for a while and at a couple of motels on the highway." Janice then began to open up.

The stories Janice told didn't surprise Buck Barton but they were fairly unusual for a town like Limite. They were stories that might have come out of the bigger cities like Dallas or Houston.

"Yeah," she said. "Gary and I have been involved in various sex clubs. We've done orgies. There's this small, exclusive group of people in the Limite area who participate in sex clubs. Even a few police officers and their wives, I might add!"

As she spoke, Janice Harrison's attitude was such that she had absolutely no problem with anything she had done. She spoke about sex openly and brazenly.

She confirmed that he'd make her dress up in the red wig and lingerie and then take Polaroids.

"He'd use the Polaroids to drum up business," she said. "Sometimes, when I was dressed up that way, he'd pretend I'm a different person and call me all sorts of *vile* names. He'd tie me up with nylon hose. He'd make me tell him about the things I did with clients while he was screwin' me. Once Gary staged a rape scene on me by gettin' three teenaged boys to tie me up and do the most *degradin'* things to me while he watched from the closet."

The woman's a nymphomaniac, Barton thought. "Did he ever try to choke you?" he asked her.

"Well, once, when I refused to do what he wanted one night 'cause I just didn't feel like it, Gary choked me until I let him do what he wanted."

Barton noted that as Janice Harrison spoke about these things, she didn't appear to be particularly put out by them. She related them matter-of-factly, as if they were things any married couple would do. It was probable that she really *did* like the bondage treatment, as well as the opportunity to have sex with men other than her husband.

Even while she described her husband as a brute who forced her to do these unthinkable, yet pleasurable, things, Janice also confirmed that Gary was a loving husband and father. He doted on the kids and cared deeply for his family.

"Why did you leave him?" Barton asked.

"I had to get away from him," she said. "I got to where I hated our life, especially here in Limite. I been married to him for over ten years. It's time to move on."

"What about your children?"

"I'll take them with me, of course. They're with my parents now. It looks like Gary's gonna have some big time legal problems. That gives me a good reason to leave him." Then she added, "Besides, he poked my goddamn' eye out."

"How did that happen?"

She shrugged. "Just one of our fights. He had an ice pick and threatened me with it. We wrestled a bit, and I fell on it. I guess it was an accident, really, but he did have it in his hand."

"You want to press charges on that?"

She shook her head. "Nah..."

A wonderful example of matrimonial love, Barton thought.

After a day of grilling Janice, they let her go. She promptly left town to rejoin the children. Gary, meanwhile, sat in the county jail and waited.

The next day, Sheriff Barton donned overalls and spent fourteen straight hours in the fields searching for Kelly White's body. It had become a personal obsession for him to find her remains.

On June 25, a judge set bonds against Gary Harrison totaling $36,000. The two felony charges added up to this amount but Harrison's lawyer immediately appealed. Four days later, another judge deemed the bond "excessive" and reduced it to a more manageable $15,000.

Harrison's lawyer, Jim Frank, personally put up the money to free Harrison. On July 1, twenty-one days after Kelly White's disappearance, Gary Harrison was released on bond. Buck Barton wasn't happy about it but there was nothing he could do. Lucas County couldn't charge him with murder due to the lack of evidence, especially since there was no body. Harrison told Jim Frank that he planned to get his family back together, try to find a job and settle down somewhere other than Limite. Sure enough, in a few days Harrison reported back to Frank that he and his family were living in San Antonio. But between August and December, the Harrisons moved around a lot. The attorney knew that they were in Lubbock for a while, then eventually moved to south Texas.

The search for Kelly White's body continued in vain. Sheriff Barton even allowed a couple of psychics to come in and try to find the corpse. Jeanne Dixon said that Kelly White's body could be found in Limite "near water."

Unfortunately, there weren't any bodies of water to speak of in Limite, Texas.

By the end of 1973, the investigation was no further along than it was in July, except that the sheriff had uncovered the rent scam that Kelly White and Sam Wynn had been operating out of the trailer park. The D.A. wanted to prosecute Wynn but the sheriff didn't think it was serious enough to pursue. Wynn got off with paying a small fine. After all, his firm had offered $1,500 reward for information leading to the . whereabouts of Kelly White.

It seemed, though, that the reward money would never be collected.

JANUARY 1999
SHANNON

After Stan finished the story, Shannon sat there in silence. "It wasn't until January 1974 that Gary Harrison came back into the Limite spotlight. I wasn't on the case then, so I don't know too much about what happened during what I call the 'second phase' of Harrison's arrest and conviction," Stan said. "That's when Sheriff Barton spent a week in Cortez, talkin' with Gary and Janice in a hospital. Gary Harrison got shot in Cortez. No one knows who the hell shot him, but someone tried to kill him at some nightclub there. At the end of nine days, Gary Harrison told Barton where Kelly White's body was and Janice Harrison was thirty-five-hundred dollars richer."

She looked at him and waited for him to elaborate.

"Didn't you say you knew the sheriff paid Janice Harrison thirty-five-hundred dollars?" he asked.

Shannon nodded.

"That came out in the pre-trial hearing," he continued. "After the money changed hands, Gary told Barton where Kelly's body was. No one but the three of them knows what went on behind closed doors. There had to have been a deal struck. My big question is why Buck Barton would even consider making a deal. Some of the news accounts say it was 'reward' money, but whoever heard of paying reward money to the guy who did it? Doesn't make sense."

Shannon sat quietly, thinking about the story she had just heard. Sex orgies? Bondage? Wife swapping clubs? Gary Harrison and his wife were part of the underbelly of society. They had lived in ways she couldn't imagine. Shannon wasn't naive but she wasn't beyond being shocked. It was unbelievable that stuff like that was going on that long ago in Limite. She had always thought it was such a backwards town; it seemed to be perpetually five years behind the times.

What really scared her, though, was the thought that her mother may have been mixed up in it.

"You okay?" Stan asked.

She snapped out of it. "Sorry. That was quite a story."

Stan shrugged. "It's as close to the truth without actually bein' there."

"What *did* happen in Cortez? Do you have an idea? Where *is* Cortez, anyway? I've never heard of it."

"It's about two hours south of San Antonio." Stan shook his head and said, "Oh, I have an idea what went on there but I can't prove it. I think Harrison was willing to confess to one of the killings if Barton provided for his family. But I also think part of the deal was that he wouldn't be charged for any of the other murders and that Janice wouldn't be charged for her part, if any."

"What do you mean?"

"In the first confessions he made regarding your mother and Grace Daniel, he implicated Janice in the murders."

"Oh, right. Do you think she helped him?"

"I doubt it. But I do believe she knew the victims prior to the murders, just like he did. There had to have been some connection there. She got indicted for two murders, you know."

"But I thought he had made it all up because she threatened to divorce him."

"That's the official story. I suppose it's true. But who really knows...?"

"Where is she now, I wonder?"

"Probably in south Texas, I would imagine," Stan said. "I could find her, if you want."

"You think she'd talk to us?"

"Who knows? She might. It's been a long time. Then again, she might not. I imagine she's a tough character. It wouldn't hurt to try."

"All right." Shannon dreaded the thought of meeting the woman face to face, especially if she did have something to do with her mother's slaying.

"In the meantime, I'll try to get hold of some of the files at the sheriff's office. I've got a couple of buddies down there who owe me some favors. I'll get copies of his confessions. Those'll tell us a lot."

"That sounds fine," she said. She looked at her watch. It was late afternoon. "I'd better go."

"Sure," Stan said, standing up.

"Don't get up, really," she said. She gathered her things and held out her hand. "Thank you."

Stan sat back down and shook her hand. "You're welcome," he said.

"When should I get back in touch with you?"

"I'll call you when I've got something for you," he said.

"Okay."

She turned, walked out into the reception room, and nodded at Merle.

"Bye bye, honey," the woman said. The phone rang. She answered it and said, "McHam Incorporated. Ask about our special this week on unfaithful spouse surveillance. How may I help you?"

* * *

Shannon made dinner and served it in silence. Carl watched her as she played with her food. When the kids wanted something, she didn't seem to notice. Carl got up and fetched Cathy's juice and Billy's catsup.

After the kids left the table, Carl said, "Look, honey, if this is going to upset you so much, maybe you better let it go."

"I can't let it go now," Shannon said. "I'm findin' out stuff about my mom that I never knew was *possible*. I've got to see it through."

"Isn't knowin' that Gary Harrison killed her enough? He's dead, too. It's not like he's gonna get out someday."

"I know... But it looks like there may have been more to it than that."

"So what?" Carl said. "What can you do about it now? It's been nearly thirty years. What could you possibly hope to change?"

She thought a minute and answered, "My own peace of mind."

Carl didn't have a reply to that.

After they had shared clean-up duties, Shannon told her husband that she was going out.

"Oh?" he asked.

"I'm just going to take a drive. I'll be back in a while. Can you get the kids to bed on time?"

She never went out in the evenings. Carl looked at her with concern.

"Sure." He watched her grab a coat and fly out the door. He sighed and called to the kids, "Hey, who's in the bathtub first?"

Shannon got in her Tempo and backed it out of the driveway. The sun had set an hour ago but it was still early in the evening. She preferred Daylight Savings Time because it became dark way too soon in the winter for her taste.

She drove to the area Stan McHam had pointed out as "the Flats." She crossed the railroad tracks and entered south Limite. That uncomfortable feeling of paranoia immediately returned. The squalor of the shacks, the garbage in the streets, and the sad eyes of the people standing in their front yards served to remind her that she lived in a completely different world.

Could her mother have had one foot here?

She drove around the block where Pal's used to be. She imagined poor Kelly White being trapped in a closet and felt her fear. Gary Harrison must have killed her at the club, then loaded her into the trunk of Greg Walker's Bonneville. He had been seen driving the car south on Mississippi Avenue. The body had been found in a vacant lot south of town, so Harrison had probably dumped the corpse that very night.

Shannon drove north back across the tracks and then west to Lucas County Road and the area where Donny's Cafeteria used to be. When her mother was cashier there, it was one of the more popular eateries in the city. There was another one on the east side as well. The building still stood today but it was vacant. Donny's had gone out of business in the late seventies.

She drove past the building and came to the intersection where the Fresh N' Dry Laundrymat once was. It was only three blocks from Donny's. Grace Daniel had been snatched from the laundrymat. Shannon's mother had worked at Donny's. Was there a connection? Did the two women know each other? Gary Harrison supposedly lived near the intersection at the time. Did he know both women before the abductions?

Shannon drove on to the Blue Mirage, a bar on the northwest side where Jackie worked. The small gravel lot was crowded, forcing her to park a block away. She got out and walked purposefully to the nightclub, out of which came the strains of Garth Brooks' latest hit.

The small club was crowded and full of smoke. The music was unnecessarily loud. Shannon almost turned around and left but she wanted to see her sister. She made her way in, nodded to the doorman who recognized her from previous visits, and snaked toward the bar past bikers, roughnecks, and cowboys.

"Hey baby," a drunken voice said in her ear as she walked past. Ignoring it, Shannon looked around the room but couldn't find Jackie. She did, however, see Travis Huffman shooting pool in the back. An ugly guy with a Marine-style crew cut was playing against him. There was a young blonde girl standing with her arm around Travis' waist, drinking a beer. Shannon took a breath and strode over to him.

"Hey good-lookin'," he said when he looked up and saw her. He immediately pushed the blonde girl away. "Chaz, did you know this is Jackie's big sister?"

"Really? Shit, she's a lot better lookin' than Jackie!" gurgled the guy named Chaz.

"Hey! You're talkin' about my girlfriend, you fuck," Travis said. Then he turned to Shannon and asked, sweetly, "What can I do for you, my dear?"

"Where's Jackie?" Shannon asked.

"She was sick tonight. She stayed home."

"What's wrong with her?"

"Beats me," Travis said. "Probably one of them female things y'all are always gettin.'"

Just as charming as always, Shannon thought.

"See ya," she said, then turned around to leave.

"Hey, stay and have a beer!" he called out.

"No, thanks," she said, striding out of the place.

She was so glad to get out of that cloud of smoke that she didn't notice the perpetual smell of petroleum in the Limite atmosphere.

She returned home two hours after she had left the house. The kids were in bed and Carl was sipping a beer in front of the television, watching *E.R.* She hung up her coat, then went into the kitchen to call Jackie.

The phone rang and rang but the answering machine didn't pick up. Shannon almost put back the receiver when someone answered.

Shannon waited for a "Hello?" but there was nothing but silence.

"Jackie?" she said. "Hello?"

"Hello?" the voice was Jackie's but she sounded as if she were talking in her sleep.

"Jackie?"

"Huh?"

"Are you awake?"

"I am now."

There was something different about her voice. At first Shannon thought she might be drunk, but this was something else.

"Are you sick?"

"Yeah."

"What's wrong?"

"Nothin'. What do you want?"

"Well, I heard you were sick so I called to see how you were."

"Who told you I was sick?"

"I saw Travis at the Blue Mirage."

"Oh." The slurring in her speech had increased since the last time Shannon had talked with her.

"Jackie, are you all right? Do I need to come over?"

"No!" Jackie almost shouted. "Don't come over."

"Where's Tyler?"

"He's asleep."

"You don't need any help?"

"No, I don't. I'm goin' back to bed."

"All right," Shannon said. "Call if you need me."

The phone clicked. No goodbye, no thanks. Shannon hung up the receiver and bit her lower lip. Jackie wasn't drunk. She was drugged.

Not knowing what she could do about it this late at night, Shannon let it go, went into the living room, and sat on the couch beside Carl. He put his arm around her but didn't say anything. They watched the show in silence, but Shannon's mind was wandering. When the commercial came on, she snuggled closer to her husband.

"Thanks for understanding," she said.

Carl kissed her on the forehead. "It's my job," he replied with warmth.

* * *

Shannon had a bad couple of nights. The first night she didn't sleep much at all. She got through the next day, a workday, on four cups of coffee and performing her secretarial job on automatic pilot.

On the second night she had a vivid dream. She was walking through the streets of south Limite. There were dozens of poor little black kids staring at her from the open doorways of their shacks. She found herself in the Flats and now the buildings were still standing. A group of men were huddled around the burn barrel, laughing and taking drinks from a jug. She wandered over to them as if she belonged there. One of the men offered her the jug. She almost refused but decided to take a drink. When she tasted the liquid, she realized the jug was full of blood.

The men started laughing at her. She looked up and saw that the man that handed her the jug was no longer a black man. He was Gary Harrison. He was holding a container of black shoe polish. He had tried to disguise himself by coloring his face.

Frightened, she dropped the jug and ran across the street to Pal's, where an attractive woman with dark hair was standing in the doorway. She was dressed in a tight black skirt and a see-through blouse. She wasn't wearing a bra.

"Wanna come in, Shannon-wannon?" the woman asked.

Shannon shuddered in horror when she realized that she was looking at her mother.

Then she woke up.

"Oh, God," she moaned when she saw that the digital clock on the nightstand read 5:48 in the morning. She slipped out of bed and went to sit in the living room until the rest of the household was up. The nightmare stayed with her for hours.

The phone rang around 9:00 a.m. after Carl had left for work and Billy was off to kindergarten.

"Good morning," Stan McHam said.

"Hi, Stan."

"Hope you're awake?"

"*Oh*, yes, I'm awake. We have two small children, remember?" She was actually dead tired.

"Right. Hey, I've got some more stuff for you. I had a long talk with a guy named Paul Rattan last night. He worked for Mike Patton, who was Buck Barton's chief deputy, you know? Mike's pretty old, and not in good shape. But Paul was pretty young at the time. He filled me in on everything that happened in 1974, after they nabbed Gary Harrison in Cortez. I figured you'd like to know."

"Yes, I do, but I'm stuck with my daughter. I can't really come to your office today."

"Well, I'm not doin' anything until later this afternoon. I have an appointment with some FBI guys on a case I'm helpin' 'em on. You want me to come over to your house?"

Curiosity won over fatigue. "Sure, if you don't mind."

He verified the address and said he'd be over soon.

When he got to the house, he carried a portfolio and limped inside. He said hello to Cathy, who was staring at him as if he was a freak.

"What's the matter with your leg?" the girl asked innocently.

"Oh, I hurt it a long time ago," Stan said, smiling.

"Run along and play, Cathy," Shannon said. "Mr. McHam and I have to talk business."

"Can I watch TV?" Cathy asked.

"Sure, just keep it down."

They went into the kitchen and Stan sat at the table. He noted the framed embroidery that stated, "God Bless This Kitchen," and the children's drawings stuck on the refrigerator. "Mom is the Best" was one of the messages in kid-scrawl. A heart-shaped frame featured a photo of Shannon and her husband with their arms around each other. In fact, there were framed photos of the Reeces with their kids all over the place. They were a family that obviously loved one another.

Shannon poured them some coffee and sat down.

"Have you heard about Buck Barton?" Stan asked.

"No, what about him?"

"He had a stroke yesterday. He's in the hospital."

"Really?"

"Yeah, Paul Rattan told me. He's incapacitated."

"Geez.... Is he going to live?"

"I dunno. The guy's what, eighty-something?"

"So I guess we're not going to find out anything from him."

"Probably not."

"He wouldn't talk to me before, I don't see why he would talk to me now."

Stan shrugged. His unique way of shrugging could indicate a number of different responses, depending on what he wanted to communicate-- "yes," "no," "maybe," "whatever you say," "don't ask me," and the old stand-by, "I don't know."

"So... what have you got?" Shannon asked.

"Oh, I forgot to tell you. Paul's gonna get those files for me. We should have some more stuff to look at tomorrow. And I've got a guy tracing Janice Harrison. He thinks there's a good possibility we'll find her."

"Okay."

Stan pulled a file folder out of the portfolio. He opened it and took out an old black-and-white photograph. It was dark and not very clear. It showed three men wearing business suits and standing at a bar. A bartender was wiping a glass dry. The room was crowded with other people in the background. A small group of men and women sat a table on the right side of the photo.

Stan pointed to one of the businessmen. "You recognize him?"

She nodded. "That's my grandfather's ex-partner."

"Yep, that's ol' Chuck Davenport," Stan confirmed. "You know who the other two men are?"

"No."

He pointed to a tall skinny man with a large Adam's Apple. "That's Guy Simms." The other man was short and overweight. "And that's Lucky Farrow. This picture was taken at the Washington Hotel Bar in 1972. I took it myself with a hidden camera. I was trying to establish a connection between the Dixie Mafia and the goings-on in the hotel. This was before we were looking into any of the abductions."

"So you think Chuck Davenport was part of this mafia?"

"Yes, I do. I know it. I'm sorry to say," he added.

"No, it's all right. I never knew him. I wonder about my grandfather, though. You think it's how my mom got involved in all this?"

"It's possible. I don't know. Now take a look at the folks at that table." He pointed to the group in the photo. "Recognize anyone?"

She was startled that she hadn't noticed before. Sitting at the table and looking toward the men at the bar was Gary Harrison.

"It's him," she said.

"Uh huh. And you know who the woman is next to him?"

"Janice?"

"That's right." Her face was partially obscured by smoke from Gary's cigarette, but Shannon could see what might have been the face of a movie star framed by sandy blonde hair cut in the style of Bettie Page, the glamour girl from the 1950s.

"Do you know the other woman at the table with them?"

There were two. One with dark hair was in profile, facing the Harrisons. The other was a blonde, and her back was to the camera.

"Which one?"

"The redhead. Well, you can't tell it's red, because the photo's black-and-white."

"I don't think so..."

"Her name is Carol Jenkins."

Shannon nodded. "She was a friend of my mom's. She worked at Donny's Cafeteria at the same time."

"That's right," Stan said. "How did you know that?"

"Uncle Fred told me about her. When I was lookin' into this before, back when I was in high school, I talked to her. She was still around Limite then. I don't know if she still is."

"She was one of your mom's good friends, right?"

"That's what they tell me. She wasn't very forthcoming when I talked to her. My dad probably knows more about her, because his hackles rise when even her name is mentioned."

"Well, look at the company she kept."

This was all very disturbing. Shannon said, "Tell me more about this Dixie Mafia. How did it operate? What exactly were they up to?"

"Well, like I told you before, the name is just a label that was laid on 'em. It's not like they got together and decided, 'We're going to call ourselves the Dixie Mafia.' The name was coined about the time I started workin' on the case-- some say by the FBI, some say by the media. For decades, though, they've been linked to vice and violence all over the South. At the time, they were a group of criminals who worked in Mississippi, Louisiana, Oklahoma, Arkansas, Tennessee, Alabama, Georgia, Florida... and Texas. They specialized in victimizing the public for a fast buck. The crimes they repeatedly committed were armed robbery, drug trafficking, burglary, safe-cracking, and scams of all kinds. They especially liked to operate gambling parlors and whore houses and pay off public officials to allow them to stay in business. People who got in their way or crossed them were killed. They often employed criminals whose careers included murder for hire.

"Their impact on crime was so great that in 1969, law enforcement agencies in the south met in Atlanta to identify and start keepin' tabs on them. They were so loosely organized that it was difficult as hell to do so. They never had an hierarchy, so to speak, like the Italian Mafia. There weren't any vows or rituals that made someone a member. It was more like a pattern of associations and behavior... and crimes. They were willin' to break society's laws and go wherever the opportunity was. And the members always did favors for each other. It was like, you know, 'I helped you do this job, so you need to help me do this one.' Actually, they called themselves 'the network' back then."

"But weren't there bosses?"

"Sure, and they were usually guys like Guy Simms and Lucky Farrow. Maybe Chuck Davenport. Maybe even your granddad. The Dixie Mafia needed confederates who stayed put in one place. The settled members did the type of networking usually associated with a fast-paced corporation, but in their case it was criminal enterprise."

"Kelly White was involved in that rent scam at the trailer home."

"Uh huh. That could have been controlled by the Dixie Mafia. Her boss may have been providing them with a kick-back. Rent scams were something they liked to do. Insurance scams were another. And embezzlement."

"Like what Chuck Davenport did."

"Uh huh. Now, like I told you before, most of the activity back then was centered in the Flats and at the Washington Hotel. Ever hear of the Bennetts?"

"No."

"They were a black family that was probably the most powerful Dixie Mafia locals in the Flats. They ran everything and took their orders from someone higher up."

"Like these men?"

"Probably. The Bennetts consisted of three brothers who were mean as hell. They all had big families and all their kids were involved in the shit, too. Pardon my French. The police were always poppin' one of the kids for something... and they never *ever* went to jail. I never understood how they always got off. I finally figured out that someone in the justice system in Limite was protecting them. I'll never forget a big gang fight that occurred in the Flats one night. It was a bunch of teenaged girls, if you can believe that. There were about thirty black girls, all kickin' and bitin' and scratchin' each other. Some of 'em had broken bottles and knives. The sheriff's department got in there to break it up. Two deputies arrested one girl and were escortin' her back to the squad car, when she was suddenly shot in the back! She was walkin' in-between two sheriff's deputies and some teenage girl shot her! Well, the deputies immediately turned around and tackled the girl with the gun and arrested her, too.

"Anyway, the girl who got shot was taken to the hospital. It wasn't a bad wound, cause the gun was just a .22. As soon as she got out, they took her to jail. The deputies wanted her parents to press charges against the girl who shot her but they wouldn't do it! You know why? The girl with the gun was a Bennett. In fact, she was Willie Bennett's kid and he was the big boss of the whole sha-bang. 'She'd just get off,' was the parents' excuse. Well, the deputies went ahead with the attempted murder charge and sure enough, the case got dismissed for lack of evidence. Lack of evidence? The damn girl was shot in front of two sheriff's deputies who could testify in court! But it still got thrown out. That just shows you how much power the Bennetts had then."

"What happened to them?"

"Well, they finally fell after several years. One of the main brothers, Abe, was arrested for a double murder. It looked like he was gonna walk, too, when someone finally decided enough was enough. They agreed to testify against him if the police put 'em in a witness protection program. You see, everyone in colored town was scared of the Bennetts. The Bennetts'd soon kill one of their own kind as look at 'em. Well, they successfully convicted Abe Bennett. And that's all it took. Once he went to jail, their mystique was destroyed. It had a domino effect. One by one, people started to come forward and testify against them. Within five years, all three brothers were behind bars. Willie was executed not long ago. By the mid-eighties, the reign of the Bennetts was no more."

"So the mafia doesn't run things now?"

"I believe they're pretty much gone out of Limite now," Stan said. "Actually, let me put it this way. It's not run like it used to be. Oh, I'm sure there are still flop houses and gambling parlors hidden away at motels and the like, but they aren't controlled by the kind of organized crime like they were then. There certainly isn't anything on the scale of what was happening at the Washington Hotel. There was an entire floor there that the elevator never stopped at if you were just a guest at the hotel. You had to have a password, and then the elevator operator would stop at the floor where all the illegal stuff was goin' on. We staged a raid there one night, and you know what? Someone had tipped 'em off that we were comin'. They had managed to clean out every single bit of evidence from the floor-- every domino, every betting chip, every deck of cards-- and they must have stored them somewhere in the hotel. It was like they had cleaned house and remodeled. Soon as we left, they pulled it all out again and it was business as usual."

"Who could have tipped them off?"

"It had to have been someone in law enforcement. Both the city police and the sheriff's office knew it was goin' down."

"Wow."

"Part of the Dixie Mafia's business was protection for those workin' for them. There's been lots of rumors over the years that the sheriff's department was in bed with 'em, if you know what I mean. No one could ever prove anything. Every now and then, the sheriff's department would do something to make it look like they were cracking down on the crime. If a bar or other nightspot was involved in illegal activity, the sheriff's office would stack the joints themselves just to get them to play by the rules."

"What do you mean?"

"Oh-- stack the joints," Stan said. "That's cop lingo for smashing up a place. Whenever a bar gets broken up in a fight or something, it's called stacking the joint. There've been a lot of cases in this town where fights have started in some honky-tonk for the sole purpose of smashing the place to bits so they can't do business. I know that Sheriff Barton and his men would stack a joint themselves if the owners got out of line. The owner would have to go down to the sheriff's office and reclaim his license from Buck in person. It's how he had some control over the places. Now, some might say that what he was doin' was runnin' a protection racket. He'd allow certain illegal activities like gambling or whatever-- if there was a kickback under the table. It's classic Dixie Mafia stuff. Whether or not Sheriff Barton was actually doin' that...? Like I said, it's difficult to prove."

Shannon shook her head. This wasn't the Limite where she thought she had grown up.

"Their reach even extended into prison," Stan said. "Their members who had already been sent to the pen were still very loyal. I believe Gary Harrison was executed by mafia hit men in Hunstville."

"Why?"

"He blabbed too much in court. He confessed to too many things. If some of his murders were actually mob hits and he *confessed* to 'em in court-- that would be enough to piss off the mob."

There was a moment of silence, then he continued. "Anyway, you asked if there was still a Dixie Mafia in these parts. Not as such, but it still exists in the south. Part of the investigative work I do now is tracing links from known Dixie Mafia control centers farther east, like in Mississippi and Alabama, and seeing if any end up here. Mostly what they do now is drugs, counterfeiting, strip clubs, and prostitution."

"Have you found anything here?"

"A couple of big time suspects have been in town for a while. I'm lookin' into a counterfeiting operation that the FBI believes is comin' through Limite. Believe it or not, one of those suspects might be the guy who shot me! But don't worry, they're known by the police, the sheriff's office, and by me. Look here, I want to show you something."

Stan pulled a manila folder out of his portfolio. It was marked "Tina Lee Peters." He opened it to a picture of a pretty blonde woman.

"This was Tina Lee Peters. She was shot to death in her apartment in Limite on or about July 5th or 6th of 1972."

He showed Shannon the photo taken at the Washington Hotel and pointed to the blonde woman sitting at the table with Gary Harrison.

"This photo was taken on July 3, 1972. That woman is Tina Lee Peters."

"Whoa!"

"During our investigation, we discovered that Mrs. Peters was working not only as a barmaid at the Tempest Club, which had Dixie Mafia connections, but as a hooker out of her apartment. You probably don't remember the old Hillview Apartments over on Mississippi Avenue?"

"I think I do."

"Well, they're not there anymore. Anyway, that's where her apartment was. We had good reason to believe that she was killed by the Dixie Mafia because she was workin' on her own."

"You said that before."

"Right. And the woman Barbara Lewis. We know for a fact that she was pimping out of her motel. Janice Harrison worked for her for a while. I'm almost positive that she crossed the mafia somehow, or was keeping money for herself. She got whacked for it."

"My mom's friend, Carol Jenkins... was she a...?"

"Hooker? Look who she's sittin' at the table with."

"There really is a connection running through all this."

"You bet your ass there is. Pardon my French."

Shannon grabbed her own file folder from the kitchen cabinet and found the clipping regarding the woman who escaped abduction in June of 1971. She showed it to Stan.

"Did you know about this?" she asked.

Stan read the article quickly. "No, I didn't. Like I said, at the time I took that photo, which was a year later, we weren't involved in the abductions. Grace Daniel was the only known one, so a pattern hadn't been established yet. It sounds like this woman may have met our friend Gary Harrison."

"Do you think she's still around? Why wasn't she questioned again after he was arrested? You'd think she might have picked him out of a line up or something." "Maybe she moved away. I'll ask my friend Paul Rattan to see if he can dig up the police report on this and we can find out who she is. Maybe we can find her." He made a note of the date on the clipping, then glanced at the folder. "You've got quite a collection there."

"Yeah. Needless to say, it's an obsession."

He noticed the clippings on the Saldañas and tapped them with his finger. "I have no doubt that if those two had been alive, they would have been in this photo, too."

"Really?"

"Richie and Laura Saldaña were regulars at the Washington Hotel before their untimely deaths."

"So tell me what happened in 1974. How did Gary Harrison come to be arrested again?" she asked.

"Well, like I said before, I don't know what went on in that hospital room in Cortez. No one knows what kind of deal was struck except Harrison, his wife, and Buck Barton. But something did, and the Kelly White case was finally broken."

JANUARY 1974 - MARCH 1975
GARY

Steve Miller's *The Joker* was playing on Sheriff Barton's portable AM/FM radio in his office when the phone rang on the morning of January 4, 1974.

"Barton," he said, gruffly.

"Buck, I think you might want to take this one," said Mike Patton on the other end.

"Who is it?"

"Sheriff of Cortez, Texas."

"Put him on."

The line clicked until Barton heard the open-air sound of the long distance call.

"Barton," he said again, just as gruffly.

"Is this Sheriff Barton?"

"Yes, sir."

"Sheriff, this is Sheriff Bill Dunham in Cortez." The voice didn't have the West Texas drawl Barton was accustomed to but the man still sounded like a small-town southwesterner.

"What can I do for you?"

"I'm requesting any information you might have on one Gary Harrison, who I understand had some dealings with the law there in Limite."

Barton almost laughed aloud. "You don't say? What's he done now?"

"Well, it's a little strange. We were told by authorities in Posse that they were looking for him for bond-jumping. He had a charge against him there a few months ago... let's see, it was Selling Mortgaged Property... and he skipped out on 'em. Anyway, we knew about him already. He was here in Cortez and was acting a little strange."

"How's that?"

"Well, Cortez is a little town. Everyone knows everybody else. Harrison aroused suspicion because he kept his car hidden in the back of his house here. I know that sounds innocent enough but in a town like Cortez, that kind of behavior is, well, considered suspicious!"

"I understand. Go on."

"Well, his wife works at a bar in town but she's been livin' with another man for the past couple of months. She's got her kids with her. This other man, well, he's one of my deputies."

Barton blinked at that one.

"Anyway, we, the deputy and me, we went over to Harrison's house yesterday to arrest him and we found him in his bedroom bleedin' like hell. He'd been shot the night before and instead of goin' to the hospital, he went home!"

"How'd he get shot?"

"We don't really know," Dunham said. "We're still lookin' into that. Witnesses say Harrison was sittin' alone at a local bar and some guy just walked in and shot him in the stomach. Harrison fell to the ground and the shooter ran off. All we know is that he was a white guy. Anyway, we took Harrison to the hospital ourselves. They operated last night and he's gonna pull through fine."

Barton shook his head in amusement. "I can tell you that Gary Harrison was... still is... a major suspect in the disappearance of a Limite woman last summer. Her body's never been found. He's also the suspect in a number of similar abductions and in those cases the bodies *were* found. I think he's one bad cat."

"Well, we got that impression from the Posse people. We're gonna put a guard on his door at the hospital and hold him on that Selling Mortgaged Property charge. I'd appreciate it if you could forward any information on him to us."

"I'll do better than that," Barton said. "Me and my captain would like to come down there and see him ourselves. I think it's time we open up the talks with Gary Harrison again."

"Be our guest."

Barton hung up and stared at the wall a moment. It was covered with a few pieces of woodworking he had recently taken up as a hobby, as well as framed newspaper accounts of his exploits in Limite. There were other photos of him with fellow officers. One picture stood out-- it showed him, Mike Patton, and Ernie Jones shining flashlights on the body of Mary Parker, who had been found eleven months ago in an oil field northwest of town. Gary Harrison was a strong suspect in that case.

Barton called Captain Jones and told him they were going to take a trip to Cortez the next day and that he should prepare to stay a few days. Then, after careful consideration, Barton made a call to Guy Simms.

* * *

Sheriff Barton and Captain Jones arrived in town late on January 5 after a nearly nine hour drive.

The next morning, Buck Barton began a routine that became the norm for the several days that he and Captain Jones spent in Cortez talking with Gary Harrison. Harrison would only talk at night. He preferred to sleep during the day and was much more willing to reveal things about himself around three o'clock in the morning. Sheriff Dunham was happy to let Barton handle the prisoner, as he was of no mind to sit up nights interrogating Harrison.

Barton sat in Harrison's hospital room, just the two of them. They spent several nights this way, talking about all sorts of subjects. Captain Jones had to sit out in the waiting room and be ready to come in to take a statement if he was needed. Most of the time he slept on a couch. After a nightly session, Barton never revealed to Jones what was said in private.

"Well, did he say much?" Jones would ask.

"Nope," Barton would reply. He would go on to say that Harrison seemed on the verge of revealing something but then he would back off.

One night, Harrison requested to see Janice. In the room. Alone.

Barton thought it wouldn't do any harm. If it would loosen the prisoner's jaw, he was willing to try anything. Captain Jones thought it to be highly unusual.

Deputy Victor Lopez, the man with whom Janice was living, was ordered by Sheriff Dunham to leave town for a day or two. Janice, who still wore an eyepatch, didn't seem to have a problem with Gary's request. She wasn't surprised. He had followed her to Cortez and would do anything to get her back.

Jones and Barton made sure that the Harrisons had privacy by pulling the curtains around the bed and making sure no one entered the room. She stayed an entire night with him. Neither Barton nor Jones knew what went on in there, but they both could imagine.

It was not quite a week after they arrived in Cortez when Buck Barton told Jones to find him the highest mountain around. Then he wanted to be taken to it.

Perplexed, but not questioning his orders, Ernie found a modest hill outside of town and drove the Sheriff to it just before sundown.

"Ernie, you wait here. I'm gonna go talk to the Lord for a minute," Barton said, and then he proceeded to climb the hill.

Ernie Jones watched the sheriff ascend the rocks carefully. He got to the top in about fifteen minutes. It was about thirty minutes later when Barton began the descent. Once he was on the ground beside Jones, Barton dusted off his pants and said, "Ernie, before we leave, Gary's gonna tell me what we want to know."

That night, Barton allowed Janice to visit Gary again. He sat outside with Jones and silently chewed tobacco. He'd spit into a large coffee cup and keep it covered with a plastic lid.

Janice came to visit the next night as well. On the 12th she just showed up at the hospital when Barton and Jones did. This time, however, Buck Barton joined Gary and Janice in the room and was there until just after midnight. At that point, he called Jones in.

"Gary's gonna tell us where Kelly White is, Ernie," Barton said. "I want you to write down the directions so you can call Mike and tell him."

And while the four of them sat around the room, Gary Harrison gave a detailed description of where the body was in south Limite. After writing it down, Jones called and woke up Mike Patton and told him to get a team together to find her.

Two hours later, Patton called back and said they couldn't find the body. Apparently the instructions that Harrison gave were not accurate. For one thing, a paved road had been put in where it had been pasture three months earlier. Barton explained this to Harrison to see if he could be more specific. This time, Jones drew a map on the back of a paper towel as the prisoner tried one more time to direct the officers to the dumping site.

Another call was made to Limite and the waiting began again. Finally, just before dawn on the 13th, Patton called and said they'd found her.

Kelly White's skeleton was underneath an old mattress in a "wash," or gully, in a vacant lot where a lot of south Limite residents dumped trash. It wasn't far from a junior high school football stadium. It had been seven months and three days since her disappearance. As was reported later that day in the *Limite Observer*, the skeleton was still wearing the white button-down dress and electrical cords were tied around the neck, arms, and ankles. No weapon was found at the site.

On January 14 Gary Harrison was discharged from the hospital and Cortez authorities released him to the jurisdiction of Lucas County. Buck Barton and Ernie Jones escorted him to their car and began the long drive back to Limite. Janice remained in Cortez with her new man, Deputy Lopez.

The media met them in full force when they got back to Limite. At last, there was a murder charge against Gary Harrison for one of the West Texas women abduction/slayings. Sheriff Dunham in Cortez was interviewed, who went on the record to say that he had never seen someone as energetic as Sheriff Buck Barton.

"I'll bet he hasn't had three hours sleep in the past three days," he said. "He put everything he had into the case and I think it's only by his perseverance that he got Harrison to talk."

Over the next several days, a few more witnesses to the June kidnapping came forward. Now that Harrison had been arrested, others were willing to talk.

A black roughneck from the trailer park reported seeing Harrison's red Chevy at Wynn's Mobile Village around 11:45 a.m. on June 10 of 1973. A black man who hung out at the burn barrel in the Flats remembered that he saw Gary Harrison leave Pal's that evening with a "long, slender object wrapped in red tablecloths." He put the object in the open trunk of a blue Bonneville backed against the front door of the club, and then drove away toward Mississippi Avenue. Harrison returned about an hour later and went into the club.

A man who lived near the Flats said that Harrison had come to his house around noon on the 10th of June to borrow a steak knife. He never returned it.

On January 19, 1974, the Lucas County Grand Jury returned an indictment of Murder With Malice against Gary Harrison in the Kelly White case. The judge denied bond.

That night, Buck Barton celebrated by taking his wife to see the new Clint Eastwood movie playing at the Parkview Cinema. It was *Magnum Force*, a modern thriller with Eastwood as "Dirty Harry." Barton enjoyed it and he identified with the character's law enforcement tactics.

But he would rather have seen a western.

* * *

The weeks dragged on as a trial for Gary Harrison was scheduled and re-scheduled. He remained in Lucas County Jail, isolated from the rest of the prisoners.

One evening in February, Buck Barton left his desk and told Mike Patton that he was going to the airport.

"What for?" Patton asked.

"I gotta pick up someone," Barton said, then left without elaborating.

Patton shrugged, picked up some paperwork, and strolled over to the detention unit. He passed Ernie Jones on the way.

"You know who Buck's meetin' at the airport?" Patton asked.

"Yeah," Jones said.

"Well, who?"

"A visitor for Harrison. You'll see." Jones grinned and walked on.

What the hell? Patton thought. He went on his way and eventually found himself near Harrison's cell. While he was there, he thought he'd look in on the prisoner.

Gary was pacing the quarters, excited about something.

"Hey, Gary, what's up?" Patton asked.

Harrison stopped abruptly and stared at Patton. Then, very slowly, he began to grin. "I got a visitor comin'," he said.

Patton frowned, then asked the guard on duty who was coming. The guard didn't know anything except that Harrison was to have an overnight visitor.

"Overnight? Are you kiddin' me?"

"No, sir," the guard said.

"Who authorized that?"

"Sheriff Barton, sir."

Patton started to speak but they heard the outer doors open.

"I think that's him, sir," the guard said, walking away from Patton to greet the sheriff.

Patton remained where he was. He heard Buck's voice in the hallway and the guard's muffled reply. The door opened and the guard returned, holding it open for Barton and a woman.

It was Janice Harrison. She was carrying an overnight bag and appeared to be exhausted. Nevertheless, Patton thought she looked great. He knew that all the other men in the place were attracted to her as well. There was something about the eyepatch that made her even more exotic.

Patton watched in amazement as the sheriff led her back to the cells.

* * *

The weeks passed. On April 15, 1974, Gary Harrison was moved to Austin on a Change of Venue motion put forth by his attorney. It was argued that the widespread publicity in the case would prohibit Harrison from receiving a fair trial. His date in court was ultimately set for November.

Sheriff Barton received a call from the Austin authorities a few days later on April 21. Gary Harrison wanted to talk to him some more.

Barton sat in his chair and rubbed his chin. This could get tricky. Was Harrison about to confess to more murders? Damn it, he thought. He was afraid this would happen. He belched loudly and threw a wad of paper at the trashcan across the room. He missed.

The next morning, he and Ernie Jones flew to Austin. When they got to the county jail, Barton asked the jailers if Harrison had received many visitors.

"No, sir," a guard said. "But his wife came to visit yesterday. It wasn't pleasant."

"What do you mean?"

"She filed divorce papers on him. He wasn't happy about that."

Barton nodded, then he and Jones met with Gary Harrison in his cell.

"Sheriff," Harrison said. "I got some things I want to clear up. I'm ready to make a full confession on this Kelly White thing. And I've got something to tell you about Grace Daniel, too."

"Are you sure, Gary?" Barton asked. "I understand Janice was here yesterday."

Harrison nodded, "Yeah but that don't matter. What I have to say involves her, too."

"You remember what we talked about in Cortez last January?" Barton asked.

Harrison considered this a moment, then said, "Yeah."

"You still want to talk to us?"

"Yeah," Harrison said, looking Barton straight in the eyes. "I do."

"All right, Gary," the sheriff said. "Go ahead then."

Harrison proceeded to give two confessions that Ernie Jones transcribed. One admitted guilt in the slaying of Kelly White. The other implicated Janice as an accomplice in the abduction and murder of Grace Daniel.

The Kelly White confession was straight-forward and pretty much how the lawmen thought it was. Harrison told Barton that on June 10 he had gone to Wynn's Mobile Village to see if his wife had left any messages there for him. She had been gone for two months, having left him to work in Posse. Harrison said he saw Kelly White in the office there and "in his mind," thought she was Janice. He pulled a knife on her and told her that she had to "come home to the children." She resisted, he struck her, and then carried her to the car. He admitted taking her to Pal's and binding her with electrical cord. He kept her in the storage room for several hours, trying to decide what to do with her. He thought about using black shoe polish to disguise himself as a black man when he hid her body. At one point she broke out of the closet but he caught her and put her back in. He claimed he never raped her. After the exchange of cars with Greg Walker, he found her unconscious in the closet. He carried her out to the trunk, wrapped in red tablecloths, then drove south on Mississippi Avenue to the vacant lot. There, he strangled her to death and left her body underneath a rotting mattress.

The Grace Daniel confession was more complicated and the contents were not released to the public. But everyone close to the case knew the gist of it. Harrison claimed that Grace Daniel was a prostitute who worked with Janice out of the Washington Hotel. One night in October 1970, he and Janice saw her in the laundrymat near where they lived. They brought her back to their house, where they robbed her and then used her for their sexual pleasure. Afterwards, he held the gun on her while Janice strangled her with a nylon hose.

A little later in the day, Gary Harrison was brought before the District Judge. There, he pled guilty to the murder of Kelly White. The judge sentenced Harrison to life in prison.

When he asked him if Harrison had anything to say, Gary nodded.

"I just wanted to let you know for the record that I plan to appeal the life sentence."

Buck Barton thought the guy was nuts.

By the end of the day on April 22, both Gary and Janice Harrison were charged with the murder of Grace Daniel.

* * *

Gary Harrison was brought back to Limite on April 24. He was officially charged in Lucas County with two counts of Murder With Malice, one for Kelly White, and one for Grace Daniel.

Janice Harrison was arrested in Cortez. Sheriff Barton spoke to Sheriff Dunham about the turn of events.

"Well, sir, she's highly upset about these charges," Dunham said over the phone. "She denies any knowledge of that murder. She's pretty emphatic about it. My deputy, Lopez, he believes her."

"He's sleepin' with her, too," Barton reminded him.

"Yeah, I know, but I trust the man. He's been with me for over ten years."

"I'm not so sure I'd trust his judgement in women," Barton said. "What else does she say?"

"Nothin' much, except she's cussin' up a storm, callin' your man Harrison all kinds of names," Dunham said. "Deputy Lopez is arranging a lawyer for her. There's supposed to be a bail hearin' later today."

"Call me back on how that goes, will you?"

"Sure will, Buck."

Barton left his office and went out to where the media had gathered in force. Newspapermen from all over the state had descended upon Limite after the word that the notorious "Oil Field Killer," as he was now called, had been caught.

"Sheriff, did Gary Harrison really do it?"

"Sheriff Barton, do you think Harrison killed Mary Parker, too?"

"What about Susan Powell? Did he kill her?"

Barton held up his hands. "I can't talk to you boys right now," he said. "We don't know nothin' about anything except what Harrison's already confessed. Now, excuse me."

He pushed his way past the reporters and made his way to the detention area. They had Harrison locked in a private cell, away from the run-of-the-mill criminals who were in jail for being drunk and disorderly or other misdemeanors.

Barton found Harrison is relatively good spirits.

"How are ya feelin', Gary?" he asked him.

"Fine, Buck," Harrison said. They had been on a first-name basis for quite some time now.

"How's the gunshot wound?"

"Healed up pretty good."

"No idea who shot you?"

"Come on, sheriff, you know who shot me."

"I do?"

"Never mind. Nah, I don't know who the fuck it was."

Barton stared at the prisoner. "Your wife's been arrested in Cortez."

Harrison shrugged. "Serves her right."

"Did she really help you in that killing?"

"I said so, didn't I?"

"Well, you can always say so but it don't mean you told the truth. She's callin' you a liar."

"That's nothin' new."

"Well, we'll see what happens..."

Barton left the jail and went back to his office.

Later that afternoon, Sheriff Dunham called back.

"Janice Harrison was released on bond," he told Barton. "It was twenty-five thousand. Deputy Lopez put up the money. She's not to leave town."

"Good," Barton said. "Keep an eye on her."

As soon as he hung up, the phone rang again. It was Lucky Farrow.

"Howdy, Lucky."

"How ya doin', Buck?"

"Can't complain."

"How about that Gary Harrison, huh?"

"What about him?"

"Well, Guy tells me that he's startin' to talk."

"It looks that way."

"How do you feel about that?"

"Well, Lucky, we've got a lot of unsolved murders on our hands."

"I appreciate that, but don't you think--?"

Barton interrupted him. "Now, hush, Lucky. Let me handle it, all right?"

"But what if he--?"

"I gotta go, Lucky. I'll see you tonight."

Farrow knew when he shouldn't press the sheriff. "All right."

Barton hung up the phone. Sometimes he wondered about the company he kept. He didn't know if they were simply ignorant or just plain stupid.

* * *

It was 2:30 in the morning on the 25th when Barton was jolted awake by the phone. His wife Naomi grumbled next to him in the bed.

He grabbed the receiver and said, "Yeah?"

"Buck? It's Mike."

The chief deputy had night duty. "What is it?"

"It's Harrison. He wants to talk to you."

"What for?"

"Hell if I know. He says it's important, that you gotta come down to the jail now."

Shit, Barton thought. Here we go again. Why did that dumb bastard like to keep late hours?

"All right, tell him I'll be there in a half-hour." He hung up and got out of bed.

"Where you goin', Buck?" Naomi asked.

"Go back to sleep, dear," he said. "I gotta go down to the jail."

When he got there, he found Gary Harrison and Mike Patton in the cell, drinking coffee and telling dirty jokes.

"Well, if it ain't Buck Barton, a hero and a gentleman!" Harrison said.

"Mornin', Gary," Barton said.

"I hope I didn't get you out of bed."

"You did. When the hell else do you think I sleep?"

"Sorry, Buck. I thought you might want to know something."

"What's that, Gary?"

"Me and Janice killed Mary Parker."

Barton took a deep breath. "You want to make a confession?"

"I sure do. Better call your man in here."

"Don't call Ernie," Patton said. "Let him sleep. I'll take down the confession."

"All right."

By the time the sun had risen, Gary Harrison confessed to the murder of Mary Parker. Again, the details were kept from the public but the contents were well-known in the law enforcement circles. On the night of January 2, 1973, Janice had left their house in Limite to bring back a couple for a wife-swapping party. She returned an hour later-- but only with Mary Parker, whom they knew from previous such get-togethers. They apparently went too far, for Janice ended up strangling Mary to death on their bed.

Barton delivered a copy of the confession to the D.A. at 9:00 sharp. The Grand Jury was scheduled to meet at 10:00.

At 1:00 p.m., they returned two murder indictments against Gary and Janice Harrison for the murders of Grace Daniel and Mary Parker.

By the end of the day, the reporters had flocked around the sheriff's office once again. Buck Barton returned from the courthouse and pushed his way through the crowd.

"Sheriff, are the Harrisons the new Bonnie and Clyde?"

"Has Harrison confessed to any of the other murders?"

"Can you tell us what was in the Parker confession?"

Barton held up his hands once again. "Sorry, boys, the confession is not public information. All you need to know is that he implicated his wife in the murder. He hasn't said anything else."

"Where is his wife?" one man asked.

"Janice Harrison is in Cortez, Texas. She's been placed under arrest but is free on bond. She ain't goin' anywhere."

"Did you know she was a killer?"

Barton said, "Now, every man and woman is innocent until proven guilty in a court of law, you know that. But in answer to your question, yes, I've been aware for several months that Janice Harrison was involved in the killings. That's all I'm going to say."

Barton left the crowd and made it to his office. He looked at his messages and saw one from Guy Simms. He could guess what that one was about. Barton elected not to return the call just yet.

* * *

On the afternoon of April 27, Sheriff Barton stormed into Gary Harrison's cell, waving a piece of paper, followed by Ernie Jones.

"Gary? Wake up. I want to talk to you."

The prisoner was asleep. He slowly stirred, sat up, and rubbed his eyes.

"Hi, Buck," he mumbled. "What time is it?"

"Never mind. Do you know what this is?"

Harrison took the paper and looked at it. He squinted and registered incomprehension.

"It's an affidavit from your wife. We just got it from her lawyer in Cortez. She says that you're making all that up about her helping you with those murders because she filed for divorce. She says you're just gettin' back at her."

"That's horseshit and she knows it," Harrison retorted.

"Is it? Listen, Gary," Barton said. "If you're lyin' about this, you can get in even more trouble. You better think real hard about this."

"Well, the bitch is tryin' to divorce me!"

"So what! You're goin' to jail for the rest of your life!"

"Not if my appeal goes through," Harrison said.

"Maybe she don't want to be with you anymore, Gary."

"She can't take my kids away from me." Harrison's voice shook when he said it. Barton could see right through the guy. The man was indeed trying to hurt his wife by accusing her of the crimes.

"Gary, you don't have a helluva lot of choice in the matter," Barton said gently.

The prisoner sat and stared at the sheriff. Ernie Jones watched the two of them as they silently communicated. He knew that something had transpired in Cortez back in January when Barton interrogated him in the hospital. Whatever it was, it now meant something to the two of them.

Finally, Harrison said, "Maybe I'll just have to talk about some more of your unsolved murders."

Barton grabbed Harrison by the collar and pulled him off the bunk. Jones couldn't believe what he was seeing.

"Listen, you little shit," Barton said. "I've done nothin' but gone to bat for you. Now you better use whatever bit of brains you got in that skull of yours and think about this before you say another word. I want you to think about what you've said regarding Janice. If it ain't true, you'd better come clean. And before you go spouting off more lies, you'd better take a good look at your ass, because you may not have one to sit on afterwards."

With that, the sheriff released him and made Jones open the cell door.

Three days later, Harrison called for the sheriff, Jones, and D.A. Rusty Franklin to visit him in the cell.

"All right," he told them. "Janice had nothin' to do with those murders. I did 'em myself."

"Gary," Franklin asked, "are you willing to make new, revised confessions in those cases?"

"Yes, sir. Oh, and another thing... I also killed Barbara Lewis."

There was a intake of breath by all three men standing over Harrison.

"Gary..." Barton began.

"No, sheriff, I want to get this off my chest," Harrison said. "I also killed that barmaid, Tina Lee Peters."

"Shit," Barton muttered under his breath. He turned to Jones and said, "Take his goddamned statements." Then he turned and left the room.

Three hours later, Gary Harrison signed revised confessions relating to Grace Daniel and Mary Parker, as well as new confessions for the slayings of Barbara Lewis and Tina Lee Peters.

Lawmen knew what the confessions contained, even though the public didn't. Harrison claimed that Barbara Lewis was a whore house madam who had employed his wife for a while. She owed them nearly a thousand dollars and he had decided one night to get it from her. He had gone to the Cowboy Courts Motel around 4:00 in the morning on October 29, 1970. He banged on Mrs. Lewis' door until she finally got up and let him in. She was furious for being awakened so early but Harrison pulled a .32 on her to shut her up. He bound and gagged the woman after making her tell him where she hid the cash box. He robbed her of all the money, which was "around $500," then shot Mrs. Lewis in the head. He left quickly and never looked back. As part of the confession, Harrison drew an accurate map of Mrs. Lewis' apartment, indicating where everything was.

As for Tina Lee Peters, Harrison stated that he knew the barmaid from the Tempest Club. He had always found her attractive and wanted a date with her. It was the "day after the 4th of July in 1972," when he followed her home one night from the club without her knowing it. He sat in his car in the parking lot of the Hillview Apartments, where she lived, and watched her go into her place. He got out of the car, holding a steak knife at his side. He knocked on her door. When Mrs. Peters realized she knew the visitor, she opened the door. Harrison burst in and threatened her with the knife. When she refused to give him any money, he got rough and hit her a couple of times. She ended up on the bed, where he claimed he strangled her with a telephone cord.

The city police investigator in charge of the two cases, Detective Bobby Gibson, didn't like Harrison's version of this story, because Tina Lee Peters had been stabbed to death, not strangled. She was also found nude.

Harrison went on to revise his stories on the earlier confessions. He admitted that he alone forced Grace Daniel out to his car. They drove out of town, where he pulled off onto a gravel county road. He admitted raping the woman, then strangling her with a nylon hose.

On the night of January 2, 1973, Harrison stated that he was sitting in his car in the Moonlight nightclub parking lot when he noticed Mary Parker drive up and park in front of the building. On impulse, he jumped out and confronted her before she could get out of her car. He opened the door, took her by force, and put her in his own car. He drove out of town and pulled off onto a gravel road, where they had "sexual relations." He then strangled her with a nylon stocking. After she was dead, he left her body there and drove home.

D.A. Franklin assembled the Grand Jury that afternoon. Harrison appeared before them and exonerated his wife in the murders of Grace Daniel and Mary Parker. He admitted that he had implicated her in the earlier confessions because she had threatened him with divorce.

Then he said something that startled everyone. Harrison told the Grand Jury that he had actually been *hired* to kill Barbara Lewis and Tina Lee Peters because they had "made some enemies." He said that his instructions had come through intermediaries and didn't know who was behind the orders.

When Sheriff Barton heard about that, he hit the roof.

* * *

Buck Barton and Gary Harrison's lawyers allowed *Limite Observer* reporter Robert Clifton to interview the prisoner at length in his cell. The results were published in the May 3, 1974, edition.

"I believe that if I'm tried, I'll get the death penalty," Harrison said. "That's why I pleaded guilty to Kelly White's murder."

"Are you planning to plead guilty to the other murders you've confessed to?" Clifton asked.

"I haven't decided. My attorney will advise me. I've made confessions. I admit it. I killed all five of those women and you can print it that way. I'll go to the penitentiary. Maybe I'll get out on parole in ten years but it's probably gonna be more like thirty or forty years."

"What made you do it?"

"Why'd I do it? There are many people inside of me. What drives me is something you could never understand. My mind is constantly in conflict. Part of me wants one thing and another part wants another. I can't control it. I've always been that way. Two of the killings were work-for-hire. Limite has a serious mob problem, did you know that?"

D.A. Rusty Franklin read the interview and shook his head. He was sitting with Buck Barton in the courthouse talking about the case and the various confessions.

With them was city cop Detective Bobby Gibson. He had been in charge of the Barbara Lewis and Tina Lee Peters cases, since the bodies had been found within Limite city limits.

"This confession on Peters just doesn't gel," he said. "The woman was stabbed to death, not strangled."

"Why would he confess to it if he didn't do it?" Franklin asked. "And what's this shit about being 'hired' to do it?"

"Beats me," Gibson said. "Do you know, Buck?"

Barton shrugged. "The guy's looney as a tumbleweed. I think he just wants the attention. I don't think he killed that girl. I'm not sure about Barbara Lewis, either."

"Me neither," Gibson concurred.

"Why not?" Franklin asked.

Gibson replied, "Because she was shot with a thirty-eight caliber pistol, not a thirty-two, which is what Harrison claims he used."

"So? He probably doesn't know the difference."

"I don't know, Rusty," Gibson said, shaking his head.

"Well, what about the map of the apartment he drew? Everything was in the right place. Wasn't it?"

"Yeah, but he could have drawn that from memory. He could have been in there before the murder. His wife did work for the lady."

"I wouldn't call her a lady," Barton said, chuckling.

"Have you asked him about Susan Powell or the Saldañas?" Franklin asked.

"Yes," Barton said, quickly. "He says he don't know nothin' about them."

"Keep at him," Franklin said. "I've given six more counties permission to come talk to him. Seems like everyone and his dog is coming out of the woodwork to interview Harrison about unsolved murders. You'd think he's been doin' nothin' but killin' people all his life."

"How many cases do you think he might be responsible for?" Gibson asked.

"Right now the count is up to twenty-eight," Franklin replied. "Every day I get another call. There was a concentration of abduction/murders in the San Antonio area around the time Harrison was there. Before he came to Limite, there were some missing women in New Mexico and Oklahoma. I think the guy's a sex pervert, that's what he is. All of those women were probably raped."

"I agree," Barton said.

"Wait a minute," Gibson said. "Those women were found in the fields partially clothed, at least."

Barton said, "The fact that they had *any* of their clothing missing indicates that his motivation was sexually oriented. The guy's a sex maniac. Hell, you've seen the witness interviews. You know what his wife did for a living. He gets off on strangling women while he's havin' sex with 'em. The guy is one sick son of a bitch. He's evil."

"Which is why I have doubts about the Lewis and Peters cases. The evidence don't match the others," Gibson said. "I'm just not sure about 'em, Rusty."

The discussion continued over the next few days while lawmen from other parts of Texas, New Mexico, and Oklahoma came to Limite to talk with Harrison in his cell. But it seemed he was through revealing things. He wouldn't say a word to any of them. He also stubbornly refused to talk to the sheriff when Barton attempted to speak to him. Nevertheless, Rusty Franklin was ready to go to the Grand Jury with the Lewis and Peters confessions. He had seen all the evidence in the cases and was convinced he could get convictions, even if the confessions were "slightly inaccurate."

On May 11, Janice Harrison was cleared of all charges against her by the District Judge. She gave a brief statement to the Cortez newspaper, saying that she planned to get a divorce and then marry Deputy Lopez. She would have custody of the two children. Then, perhaps, she could put her past behind her and look forward to the future.

Reporters interviewed Detective Gibson on May 12 but he declined to say whether or not Harrison would be indicted for the Lewis and Peters murders.

"We're not so sure he really did it," Gibson said. "We do know that Janice Harrison worked for Barbara Lewis at one time, though. We're still investigating."

On May 28, Gary Harrison was brought before the Grand Jury to testify in the Lewis and Peters cases. Rusty Franklin argued strongly in favor of indictment but the testimony of Detective Gibson and other investigators aroused enough reasonable doubt that the Grand Jury, in the end, elected not to indict Harrison for the two murders. What really clinched it for them was Harrison's claim that he had been "hired" to kill the women. They just couldn't buy that.

The same day, Harrison was brought into District Court to make a plea in the Grace Daniel and Mary Parker cases. Everyone, including Buck Barton, expected him to plead guilty. His attorney had even forewarned the D.A. that Harrison planned to do so.

The judge went through the standard legal admonishments, then asked Harrison how he pleaded in the murder of Grace Daniel.

Harrison stood up and surprised every person in the room by saying, "Not guilty!"

The judge asked how he pleaded in the murder of Mary Parker.

"Not guilty!"

As he was led away, Franklin silently cursed. He was hoping he wouldn't have to go to trial on the cases but now it looked inevitable. At least they had confessions, which made the job a lot easier. Harrison's attorneys had also appealed the life sentence he had received for the Kelly White slaying, which meant even more work.

The next day, Gary Harrison was officially charged with two more counts of Murder With Malice. His picture appeared on the front page of almost every major newspaper in Texas. Harrison *was* the "Oil Field Killer," and he seemed to like the attention. He was a celebrity now. When the prisoner was moved to Austin on June 22 on another change of venue motion, Sheriff Barton had to use a four-man team to escort Harrison so that he could be protected from the hordes of media personnel who wanted a piece of him.

BUCK

The paperwork crossed his desk in August. Buck Barton looked at it and winced. Gary Harrison's lawyers had arranged for a pre-trial hearing in Austin. Harrison was now claiming that his confessions had been coerced and were made under duress. The hearing was tentatively scheduled for September 5.

"Goddamn it to hell," he muttered. He picked up the phone and called Rusty Franklin.

"Rusty, you've seen this shit about a pre-trial hearing for Harrison?" he asked the D.A.

"Buck! How are you? Yeah, I've seen it. I was gonna call you this afternoon."

"What's this all about?"

"Well, it's in the report, Buck," Franklin said. "Harrison claims that last January you coerced him into revealing where Kelly White's body was and that the further confessions were made against his will."

"Aww, Jesus, that's a damned lie!"

"Well, of course it is but we're gonna have to prove it. You'll be able to testify?"

"Damn right I can."

"What about Captain Jones?"

"He'll be there."

"I'll make sure Gibson is there, too."

Barton hung up the phone and went to the men's room, passing Mike Patton on the way.

"Harrison says we coerced the confessions out of him," Barton said.

Patton wrinkled his brow. "That don't make sense."

"That nut'll try anything to delay the inevitable." He shook his head and went on.

Barton entered the restroom and looked at himself in the mirror before stepping up to the urinal. He was gaining weight at an alarming rate. Too much Mexican food. If he didn't watch it, he'd end up like his two brothers. They both had bad hearts and one had been briefly hospitalized.

He was supposed to meet Guy Simms and Lucky Farrow at the hotel that night but Barton thought he'd reschedule the meeting. He was pissed off at them. It was their fault that he was in this mess with Gary Harrison, he thought. Now everything was completely fucked up.

If he got out of this without tarnishing his reputation, it would be a miracle.

* * *

The hearing took place in Austin on September 5, as planned. District Judge Roy Kennilworth presided over the matter. Present were the defendant and his attorneys, Sheriff Barton, Captain Jones, D.A. Franklin, and Detective Bobby Gibson.

Barton was called to the stand by Bill Childs, Harrison's lead attorney. The sheriff was dressed in full uniform and exhibited an authoritative, commanding presence. When he spoke, his voice boomed in the small courtroom. There was no mistaking that Buck Barton was a giant of a man.

"Sheriff," Childs began, "can you tell the court in your own words what went on in Cortez City Hospital last January of 1974 between you and the defendant?"

Barton proceeded to tell his side of the story. "We had several unsolved murders in Limite and Gary Harrison was a suspect in them. He was a major suspect in one, the Kelly White case, and we felt we had a pretty good case against him-- but we didn't have the body. I received a call from Sheriff Dunham in Cortez that Harrison was in the hospital there, so Captain Jones and I made the trip to go and talk to him. At first, Gary didn't want to talk but I was persistent and patient. We spent several nights in a row, talking in his hospital room. I finally persuaded him to tell me where Kelly White's body was."

"And how did you do that?"

Barton shrugged. "Just by talkin'. He finally saw that he wasn't gonna get out of it and that he was caught."

"Was it true he had been shot?"

"Yes, sir."

"Do you know who shot him?"

"No, sir."

"Mr. Harrison claims that someone you knew shot him."

"I'm completely unaware of that. I have no idea who shot him."

"Sheriff, did you allow the defendant's wife, Janice Harrison, to visit him in the hospital room?"

"Yes, I did."

"Why did you do that?"

"He asked for it. I thought if it would help loosen his tongue, then I didn't see the harm. This was before she had been charged with anything."

"Is it true that Mr. and Mrs. Harrison had sex in the hospital room the nights she visited?"

"I have no idea. I wasn't in the room."

Childs consulted his notes. "According to Mr. Harrison," he said, "you paid thirty-five hundred dollars to the defendant."

"That's correct."

"Why did you do that?"

"There was a reward that had been put up by Wynn Mobile Village, as well as by myself, out of my own pocket, for information leading to the whereabouts of Kelly White's body."

"So you paid the reward money to the defendant?"

"No, sir."

"You didn't?"

"No, sir."

"Who did you give it to?"

"I gave it to his wife, Janice."

"Why did you give it to her? Did she provide the information?"

"No, sir. Gary Harrison said that he would tell me where Kelly White's body was if I made sure his wife and kids were taken care of. I didn't see how I could do that unless I offered the reward money to him. It really went to her, but I guess you could say that he got the reward money for tellin' us where the body was."

"That's highly irregular, isn't it, sheriff?"

"I was determined to find that body," Barton said sternly.

"Is it true that you flew Mrs. Harrison from Cortez to Limite several times between January and April, when Mr. Harrison was in Lucas County Jail?"

"Yes, sir."

"Where did the money for that come from?"

"It came from a fund that is supplied by the city for purposes of travel expenses related to cases."

"Who authorized you to do that?"

"No one. I have the authority to use it any way I see fit."

"Why did you allow Mrs. Harrison to have overnight visits with her husband in jail?"

"Again, I thought if Gary got some things he wanted, then we'd get some things we wanted."

"Isn't it true, sheriff, that you made a deal with the defendant? That you promised Mr. Harrison special treatment and favors in return for confessions?"

"No, that's not true. I never promised him anything."

Childs consulted his notes, then asked, "Sheriff, how did Mr. Harrison reveal where the body was?"

"I beg your pardon?"

"How did he lead you to the body?"

"He gave directions, and then Captain Jones relayed them over the phone to my chief deputy in Limite, Mike Patton."

"You didn't already know where the body was?"

"Of course not!"

"Sheriff, did you give Mrs. Harrison some money to buy a used car?"

"Yes, sir, I did. It was a loan, actually, but she never paid it back."

"How much was that?"

"Uhm, three hundred dollars, I believe."

"Was that part of the deal you made with Mr. Harrison?"

"There weren't any deals made."

"It sure sounds like a deal was made to me!"

D. A. Franklin stood up. "Objection, your honor."

"Sustained," Judge Kennilworth said.

The testimony didn't look good. After a short recess, Captain Jones testified, which proved to be utterly useless. Since he had not been privy to anything that had gone on in the hospital room, there wasn't much he could say. He did concur that Mrs. Harrison had visited the defendant in the Limite jail "two or three times."

"And what was the purpose of those visits, Captain Jones?" Childs asked.

Jones shrugged in his good-old-boy way. "I imagine that they had sexual relations. That's just my opinion."

"Did Sheriff Barton promise Mr. Harrison such visits in exchange for confessions?"

"Not that I know of."

Detective Bobby Gibson testified to interviewing Harrison several times in his cell in Limite. He admitted knowledge of Janice Harrison's visits, but didn't think it was unusual.

"You didn't think it unusual for a confessed murderer to get an overnight visit in jail from his wife?" Childs asked.

"No, it's not the first time." Gibson went on to explain that it's a common practice in some small towns. Things were "looser."

"Are you aware, Mr. Gibson, of Mr. Harrison being mistreated in any way?"

"No, sir."

After lunch, Gary Harrison was put on the stand. He was dressed in a new suit and tie, the first time Barton had ever seen him wearing more than blue jeans and a work shirt.

"Mr. Harrison," Childs began, "what happened in Cortez when Sheriff Barton came to visit you in the hospital?"

Harrison cleared his throat. "We'd sit up at night and talk about a lot of things. My childhood, his childhood. He talked a lot about the war. We talked about our kids, that kind of thing. He was trying to be friendly, I guess."

"Did he ever ask you about the Limite murders?"

"Oh, sure. Lots of times. I kept tellin' him I didn't know anything about 'em."

"But you eventually told him where Kelly White's body was hidden?"

"Well, not exactly."

"Could you elaborate on that, Mr. Harrison?"

"Sheriff Barton knew where the body was. In fact, he had the directions to where she was written down on a piece of paper. There was a map drawn on a paper towel. He wanted me to read off the directions, just as he had written them, and say that I was the one who came up with the directions."

Barton and Franklin looked at each other with incredulity.

"Lyin' son of a bitch," Barton muttered.

"So it's your testimony that you simply repeated what Sheriff Barton wanted you to say?" Childs asked.

"That's right."

"Mr. Harrison, who shot you in Cortez?"

"I don't know who it was, but I'm pretty sure it was someone workin' for Sheriff Barton."

Franklin stood up. "Objection! Your honor, this is outrageous!"

The judge nodded. "Counsel approach the bench." Both Childs and Franklin stepped up to the judge, where they whispered animatedly for a few minutes. When they were done, the judge said, "Objection sustained." The questioning resumed.

"Mr. Harrison, did Sheriff Barton promise you anything in return for confessions?"

"Yes, sir, he did."

"What was that?"

"Well, he wanted me to confess to the Kelly White murder really bad. That was the one I guess he wanted to close the most. He offered me the reward money if I would take the fall for the murder and relay the directions to the body. He knew my family was desperate for money and it was quite a temptation. I guess I was willing to go to prison for a while so that my family could get back on their feet. He promised that I wouldn't get the death penalty."

"And what was the amount of the reward money?"

"Thirty-five-hundred dollars."

"And he paid you that money?"

"No, he gave it to Janice, my wife."

"Mr. Harrison, did Sheriff Barton promise you visits by your wife in Limite?"

"Yes, sir, he did."

"That was part of the deal?"

"Yes, sir."

Franklin jumped up again. "Objection! The use of the word 'deal' is inappropriate and--"

"Sustained," the judge said, interrupting him. "Go on."

"How were you treated in the Limite jail?" Childs asked.

"Well, at first, I was livin' like a prince. I got everything I wanted."

"And what happened when your wife came to visit?"

"They'd tape up some blankets over the bars of the cell so we could have some privacy."

"And did you and your wife engage in sexual relations in the jail cell?"

"Yes, sir."

"What else did you do?"

"Just talked about business and our family situation."

"You said 'at first' you lived like a prince. What happened to change that?"

"The visits stopped before I was transferred to Austin in June. Actually they stopped around April. Then, one night, before I was moved to Austin in June, two or three deputies came into the cell and beat me up."

"Why did they do that?"

"They wanted me to confess to more of the murders."

"Do you know their names?"

"No, sir. I'd never seen 'em before."

"They were wearing deputy uniforms?"

"No, sir."

"They were civilians?" Childs asked.

"They were dressed like civilians."

"Who let them in?"

"The jailer."

"No further questions."

While waiting on the judge's decision, Franklin and Barton stood outside the courthouse. Barton stuffed a wad of Redman into his mouth and scowled.

"This don't look too good," Franklin said. "What a lying piece of work."

"He wasn't very convincing," Barton commented.

"No, he wasn't. I just hope the judge thought so, too."

They were summoned back into the courtroom thirty minutes later. Judge Kennilworth called the proceedings to order and said, "I'm not going to make a ruling on the validity of Mr. Harrison's confessions at this time. Mr. Harrison's trial for the murders of Grace Daniel and Mary Parker is scheduled for November third. I would like to resume this hearing shortly before then. In the meantime, I suggest that both parties gather relevant evidence and witnesses to corroborate your cases. I cannot make a fair assessment of all this on testimony alone."

He banged the gavel and it was over. For a while.

* * *

The rest of the summer passed without incident. It was over a hundred degrees, the usual suspects were arrested for raising hell and stacking the joints, and Buck Barton counted the days before Gary Harrison's pre-trial hearing resumed.

It wasn't that he was afraid of anything. It was simply that he hated to be made to look foolish. Gary Harrison had made him look foolish. The hearing in September was reported in the paper. The public knew that something odd had gone on between the sheriff and the Harrisons in January of 1974. Perhaps it was his imagination, but Barton thought his fellow officers and colleagues seemed to treat him differently now. It was as if he had somehow pulled the wool over their eyes.

Damn you, Harrison, he thought. What kind of trick are you going to pull next time?

Barton found out soon enough when the hearing resumed on November 1 in Austin. The same people were present, except that Janice Harrison, now Janice Lopez, was there to testify.

As soon as the proceedings began, however, Bill Childs requested that they be allowed to present physical evidence proving that Gary Harrison had been coerced into making confessions. The judge agreed. Childs called Harrison to stand. Today the prisoner wasn't wearing a suit; he had on a loose-fitting white dress shirt and trousers.

"Mr. Harrison, would you remove your shirt, please?"

Franklin, clearly bewildered, stood and said, "Objection, your honor?"

"Your honor, as you know, I'm about to display physical evidence of abuse to my client," Childs said.

"Objection overruled," the judge said. "You can remove your shirt," he said to Harrison.

Harrison did so. Everyone noticed red marks on his upper arms.

"Mr. Harrison, what's that on your upper arms?" Childs asked.

"They're scars."

"How were they done?"

"With a lit cigarette."

"Who did this to you?"

What Harrison said caused everyone in the room to gasp aloud. "Detective Bobby Gibson and three other deputies."

"And when did they do this?"

"The day before I was transferred from Limite to Austin. June twenty-first, 1974."

"Why did they do it?"

"They wanted me to plead guilty to all the murders."

"How did they do it?"

"They came in and held me down. I don't remember who actually did the burning, maybe they took turns. I was in agony."

Franklin stood and said, "Your honor, I object! This is ridiculous!"

Several people spoke at once until the judge banged the gavel. The judge spoke to the lawyers at the bench. Barton sat there in disbelief and anger. He glared at Harrison, who eventually met his eye. Harrison stared back, then grinned slyly.

It was no use. The judge allowed Harrison's condition to be noted for the record and had a bailiff take Polaroid pictures of the wounds.

Of course, Bobby Gibson testified that he never touched Gary Harrison in his cell. He did admit to getting into a fist fight with the prisoner one day when Harrison started it for no reason. The guards had to pull Harrison off of him. This had occurred shortly before Harrison's transfer to Austin.

After a short recess, Janice Harrison Lopez took the stand. She was dressed in a tight, black dress that was more suited to dinner out on a Saturday night. She looked gorgeous and exuded a blatant sexuality that caught the attention of every male in the room.

D. A. Franklin began the questioning. "Mrs. Lopez, you were married to the defendant, Gary Harrison?"

"That's right."

"How long were you married?"

"Fifteen years."

"When did you get divorced?"

"In June."

"And when did you marry your present husband?"

"Three weeks ago."

"Mrs. Lopez, you were still married to Gary Harrison in January of this year, is that correct?"

"Yes, sir."

"Tell us what happened in the hospital in Cortez?"

Janice Harrison told her side of the story. "Gary wanted to see me. I really didn't want to see him, I was livin' with my future husband. I had left Gary. I finally agreed to see him, though, after Sheriff Barton asked me to."

"And was it for sex, Mrs. Lopez?"

"No."

"You didn't have sex with him at any time when he was in the hospital in Cortez?"

"No."

"What did you do all night?"

"He mostly just wanted me to be with him. He knew he had lost me. He did ask me to smuggle in a hack saw for him so he could try to escape. I didn't do it."

"Did Sheriff Barton give you money?"

"Yes, he did."

"How much?"

"Thirty-five hundred dollars."

"What was your understanding of why the money was given to you?"

"It was reward money for information leadin' to the body of Kelly White."

"And did that information come from you?"

"No."

"Who did it come from?"

"Gary."

"Were you present when Gary told Sheriff Barton where the body was?"

"Yes, I was."

"What happened?"

"Gary told the sheriff where the body was. That other man, the deputy, he wrote it down."

"So Sheriff Barton never told Gary Harrison where the body was? Mr. Harrison gave the directions with his own free will?"

"That's correct."

"Mrs. Harrison, did Sheriff Barton fly you from Cortez to Limite to visit the defendant any time between January and April of this year?"

"Yes, sir."

"How many times?"

"Four."

"And why did he do that?"

"Same reason. Gary wanted to see me. Actually, he had threatened to involve me in his crimes because I had asked him for a divorce. He kept sayin' that if I didn't come to visit him, then he'd say I helped him do it."

"Is this what ultimately happened?"

"Yes, sir."

"Tell us how that happened."

"When I filed for divorce, Gary made false confessions involving me in two murders. I was arrested and charged with them."

"But you've been cleared of all charges, is that correct?"

"Yes, sir."

The other side didn't have much to add, except that they got Janice to admit that more went on in the Limite jail cell than "just talking."

Finally, Gary Harrison testified again regarding the arm-burning incident and how the confessions had been made under duress and while intoxicated.

"My doctor had given me 'red birds' for my nerves," he said.

"What are those?" Childs asked.

"Drugs for nerves."

"And you think those had an influence on your thinking?"

"Definitely."

"So all that-- the arm-burning, the drugs, the constant pressure-- these all contributed to your duress?"

"Yes, sir."

"Mr. Harrison, did you voluntarily make any of those confessions?"

"No, sir."

That goddamned liar, Barton thought. If he could only get his hands on the scumbag...

Judge Kennilworth took an hour before gathering the parties involved.

"I'm ordering a full investigation into the arm-burning matter," he said. "These are serious charges. I'm turning it over to the FBI and the Texas Attorney General's Office. The trial scheduled for November Third is postponed pending the results of the investigation. Furthermore, I rule that due to the unusual circumstances surrounding the defendant's interrogation and subsequent confessions, all of the defendant's said confessions are inadmissible."

He banged the gavel. Rusty Franklin and Buck Barton felt their hearts stop.

Inadmissible? Was the judge mad?

"Your honor," Franklin said, "We appeal that decision on the grounds that these confessions may be the only evidence we have to convict this man of these terrible crimes."

"I understand, and your objection is noted." The judge went on to cite reasons justifying his decision but his words blurred in Buck Barton's ears. All he could hear was the high-pitched shriek that blocked out everything else whenever he was under too much stress.

* * *

The next month contained a flurry of activity in the Limite Sheriff's Office. FBI agents, investigators from the Texas Attorney General's office, and even the Texas Rangers got involved in the investigation into Gary Harrison's allegations that he was burned by a cigarette in Lucas County jail. D. A. Franklin ordered the Lucas County Grand Jury to conduct a separate investigation on their own. Deputies and jailers were interviewed at length and Buck Barton gave no less than thirty statements to thirty different officials. D.A. investigator Bobby Gibson was especially under scrutiny, as it became known during the investigation that he had been "run out" of New Orleans when he had been an assistant D.A. there in the late sixties. Apparently he had been charged with unethical conduct and was removed from office.

The days turned into weeks. Approximately a month later on December 1, 1974, the Lucas County Grand Jury and the Texas Attorney General's Office returned their reports on the investigations. All of the relevant parties gathered in Judge Kennilworth's courtroom in Austin once again to hear the outcome.

A representative from the Attorney General's office read a summary statement that accompanied the sixty-eight page report.

"We find that the allegations made by Gary Harrison regarding coercion and mistreatment by Lucas County law enforcement officers and personnel during his stay in the Limite jail between January and June, 1974, to be unfounded. We hereby exonerate the Lucas County Sheriff's Office and the Limite District Attorney's Office of any wrongdoing. Furthermore, we find that Gary Harrison invented the story of burning charges and that the wounds on his arms were self-inflicted. A fellow inmate in Travis County Jail assisted Harrison in burning his arms on or around July 1. We believe the wounds were such that they would have required cooperation from the subject to receive them, due to the pain involved."

Buck Barton and Rusty Franklin breathed a sigh of relief. Harrison's trial for the murders of Grace Daniel and Mary Parker could go forward, if the Lucas County D.A. felt they could win without the inadmissible confessions. Franklin thought it was pretty hopeless. On January 5, Rusty Franklin asked that the murder charges against Gary Harrison in the Daniel and Parker cases be dismissed in District Court. There simply wasn't enough evidence to convict Harrison without those confessions.

That left Harrison's appeal on the life sentence for the Kelly White murder, which was scheduled to take place in early 1975.

"It's a goddamn shame," Franklin told Barton, as they ate lunch at the Tamale Shop. "We gotta hope that he doesn't win on appeal, or he's gonna be a free man."

"Oh, he's never gonna be a free man, even if he gets out," Barton said.

"What do you mean?"

"Never mind."

The music on the restaurant's loud speakers switched from Ronnie Milsap's *Please Don't Tell Me How the Story Ends* to Eric Clapton's *I Shot the Sheriff*.

"I fuckin' hate that song," Barton said. He finished his meal, then stood and walked away from the D.A. He got into his car and drove toward his office. The smell of petroleum was once again in the air. Sometimes it made Barton want to gag. He looked out at the stinking town around him and, for once in his life, wished he was somewhere else.

Gary Harrison had been nothing but a thorn in his side since he first heard the man's name. It was going to have to end soon.

On March 16, 1975, the Texas Court of Criminal Appeals heard arguments from Gary Harrison and his lawyers that the District Judge had not properly admonished him and tell him that he did not have to plead guilty in the Kelly White case. Fortunately, the court upheld the life sentence, ruling that the judge had given sufficient warning and had complied with the law. The next day, Gary Harrison left Travis County Jail and was sent to the state penitentiary in Huntsville. For life.

That night, Buck Barton got together with Lucky Farrow, Guy Simms, and Chuck Davenport to play a game of poker. Ever since the Washington Hotel had been sold and turned into the Lodge of the Western Plain, they had begun to meet at one another's home. As they played, the conversation turned to the Harrison case, as it had been of intense interest in Limite since it started. Simms had an interesting suggestion about what could be done about Gary Harrison, given all the grief he had caused.

Buck Barton off-handedly replied that he'd like nothing better.

Four days later, on March 20, Buck Barton got a phone call from Rusty Franklin.

"Buck, you're not gonna believe this," he said.

"What's that?"

"Gary Harrison is dead."

"What?"

"Yep, it happened in the prison exercise yard. He was attacked by unknown assailants and his throat was slashed. It happened this morning."

Barton nodded. "It's not surprising."

"It's not?"

"Nah," Barton said. "The guy was an asshole. He'd insult anybody and everybody. He had a big head. His ego was bigger than he was. I knew it wouldn't be long before he stepped on the wrong toes or bragged too much or something. Do they know who killed him?"

"No, they're investigating the matter. I'll keep you informed."

"You do that. Thanks, Rusty."

Barton hung up the phone and looked at his wall of memories. He had added a photo of Gary Harrison displaying the burn scars on his arms in court.

The sheriff suddenly felt very tired. He had been at the job far too long. He wondered if it might be time to retire. He enjoyed woodworking. Maybe he could open up a little crafts shop somewhere and take it easy for a while. He wasn't getting any younger.

On March 26, the investigation in Huntsville revealed that Harrison had been killed with a makeshift knife created out of razor blades and masking tape. The assailant or assailants had not been caught, for no one betrays anyone else in Huntsville. Sheriff Barton had been right about Harrison. The prisoner had entered the pen boasting of his notoriety, insulting other inmates, and "looking for trouble." One jailer commented that he had placed a bet with other officers on the day Harrison arrived that he "wouldn't last a week."

It was over. Gary Harrison was dead. He had answered, perhaps, for the murder of Kelly White. Sadly, there were at least five other victims who were left behind, totally forgotten by the judicial system.

Sheriff Barton, however, had not forgotten them. What happened to those victims weighed heavily on his conscience.

JANUARY 1999
SHANNON

Stan promised Shannon that he'd be in touch. He left after he had related the long story and she felt very alone. She slowly paced the kitchen and living room, ignoring her two children parked in front of the television. Billy had come home from kindergarten halfway through Stan's story. She had made the kids' lunch on autopilot.

A wave of depression hit her and she had an urge to cry. The emotion turned to anger as she thought about it all.

Was this a completely useless waste of time? Did she already know everything she needed to know, or could possibly know? It looked as if there was indeed a connection between all of Gary Harrison's victims, and that perhaps Stan's theory of involvement with the so-called Dixie Mafia was real. How much did Buck Barton really know about Gary Harrison before he was arrested? The strange deal made in Cortez was the key to it all. But what could she do about it?

What she wanted to do was confront Buck Barton and see if he had anything to say. Unfortunately, he was in the hospital.

She stared at the pile of newspaper clippings that were spread over the kitchen table. If she didn't do something soon, she was going to explode.

Damn it, she thought. If what Stan thinks is correct, then Buck Barton could have prevented her mother's murder. If he knew that Gary Harrison was a killer beforehand, why wasn't he arrested sooner?

Shannon decided she would go to the hospital and see if she could talk to the former sheriff. If he was a vegetable, fine, then she wouldn't be able to. She knew, though, that if she didn't *act* this very minute, she would scream.

She picked up the phone and called her sister to see if she could drop off Cathy and Billy.

"Hi! You've reached Jackie! I can't come to the phone right now..." began the answering machine, but Shannon hung up without leaving a message. She would just have to take the kids with her.

Fifteen minutes later, the kids were buckled into their seats. They whined about being torn away from the television but they shut up when Shannon lost her temper and shouted at them.

"Hush! You're comin' with me, and that's final!"

They weren't used to mommy yelling. Cathy started to cry and Billy began to suck his thumb, a habit he had grown out of but resorted to when he was frightened.

"Oh, I'm sorry," Shannon said, trying to control herself. "I didn't mean to yell. But you gotta understand that when mommy needs to do something, she can't just leave you alone at home. You don't want to be left alone at home, do you?"

Both kids shook their heads.

So they were off to Limite Hospital, a short drive downtown. It was an eight-storey structure built in the fifties. Additions and remodeling had been done here and there over the years, resulting more in a patchwork quilt than a building. She parked the car, then held the kids' hands as she entered.

Shannon hated hospitals. They smelled of death and pain. It was a sad, depressing place-- except perhaps on the maternity ward, where life was a joyous beginning. She allowed herself a smile as she remembered the births of her two children. Carl had been nervous as hell. He had waited outside when Billy was born but he had been in the delivery room when Cathy emerged. Shannon considered herself lucky that she had two healthy children and one of those rare husbands who cared.

It was amazing to her that such a thing could be taken for granted by so many people.

Shannon approached the Information Desk and inquired about Buck Barton.

"We have a B. D. Barton, is that him?" a woman with blue hair asked.

"Yes."

"He's in three-thirty-five, third floor."

Shannon took the kids to the elevator and let Billy press the Number 3 button. When they reached the floor, Shannon was overwhelmed by the smell of bedpans and cleanser.

There was a waiting area to the left. A nurse's station was just down the hall to her right. Barton's room, 335, was directly across from the station. Shannon composed herself, took her two children by the hands, and walked to the door as if they were family.

The door was slightly ajar. She could hear a woman's voice inside. Shannon gently pushed the door open and looked in.

Shannon guessed that she was in her seventies, probably Barton's wife. She was a small woman, and Shannon wondered how she got along physically with such a huge man. She had white hair, glasses, and large blue eyes magnified behind the lenses. Mrs. Barton was sitting next to bed, reading aloud from the newspaper. Buck Barton was hooked up to what seemed like a hundred tubes and wires, but he was awake and listening to her.

"...And the Limite Lynxes won their basketball game against Prescott," the woman was saying. She had that distinctive cheerful West Texas Old Lady drawl that can be sweet and irritating at the same time. She stopped, looked up and saw Shannon and the two children. "Oh, hello. Can I help you?"

Shannon suddenly didn't know what to say.

"Oh, uhm, I just wondered how Mr. Barton was doin'," she said.

"Well, he can't really talk yet, but the doctor thinks that his speech is going to come back real soon. Otherwise he's alert and knows what's goin' on. I'm sorry, do I know you?"

"No, ma'am. My name is Shannon Reece. And this is Billy and Cathy."

The woman baby-talked at them. "Well, *hello* there! How are you doing?"

The kids were staring at the old man in the bed. They were clearly frightened by the strange surroundings.

"They've never really been in a hospital before," Shannon explained nervously.

"Well, that's all right, come on in. Do you know my husband?"

"Well, we've met before, a long time ago," Shannon said, stepping inside the room with the two kids at her side. She felt as if she was standing in front of a thousand spotlights.

Buck Barton's gaze shifted over to her. He studied her but there was no recognition in his brown eyes.

This wasn't her place after all, she thought. She had to get out of there. She had made a mistake.

"I'm sorry, I really should leave y'all alone. I didn't mean to interrupt you," she stammered, backing away with the children in tow.

"Oh, don't go on our account," Mrs. Barton said. "I'm Naomi Barton. You're welcome to stay and visit. What did you say your name was? Do I know your mom and dad?"

"No, I don't think so," she said, continuing to back slowly toward the door. "I gotta go, really. I just... stopped by to see how our former sheriff was doing, that's all. You don't know me. Sorry. Y'all take care..."

And she was out of the room.

* * *

The Reeces went to Forest Grove Christian Church nearly every Sunday morning. (Why it was called "Forest Grove" was mystifying to Shannon, seeing that there was nothing like a forest anywhere near Limite.)

Shannon considered herself fairly religious-- at least she believed in God and Jesus and all that. Carl was apathetic about it but didn't mind going. Like her, he had been raised in a Protestant household. The church itself was a branch of the Disciples of Christ, which held a somewhat more liberal doctrine than the Baptists and Methodists. The kids were at an age when Sunday School was fun, and the Reeces genuinely liked the minister, Reverend Wayne Wyatt. He was young, in his thirties, and he seemed kind and compassionate. The only thing Shannon didn't like about the church was the snobbishness of some of the people. She had been welcomed with over-enthusiasm to the women's club when they had first joined the church seven years ago. Shannon was pregnant with Billy at the time. Mrs. Cooper, a forty-something busybody who was in charge of the group, found out that she was Mary Parker's daughter and must have spread it around. Soon, Shannon felt as if the other women were embarrassed to be seen talking with her. Finally, one of her only friends, Jeannie Stevens, told her that some of the women had been discussing her mother, trying to remember the details of the murder. Hearing that brought back memories of being in school, where Shannon had learned to toughen her skin. Some of the other children were cruel and would discuss the fact that Shannon's mother had been killed by a "sex maniac" right in front of her. It had sometimes made Shannon believe her mother had somehow been at fault, even though she knew it wasn't true. She *still* knew it wasn't true... yet, after hearing some of Stan McHam's stories, she was beginning to wonder who her mother really was. The picture of Mary Parker that she had conceived in her mind and heart so long ago had been shattered. Over the past several days, her mother had become some kind of monster. Shannon felt confused and anxious, not knowing quite what to do with herself.

It was for this reason that Shannon found it difficult to pay close attention to Reverend Wyatt's words or sincerely concentrate during the silent prayers. The sermon was about the same old topics-- faith, salvation, love—but with the spin-of-the-week on them. Her mind wandered, imagining dozens of possible scenarios involving her mother and Gary Harrison, her mother and Buck Barton, her mother and Kelly White...

Then, something Reverend Wyatt was saying slowly pulled in Shannon's focus.

"Faith in God is one thing. Faith in ourselves is something else," he said. "In order for anyone to fully accept God's love, you gotta have faith in those around you whom you love-- your family, your parents-- and ultimately, yourself. If you don't have faith that you were brought into the world through love, if you don't have faith to realize that you are a *product* of love, how can you love yourself, or expect to love someone else, including God? I was speaking with a young man the other day, and he was telling me what a terrible childhood he had had. He said both his mother and father used to beat him. He was often sent to bed without supper. They had both died in a car accident involving drunk driving, then he lived with a foster family who was good to him. I asked him if he loved his real parents anyway, and he replied that he wasn't sure, probably not. I told him that he had to look deep in his heart and forgive them, whether he expressed it verbally or not. I told him that human nature can make people do things they don't want to do, or never thought they were capable of doing. Jesus knew that. That's why he told us that if we have faith, then all would be forgiven. I ask you all... do you love your father? Do you love your mother? Answering yes to those questions is the first step toward loving God."

It was now clear to her. Shannon realized what it was that was keeping her in torment.

After the Benediction, the preacher stood at the back of the sanctuary, greeting the congregation as they exited. The Reeces moved slowly along the line toward the doors. Shannon thought about asking the preacher if she could talk with him about her problem.

"Hi, Shannon," came a familiar voice. It was Frieda Williams, with her husband, Sam, and little boy, Sonny.

"Hello, Frieda," she said.

"We enjoyed the evening at your house the other night," Frieda said.

"We did too. We'll have to do it again sometime."

"We'll have to have y'all over our house next time," Frieda said. "We won't have the Super Bowl on, but we'll find somethin' to entertain us. We can play Trivial Pursuit or somethin'. I must admit I was fascinated learnin' about your mother. Oh my lord, it gave me nightmares two nights in a row!"

Shannon swallowed and almost choked. She knew Frieda hadn't meant anything by it, but somehow the words hurt her deeply. Frieda could see by the look on Shannon's face that she had said the wrong thing.

"Oh, honey, I'm sorry, I didn't mean--"

"It's all right," Shannon said. Her voice cracked, and it was enough to trigger an outpour of pent-up emotion. She released her children's hands, leaving them with Carl, then walked quickly through the crowd, past the minister, and into the foyer to the ladies' room. She stepped quickly into one of the stalls and began to cry.

Her problem was that she didn't know if she could love her mother again.

* * *

That night, Shannon dialed a number in Denver, Colorado. He answered after four rings.

"Hello?"

"Uncle Fred? It's Shannon."

"Shannon! How nice to hear from you!"

She had really liked her mother's brother when she was a little girl because he often looked after the kids. He was a little younger than her mom and had the same kind of energy and love of life-- but he wasn't as reckless. At the time of the murder, he had lived a few blocks away from their house. He had worked as a manager of a fast-food hamburger joint. Now he was a regional manager for McDonald's, or Burger King, or some such corporation-- Shannon couldn't remember which one. She hadn't seen him in five or six years.

"It's good to hear your voice, too," she said. "How are Penny and the kids?"

"They're just fine. Cheryl is eighteen and is at Colorado University. Michael is twenty-three and is supposed to graduate this year."

"That's wonderful!"

"Well, he's still not sure what he's gonna do. He's majoring in philosophy. I don't know what the heck you do with a degree in philosophy."

"I'm sure he'll find something. I have smart cousins."

"How's your family?"

"Great. Couldn't be better."

Fred must have detected a hesitation in her voice. "So what did you call about, honey?"

"Do you have a minute to talk?"

"Sure do."

"Well, I'm lookin' into mom's case again."

"Somehow I knew that. Don't know how."

"Well, I was wonderin' if you might be willing to tell me more now. You know, I'm all grown up and everything. I mean, am I right that you knew a lot more that you never told me?"

She heard her uncle sigh deeply. "Shannon, are you sure you want to go into this?"

"Yes. I've even hired a detective to find out some stuff for me."

"Why don't you talk to your dad?"

"You know my dad. He won't say a word about it."

"Well, honey," Fred said, "that's 'cause he knows a lot more than he's ever let on."

"What do you mean?"

"My sister... your mom... she was pretty wild. You knew that. In a way, I'm surprised she didn't get in trouble before she did. She hung out with the wrong kind of people. She liked to party."

"What about dad?"

"Well, he did, too. They were both... aw hell, I hate to tell you this... I don't know if I should..."

"Come on, Uncle Fred, I'm a big girl. Please tell me."

"Your mom and dad were swingers."

"Swingers?"

"You know-- they messed around with other married couples. They swapped spouses at parties and stuff. I never approved. I told Mary that she was going to meet the wrong person some night, and sure enough she did."

"Do you think Gary Harrison was one of the people they... you know... ?"

"That I don't know. I really don't know the whos, whens, wheres, or hows. I just know the whys-- and it's 'cause they liked it. You know Limite. It's boring as hell. Mary wasn't the smartest girl. She had common sense but she didn't use it much. All she was interested in was having a good time."

"Do you think she wanted to get away from us? The kids, I mean?"

"Well," Fred said, "I do know she loved y'all very much. But she also missed her single lifestyle. She married way too young, Shannon. And I hate to say bad things about your dad, but I always thought he was not very good for her. He let her run all over him and I think it was she who eventually dragged him into that stuff."

Shannon let that sink in for a moment then thought of something else to ask. "Do you remember Carol Jenkins?"

"Yeah, I do. I went out with her a couple of times when I was in high school." He chuckled. "It was an 'older woman' kind of thing. She was pretty wild, too."

"Do you know where she is?"

"Haven't the foggiest idea."

"Uncle Fred?"

"Yeah?"

"Do you know if my mom was ever... well... a prostitute?"

Her uncle gasped. "Shannon..."

"Well?"

"I don't think so. At least I don't know it if she was... I like to think that she didn't do that."

"But you don't know for sure that she didn't?"

"No, I don't. Look, she ran around with a wild crowd. There's no tellin' what they did. They were into orgies and drugs and stuff like that. Your mom liked to smoke pot and take speed, and she liked to drink, too. But prostitution? I suppose it's possible, but I don't believe it. I won't believe it."

"What do you know about Sheriff Barton?"

"That mean old cuss? All I remember about him was that when I was in high school, we all would say that if you were gonna get stopped on the road, you'd better pray it's a city cop and not the sheriff's department. We were all scared of Buck Barton."

"How come?"

"I don't know. He had a reputation of bein' a tough bastard. It's probably all rumors and stuff, you know how kids are. There were all kinds of stories goin' around that he beat a prisoner senseless when the guy tried to pull a knife on him. There were rumors of him running whorehouses and stuff..."

"Wait. Tell me about that."

"I don't know anything, Shannon!"

"No, about the whorehouses..."

"It was just rumors, you know, that kids spread. Supposedly the sheriff ran whorehouses out of motels and hotels downtown and stuff. He made money off of 'em."

"You can't prove it, though."

"Hell, no. I doubt anyone could."

"Uncle Fred?"

"Uh huh?"

"What happened to my dad? After the murder, I mean. He changed, didn't he? Was he different before?"

"Yeah, I guess he was. He became a different person. Not a very pleasant person, either. I always thought we got along, you know, brothers-in-law and all that, but after the murder, he avoided me. I guess he thought I knew more about it than I did and he was ashamed or something. You gotta remember that he was under a microscope right after the murder. The police department *and* the sheriff's department were grilling him like there was no tomorrow. They followed him for weeks. He was the number one suspect. I guess no one knows what that's like unless they've been there. To be suspected of killing your own wife... He lost all his friends. He lost his job-- they wouldn't let him be a bail bondsman anymore. He had trouble getting work for over a year. It was a very bad time for him. He started drinkin' pretty bad."

Shannon had only vague memories of feelings from the time. They weren't pleasant. She remembered being moved around a lot from relative to relative until her father got back on his feet.

"What do you think he knows?"

"Shannon, you're gonna have to ask him," Fred said. "I don't know. He's the only one who can tell you. Maybe after all this time, he will."

"I doubt it. He's Mr. Stonewall when it comes to stuff like that."

"Well, I do know one thing."

"What's that?"

"He loved your mother very much. She was the love of his life."

Tears filled Shannon's eyes involuntarily.

"Thanks, Uncle Fred. I guess I'll let you go."

"Sure thing, honey. Call anytime. Hey, don't let this get you down. I know it's hard for you to remember your mom, but I sure remember her. I remember her as bein' sweet, pretty, and fun-lovin'. We never fought when we were growin' up. We stuck by each other. That's how I remember her. I hope that helps."

"It does. Thanks."

"You take care now. Keep in touch more often!"

"I will," she said. "Bye."

She hung up the phone and sighed. It had been a long, emotionally-draining day. She was ready to get in bed.

But there were the children's nightly rituals to attend to-- bathing, pajamas, book reading, snack, and then bedtime story. It seemed to take forever each night. She loved her children dearly, but some nights she just wasn't in the mood.

Shannon steeled herself for the chore, walked into the hallway, and heard splashing in the bathroom. The door opened and Cathy ran out, naked and giggling.

"Cathy?" The little girl ran into her room and slammed the door. Shannon stuck her head in the bathroom and saw Carl helping Billy get into the tub.

"One down, one to go," he said, smiling.

Shannon leaned over, kissed her husband on the cheek, said, "Thanks, sweetheart," and then went to their bedroom to lie down.

* * *

On Monday, Shannon had to work. Cathy went to a day care center and Billy joined her there after kindergarten until Shannon got off at 5:00 p.m. When she got home with the kids, there was a message on the machine from Stan McHam. She called him back at the office.

Merle put her through in a flash. "Shannon?" he answered.

"I hope I'm not catchin' you walkin' out the door?"

"Nah, I practically live here now. How are you?"

"Fine, you?"

"Rosy. Listen, I got some stuff. Janice Harrison is in San Antonio. Her name is still Janice Lopez but I think she's divorced again. I'm workin' on a home address but I have the address of some fancy nightclub where she works. It's called the Caribbean. If you're interested, you can check that out."

"All right."

"I also found out the name of the woman who was attacked in the parking lot of the Fever club in June of 1971. She lives in Dallas now. Her name is Kim Clark. My buddy Paul Rattan dug her name out of an old case report."

"I wonder if she'd have anything useful to tell us?"

"Well, I called her up and talked to her myself. She left Limite shortly after that incident. No one from Limite ever followed up on it after Harrison was arrested. She had never heard of Harrison. I mailed her a picture of him but she said it's been so long that she might not be able to remember what the guy looked like. I'll talk to her again later in the week."

"Thanks."

"No problem. And I've also got copies of Harrison's confessions. They're pretty much what I thought they were. You can take a look at 'em at your convenience."

"Thanks. Oh, what about Carol Jenkins? Have you tried to find her?"

"No, I'll get on that tomorrow."

"Okay. I'll try to come by the office sometime tomorrow, is that all right?"

"Sure. Anytime... well, call first. The FBI got a break in that counterfeiting case I was helpin' 'em on. I may be out checkin' a couple of things for 'em."

"Okay, thanks, Stan."

She hung up and began to prepare dinner.

At around 9:30 that night, after the kids were in bed, the phone rang. Carl answered it in the kitchen and handed it over to Shannon. "It's Jackie," he said.

Shannon, who had just sat in the living room and put up her feet, groaned and got up to take the receiver.

"Hello?"

"Shannon, I need a big favor." Jackie sounded out of breath. Something wasn't right.

"What is it?"

"Can Tyler stay with you tonight? I'll pick him up in the morning."

"What's wrong?"

"I-- I gotta go somewhere. Out of town, overnight. With Travis."

"Jackie, tell me what's going on." Shannon attempted to sound like the older sister disciplinarian.

"Nothing's going on! I just have to do something. Please."

Jackie was clearly frightened about something.

"Jackie, are you in trouble?" This time Shannon tried the voice of the concerned older sister.

"No. Please, just let me bring him over now, I gotta do this!"

She sounded so desperate that Shannon couldn't say no.

"All right, but you'd better tell me what's goin' on when you get over here."

"See you in a minute," her sister said, then hung up.

Carl could tell by the expression on his wife's face that trouble was brewing. "What now?"

"She's bringing Tyler to stay overnight."

Carl rolled his eyes. "What for?"

"I don't know. Yet."

Carl did his famous Sigh of Resignation, picked up the paper, and went to the bedroom.

A few minutes later, the bell rang. Shannon opened it and found Jackie, Tyler, and Travis Huffman standing on the porch. Tyler was sobbing, his hand clutched tightly by his mother.

"There's Aunt Shannon," Jackie said. "Now stop crying."

"Jackie, *what* is going on?" Shannon asked, opening the screen door.

Tyler ran inside. Jackie and Travis followed him. Travis was carrying a fairly large, stuffed overnight bag. Jackie ignored Shannon and squatted down to whisper to Tyler.

"Here's his stuff," Travis said.

"Wait a minute," Shannon said. "That's just for tonight?"

"It might be longer," he answered.

"Jackie, you didn't say anything about--"

It was then that Shannon noticed a red welt on Jackie's left cheek. She had been slapped recently.

"Jackie, what happened to you?" she asked.

Jackie stood up and faced her. Her eyes were droopy and bloodshot.

"Nothin', I, uhm, hit myself with the cabinet door, can you believe it?"

"No, I can't." Shannon turned to Travis. "Did you hit her?"

"No way. Look we gotta get goin'," he said. "Come on, sugar." He took hold of Jackie's arm and pulled her toward the door. Tyler started howling.

"We'll be back, honey," Jackie said. "Don't worry. You'll have fun with your cousins."

"Jackie! Where are you going?" Shannon shouted.

Neither of them answered her. Travis pulled Jackie outside and they got into the black Mustang.

"Jackie!" Shannon followed them, shouting.

As the car pulled out of the driveway, Jackie rolled down the window and yelled back, "Don't worry, I'm fine! I'll talk to you tomorrow!"

The car screeched and sped off down the street.

Carl, in his pajamas, joined Shannon outside. He was holding Tyler, who was still bawling.

"What the hell is going on?" he asked.

"I don't know," Shannon said, fearfully. "Something's wrong."

"Should you call the police?"

"I don't know. She seemed like she was okay, but he's making her do something."

"Maybe you should call the police."

They went back into the house. Tyler started to settle down after Shannon gave him some graham crackers and milk. He'd be fine.

"I have a feeling that I'm not going to hear from her tomorrow like she said," she muttered.

"Maybe you should call the police," Carl said again.

"I'm not goin' to. Not yet."

Carl looked at her for an explanation.

"I'll see if she comes back tomorrow first. I'll give her the benefit of the doubt."

Carl waited a moment, then gave another Sigh of Resignation. He went back into the bedroom.

Shannon sat down at the table across from her nephew and watched him dip the crackers in the milk. He ate graham crackers just like she did.

"Can I have one?" she asked him.

Tyler nodded and handed her a nice mushy one. It fell apart as she took it.

"Uh oh," she said. "Why don't I take a fresh crispy one and dip it myself, how's that?"

"Okay," Tyler said.

Shannon smiled warmly at him and he grinned back. He's a cute kid, Shannon thought. Smart. So what the hell was wrong with his mother?

She got up and took a look at the stuffed travel bag. She unzipped it and allowed it to fall open on the floor. It was, as she expected, full of clothes and toys. A number 10 sized envelope was lying amidst the mess. It had "Shannon--Thank You" written on it in Jackie's hand. She picked up the envelope and opened it.

Inside were ten crisp $100 bills.

CONFESSIONS

By noon the next day, Shannon hadn't heard a word from Jackie. Carl still thought she should call the police. She called her father instead.

Larry Parker answered the phone in the noisy warehouse office.

"Dad? It's Shannon!"

"What?" He was shouting over the rumble.

"Dad?"

"Shannon?"

"Yeah. Listen-- Jackie's gone off with that thug and left Tyler with me. I don't have a clue where she is or when she's coming back!"

"What?"

"Did you hear me?"

"Yes," he shouted. "I just want to make sure I heard it right. Jackie's gone out of town?"

"Well, I think it's more than that, dad. She's run off like she doesn't plan to come back for a while. She left Tyler here with a big bag of clothes and toys. That Travis Huffman was taking her somewhere, and not only that, she gave me a thousand dollars!"

"A thousand dollars? Where did she get a thousand dollars?"

"Well, that's what I'd like to know, too!" Shannon knew he wasn't going to be able to help.

"What do you want me to do?"

"I don't know. Should I call the police?"

"Do you really think Jackie'd run off and leave her son?"

"Well, no..."

"She'll be back, Shannon. Just sit tight if you can. It'd be best not to involve the police yet. You don't want your sister to have a run-in with the law."

"I don't know, maybe it would scare some sense into her. What about Travis? He's up to no-good, I just know it."

"Give it a couple of days. That's my advice. Jackie's a tough girl. She can handle herself."

Shannon still didn't know what to do.

"Shannon?" he asked.

"Yeah?"

"Just makin' sure you were still there. Can you wait? Is Tyler gonna be all right there with you for a couple of days?"

"I guess. It just puts a bigger burden on us, but it'll be all right. I think he's happier being over here anyway."

"Okay, look, I gotta go. Keep me informed, all right?"

"All right."

Shannon hung up and felt one of her infamous panic attacks threatening to ruin her day. She retrieved a Klonopin tablet from the bathroom, swallowed it with water, then went back into the kitchen to use the phone again.

Stan McHam was in, as she suspected.

"Hi, Stan, it's Shannon," she said.

"Howdy howdy. How are you today?" There was something about his drawl that was extremely comforting. She felt better just hearing him on the other line.

"Oh, not so great, really. Last night, my sister ran off with her crazy boyfriend and left her son with me. I have no idea where they've gone or when they're gonna come back."

"Geez," he said. "That's rough. I take it you're not comin' by today, then?"

"Not unless I can find someone to watch the kids."

"Mmm, I see. I'd come over there, except I'm up to my neck in some other stuff at the moment... There was a murder last night in town that's connected with the case I'm workin' on for the FBI."

"Oh." Shannon was hoping he could come over again so that she could stay close to home.

"I tell you what," he said. "If you can wait until late afternoon, I may be able to swing by for an hour. Is that all right?"

"That would be great," she said. "Don't trouble yourself, though."

She hung up the phone and tried to think. She didn't have much patience when she was nervous or upset. She hated the feelings of helplessness and despair that accompanied her anxiety attacks. They didn't occur often, but they were debilitating when they did.

"What are you doing, mommy?" Cathy asked. Her daughter was sitting in front of the television with Tyler. She had caught her mother pacing from the living room to the kitchen and back for several minutes.

"Oh, nothin', honey, I'm just thinkin' about a lot of things. I tend to walk around when I'm thinking," Shannon explained.

"Maybe you should lie down and take a nap," Cathy suggested.

Great idea!

"You know, Cathy, that sounds wonderful. I think I will. Do you and Tyler need anything before I go lie down?"

"No."

"All right. Wake me up if you need me."

She went into the master bedroom and flopped onto the bed.

Who was she kidding? she thought. She'd never be able to go to sleep in this state. She was much too worried about her sister and concerned about the things she was learning about her mother.

But in fifteen minutes, she was asleep.

* * *

Once again, Shannon was troubled by disturbing dreams. This time, she found herself at a table, looking through a stack of Polaroid photos. The first photo was what she imagined Janice Harrison looked like in her red wig and garter belt get-up. Janice was wearing the black eyepatch in the photo, which made her look positively evil. Of course, Shannon knew that Janice didn't have the eyepatch when the real Polaroids were taken. In her dream state, however, Shannon convinced herself that this was a new photo.

She thumbed through more of the photos. There was Grace Daniel, standing at an ironing board wearing a skimpy top and shorts. Barbara Lewis was standing by a motel swimming pool, drink in hand, and smiling at the camera as if the shot had been taken on vacation somewhere. Tina Lee Peters was dressed in a bra and panties and was serving drinks to men at a table. Richie and Laura Saldaña were at their wedding-- she was in a beautiful white bridal gown and he was wearing a tuxedo. Susan Powell had her back to the camera, posed provocatively across a sewing machine, and was looking back with a smile. She was wearing a dress that had been slashed to ribbons. The next Polaroid was of her mother, swaying in the middle of a dark dance floor in a smoky nightclub. She was surrounded by a circle of men and she was the center of attention. Kelly White was next, sitting at a cash register with neat stacks of currency on the table in front of her.

The next picture was a shot of Shannon and Jackie. They were sitting at a table, smiling and waving at the camera. Shannon recognized the picture. It had been taken on Jackie's 21st birthday. They were at the Western Saloon, one of the more upscale restaurants in Limite. Bouquets of balloons surrounded the table and a half-empty pitcher of frozen margaritas sat in front of them.

The memory brought a smile to Shannon's face and she decided to go through the stack of Polaroids again. This time, however, they were different.

The picture of Grace Daniel was a gruesome tableau of lawmen standing over a skeleton in an oil field. The corpse was lying incongruously on an ironing board.

The sight terrified Shannon and she began to flip through the photos quickly.

The photo of Barbara Lewis was bloody and horrible. She was lying on a bed, a gunshot wound in her head. The drink she had earlier was still in her hand.

Tina Lee Peters' nude body was covered in blood and was lying across a bar in a nightclub. Patrons stood at the bar drinking, oblivious to the corpse in front of them-- or perhaps they were just ignoring it.

Richie and Laura Saldaña were lying in side-by-side coffins. Richie's face and chest were bloody. Laura was nude and covered in leaves and sticks. She was still holding her bridal bouquet.

Susan Powell was unrecognizable as a pile of bones scattered around a sewing machine. The machine was outdoors, sitting in the middle of a patch of tumbleweeds.

Mary Parker's photo was exactly like the earlier one. She was dancing at a nightclub, with men surrounding her in a circle. The only difference was that she was a mummified corpse.

Kelly White's skeleton was recognizable only because the stacks of money were placed symmetrically around the body.

Shannon came to the last photo once again, expecting to see herself with Jackie at the birthday celebration. Instead, it was a picture of Jackie alone. She was lying in a hospital bed, covered in bloody sheets. Her eyes were open but were glazed over.

"Mommy, mommy!"

Shannon screamed aloud and dropped the photos.

"Mommy!"

She raised from the bed, gasping for air. Cathy, Tyler, and Billy were standing at the foot of the bed.

"Mommy? Were you having a bad dream?"

Shannon closed her eyes with relief. She was in a sweat and felt shaken.

"Yes, honey, I guess I was."

"Was it scary?"

"I guess it was."

"What was it about?"

The dream had faded by now and all she was left with was a vague mixture of emotions that had accompanied it.

"I... I don't remember," she said. "Go on in the living room, kids, I'll be out in a minute."

"Mommy, that man is here. The one that walks funny."

"Stan?"

Cathy nodded. Shannon looked at the clock. It was 3:45 in the afternoon. Of course it was, Billy was home. Cathy had let him inside.

"Go tell him I'll be right there, okay?"

The kids nodded and ran out of the room.

Shannon took two minutes to pull herself together, then went to greet the detective.

"I didn't catch you at a bad time, did I?" he asked.

"No, I had fallen asleep," she said, still a little fuzzy-headed. "I slept for hours, I normally don't do that. I had a bad dream that shook me up. I'm all right, I think."

"Want me to come back another time?"

"No, no. Please. I'm going to make some coffee, you want some?"

"Sounds good."

He was carrying a briefcase this time. He set it on the kitchen table and opened it while Shannon used the coffee maker. The briefcase was full of various manila folders stuffed with papers and photos. The briefcase also contained a camera and handgun.

"Don't let my thirty-eight special bother you," he said. "I have a permit."

Shannon nodded.

"I'm working on six different cases," he said. "A couple are really interestin' and the rest bore me to tears. The big one is the thing I'm doing with the FBI. Yours is pretty interestin'. The rest are bullshit adultery cases. Pardon my French."

"That's okay, just don't let the children hear you."

"Right." He opened a folder and pulled out some documents. "Anyway, here are Gary Harrison's confessions on the Grace Daniel case and your mother's. They shouldn't take you long to read 'em."

He handed them to her one by one-- the first Grace Daniel statement that implicated Janice, and the second one made over a week later that exonerated her. These were followed by the two Mary Parker confessions-- the first with Janice, the second without.

* * *

Statement made on April 22, 1974.

"I would like to say that on October 10, 1970, my wife Janice and I were driving home from the Washington Hotel. I think it was a Saturday night around 11:30. I had been drinking a little, so I was kinda high. Janice was mad about not making much money that night and wanted to stay at the hotel. She was working there as a hooker. I sometimes worked as a bouncer there, and I was that night. It had been a slow and quiet evening, so I drank about six beers. She had gotten pretty drunk that night, a lot more than me, so I made her come home early. I had to drag her out of there, and she was in a mean mood.

"Anyway, we were driving home on Lucas County Road. We were living on Chestnut Street, which is two blocks west of the intersection of Lucas County Road and Twelfth Street. You know there's that big shopping center there at the intersection, and there's this laundrymat there. I think it's called Fresh N'

Clean or Fresh N' Dry or something like that. Janice did our laundry there, so I'd been in there before and knew about it.

"Anyway, Janice pointed to the parking lot as we drove by. 'Look, I think that's Grace's car,' she said. I looked over and saw a yellow VW all by itself in front of the laundrymat. I slowed down and stopped at the red light.

"Grace Daniel was this other hooker who worked at the Washington Hotel sometimes. I seen her there. She was a pretty, blonde haired lady. I think she had one kid, but no husband. She also worked at this drive-in, you know, one of those places where the waitresses come out to your car and put the tray on the window. I had first met her there, at Shelly's Drive-Inn. Everyone goes around Shelly's, it's a big place to hang out at night.

"Anyway, Janice says, 'That bitch owes me money. Let's go see if she has it.'

"I says, 'What do you mean, she owes you money?' So Janice tells me that Grace borrowed a hundred dollars from her over two months ago or somethin' like that, and she hadn't paid her back. 'Every time I ask her about the money, she puts me off,' Janice said.

"So I turned left onto Twelfth Street, then pulled into the shopping center from there. We drove up to the laundrymat and looked inside first. Grace Daniel was in there, ironing. I think she was wearing shorts and a t-shirt. Nobody else was in there, and there wasn't anyone else in the parking lot. Janice tells me to stop the car and get out. So we did.

"We went inside the laundrymat and Grace seemed surprised to see us. I remember that there was music playing on a transistor radio that Grace had. It was that Carpenters song, 'We've Only Just Begun.'

"Janice asked her for the hundred dollars, and Grace didn't have it. I had a gun with me. It was a thirty-two caliber Smith and Wesson. I took it out and pointed it at her, and she got frightened. Janice told her to come with us. When Grace resisted, Janice said, 'Leave all your stuff and come with us now or Gary will shoot you.' So we took her out to our car. We put her in the front seat by me, and Janice got in the back seat. We drove away. No one saw us.

"We drove to our house, which was just a minute or two away from there. We made her get out of the car and come inside. I put the gun away and warned her not to try anything funny or I'd get it out again. She was pretty scared of the gun.

"Janice went through her purse and found some money, I don't know how much, thirty dollars or somethin'. Janice took the money then threw the purse back at her. Then Janice asked me if I wanted to fuck her. Janice knew I kinda thought Grace was pretty. I said, sure. So we made Grace take off her clothes. I got some electrical cord that I had in the closet and tied up Grace's hands with them. Janice watched me and Grace together, and then Janice and Grace did some stuff together while I watched. My wife and I are pretty open about our marriage. We like the same kinds of things, you know what I mean?

"After we were finished, we let Grace put her clothes back on. We left her in the bedroom, then Janice and I talked about what we should do about her. Janice was afraid she might go to the police or something. I agreed, so we thought the best thing to do would be to take her out of town somewhere and kill her.

"We went back to the bedroom and told her we were all going for another drive. We took her out to the car and put her in the front seat again. We drove out north of town, way out, about ten miles or so. We pulled off onto a dirt road that led out to an oil field I worked at once. It was the middle of the night so no one saw us. We stopped the car and made Grace get out and walk out into the field. I guess we walked for about five minutes .

I had the gun out, so I made Grace get down on the ground. I think I did something else to her, like make her take off her top, or I tore it off or something. Oh yeah, I had her panties that I had taken off at the house. I stuffed 'em in her shorts. I had this nylon stocking in my pocket that I got at the house, and I gave it to Janice. She put it around Grace's neck and started to strangle her. I held her. Finally, she was dead and we left her there. We walked back to the car and got in and drove away.

"About a minute later, Janice threw Grace's purse out the window, and it landed somewhere off the side of the road. We drove back to the highway, then went home.

"This is a true statement and I make it with my own free will."

* * *

Statement made on April 30, 1974.

"I would like to say that this is a corrected, amended statement concerning the events of Saturday night, October 10, 1970. The first statement that I made was not true and was not correct, but this statement is true and is correct. The reason the first statement was untrue is that I involved my wife Janice and this is not correct. I had just received a divorce summons from my wife and for some illogical reason thought that if she didn't drop the divorce action, I would involve her in some cases and enter a guilty plea.

"Furthermore, my wife will not appear as a witness for me in the pending White case. To do so, she would give testimony that would involve perjury by my wife concerning Sheriff Barton. The testimony would have been in effect that my interrogation in Cortez, Texas, was psychologically coerced. My wife, in all consideration and treatment given us by Sheriff Barton could not commit perjury even though it meant that she could not appear in my defense in the White case.

"On the night of October 10, 1970, I was driving home from the Washington Hotel around 11:30 p.m. I passed by the laundrymat at the intersection of Lucas County Road and Twelfth Street and noticed a yellow Volkswagen by itself in the parking lot. I thought I recognized the car as belonging to Grace Daniel. I knew Grace from the hotel because I worked there as a bouncer sometimes and she was a cocktail waitress. She also did

some hooking from time to time. I also knew her from Shelly's Drive-Inn, where I sometimes went for a hamburger. Grace was always friendly to me and I thought she was attractive.

"I was a little drunk from drinking beer at the hotel, and I had also taken some speed pills. I was feeling high and thought I could get away with something. I pulled into the parking lot and drove past the laundrymat real slow so I could see inside. Sure enough, it was Grace Daniel. She was ironing, or something, and was wearing shorts and a t-shirt.

"I drove home, which was only two blocks away, and went inside the house. I got my thirty two caliber Smith and Wesson and some electrical cord, then went back to the laundrymat. It was probably about 11:40 by now. I parked next to her car and went inside.

"I remember that the music playing on her transistor radio was the Carpenters new song, 'We've Only Just Begun.' I thought that was funny. I started singing along with it as I walked in.

"Grace recognized me and was friendly at first until I pulled out the gun. Then she got scared. I told her to leave her laundry and get in my car. She wouldn't do it, so I threatened to hurt her. I said that if she screamed I would kill her.

"She got in my car, and we drove away. No one saw us. I drove north toward Mitchell and after about ten miles out of town I pulled off onto a dirt road that led to an oil field where I used to work. I went down another road and parked the car. We were all alone out there.

"At that point I tied her hands with the electrical cord and then made her have sexual relations with me. I used a nylon stocking around her neck to get her to do what I said. When we were done, I made her put her shorts and shirt back on, then told her to get out of the car. I still had her panties in my hand, so I put them in my pocket.

"I walked her away from the car out into the bushes where all the tumbleweeds were. It was pretty dark, but the moon gave us a little light. I don't know how far we were from the car when I told her to lie on the ground. I put the stocking around her neck again and choked her until she was dead. I think I tore open her shirt then, or I may have done it in the car, I can't remember. I started to walk away, but I remembered that I had her panties, so I stuffed them in her shorts.

"I ran back to the car and drove away. Her purse was in the seat, so I threw it out the window as I drove. It went over the barbed-wire fence, I know that. I got back to the highway and drove home. No one saw me. When I got home, my wife was there asleep. The whole thing probably took me an hour and a half.

"This is a true statement and I make it with my own free will."

* * *

Statement made on April 25, 1974.

"I would like to say that on January 2, 1973, I was living with my wife on Chestnut Street. I remember the date because the day before was New Year's, and I had got pretty sick on New Year's Eve at a party at the Washington Hotel. I had too much to drink and was in bad shape on New Year's Day. But on January 2nd, I felt pretty good.

"My wife and I belonged to several wife-swapping clubs at the time. We knew a few Limite policemen and their wives, and about six or seven other couples who we would have sex parties with. We both knew Mary Parker and her husband from a couple of these parties. Mary had been to the Washington Hotel a few times, and I also knew her from the cafeteria where she worked. It's called Donny's. I ate at the cafeteria a lot, so we were friends.

"This night, I can't remember what day of the week it was, Janice went out of the house to go pick up a man and woman for one of our sex parties. Apparently the couple didn't show up at the meeting place, so Janice went to some of the nightclubs outside of town where we usually met swingers. She was gone longer than I expected, and I was starting to get worried. But she eventually showed up around 11:00 with Mary Parker. Janice told me that she had found her at the Moonlight Club, all by herself, and asked her if she'd like to come over. Her husband, who I know was a bail bondsman, was out of town on business or something.

"The three of us started drinking, smoking pot, and taking pills, and one thing led to another, you know? We all three ended up in bed together. We had the radio on, and I know I heard that Roberta Flack song, 'Killing Me Softly.' First Mary and I had sexual relations together while Janice watched. Then Janice and Mary did a lesbian thing while I watched. Mary kinda liked rough stuff, the same as Janice, so Janice got some nylon hose and we tied Mary's hands together. Then we both started doing stuff to her and she liked it a lot. Mary kept asking us for more pain and stimulation, so Janice put a nylon stocking around Mary's neck. Janice and I sometimes did this ourselves, because when you choke someone during sex, it makes the orgasm more intense. Mary wanted to experience that, so Janice did the choking while I fucked her. Mary passed out and wouldn't wake up. Janice said, 'Uh oh, I think we killed her.' At the time we were so drunk and high that it seemed funny. I know it's not funny now, but we both started giggling and couldn't stop.

"Anyway, we got hold of ourselves and realized that Mary was really dead. So we put her clothes on her and decided to do what we did with Grace Daniel-- take her out in the oil fields and leave her. So we put her in the back seat of my car and drove out north again to a different oil rig place that I knew. I pulled off the highway and onto the dirt road that went into the field. It was pretty dark 'cause I wasn't using my headlights. We didn't want anyone to see us. We stopped the car, I don't know, about a mile from the highway, then Janice helped me carry Mary out of the car and into the bushes.

Janice laid her coat on the ground and I put the body on top of it. Janice had gotten a bolt out of my glove compartment. To make sure she was dead, Janice wrapped the bolt inside the stocking and twisted the stocking around Mary's neck with it. While she was doing that, I think I might have taken Mary's top off again. Maybe it was already off, I don't remember. Anyway, once we were sure she was dead, we went back to the car and left. We didn't turn on the headlights until we got to the highway.

"This is a true statement and I give it of my own free will."

*   *   *

Statement madb on April 30, 1974.

"I would like to say that this is a corrected, amended statement concerning the events of the night of January 2, 1973. The first statement that I made was not true and was not correct, but this statement is true and is correct. The reason the first statement was untrue is that I involved my wife Janice and this is not correct. I had just received a divorce summons from my wife and for some illogical reason thought that if she didn't drop the divorce action, I would involve her in some cases and enter a guilty plea.

"Furthermore, my wife will not appear as a witness for me in the pending White case. To do so, she would give testimony that would involve perjury by my wife concerning Sheriff Barton. The testimony would have been in effect that my interrogation in Cortez, Texas, was psychologically coerced. My wife, in all consideration and treatment given us by Sheriff Barton could not commit perjury even though it meant that she could not appear in my defense in the White case.

"On the night of January 2, 1973, I was at a beer joint on Mitchell Highway. I think it might have been the Fever club, I really can't remember. Anyway, I guess it was around 10:30 or so when I left and went to the Moonlight nightclub. I pulled into the parking lot and sat in my car, just watching who was going in and coming out of the joint. After a bit, I saw this old car pull up into the parking lot with a pretty girl in it. She had black hair and I recognized her from Donny's Cafeteria. Her name was Mary Parker. I guess I just had a crazy impulse, so I jumped out of my car and ran over to hers before she could open the door. She saw me and asked how I was doing. She knew me and recognized me. We had seen each other at the Washington Hotel before, too. In fact, we had been to a sex party at the same time, but I had never had sexual relations with her. But I wanted to. She was real good-looking, you know? Anyway, I asked her if she'd like to have a beer in my car. She didn't really want to, but I said let's just go for a drive. She said she was looking for someone in the club and had to go inside. I guess I kinda lost my temper, so I opened the car door and pulled her out. I think I might have had a knife. Yeah, that's right, I didn't have my gun, I had a kitchen knife. I put it up to her throat and told her that she had to come with me. She was scared now, I guess, so she shut up and went with me. I made her get into my car. It was a miracle that no one saw us. No one came out of the club during that

123

time, and no one drove up in another car. Anyway, we were in the car, and I drove away. I put on the radio, and they were playing that Roberta Flack song, 'Killing Me Softly.' I remember that 'cause I like listening to the radio and usually I can remember songs and what I was doing when I hear them.

"After I put the knife away and told her I wouldn't hurt her, she relaxed and said something like, 'I've never been taken by force before.' Actually I knew that wasn't true, because I watched two men do her at a party once, and they were pretending to take her by force. I think Mary warmed up to the possibility of having sex with me, because she took her top and bra off while we were driving. She let me touch her breasts while I drove with one hand. We finally got way out in the country, and I pulled off the highway onto a dirt road. We drove a mile or so, then I stopped the car.

"We got in the back seat and had sex twice. I wrapped a nylon hose around her neck to apply pressure during the sex act. She was going in and out of consciousness but I'm pretty sure she enjoyed it. I think I might have gotten carried away, 'cause I started getting rough. She complained that I was hurting her, so I hit her a couple of times. I thought it's what she really wanted. She screamed and that made me mad. I hit her again and told her to shut up. Then I made her put her clothes back on and pulled her out of the car. Before I got out, I opened the glove compartment and got a bolt out of it that I knew was in there.

"We walked a ways, then I told her to take off her coat and lay it on the ground. It was pretty cold outside, I remember that. I made her lie on the coat, then I got on top of her. I think I tore her clothes open then. I wrapped the nylon stocking around her neck again, this time with the bolt stuck in the knot so I could twist it tight. Did I tie up her hands? Yeah, I think I did. With electrical cord, I think. I had some in the back seat of the car and I brought that along with us on the walk. Anyway, I strangled her there on the ground, then left her and went back to my car.

"As I drove away, I threw Mary's purse out the window, just like I did Grace Daniel's. I felt kinda bad about this because I liked Mary and I was sorry that she had screamed and gotten scared. That had ruined it for me. I got mad, then I got rough, and so I had to kill her.

"That's the true statement of what happened that night."

* * *

Reading the two confessions regarding Grace Daniel were bad enough. When Shannon read the two about her mother, she felt ill. She stood up, ran out of the kitchen, bolted into the bathroom, and vomited into the toilet bowl.

Minutes later, she dragged herself back into the kitchen and flopped down into the chair. She looked pale and felt weak.

"Are you all right?" Stan asked.

She nodded. "I will be."

"Sorry about that. I guess I should have warned you."

"No, I actually expected it to be worse."

"He's a piece of work, ain't he?" Stan said, taking the confessions and replacing them in the folder.

"The thing is, both versions of each confession sound plausible," Shannon mused.

"I agree. In fact, there are some things that just don't click in the second versions of each one. For example, I don't buy your mother taking off her shirt and bra in the car after he pulled a knife on her. She would have been scared to death, even if she *had* been friends with Harrison."

"So, do you think the first confessions were what really happened?" Stan shrugged. "Who knows?"

Shannon answered that one. "Janice Harrison does."

He nodded. "I can't see her confessing to you, though."

"I'll be lucky if she'll talk to me at all."

"You thinking about going to San Antonio to see her?"

"I might, I don't know. Maybe I can get my brother to go with me. He lives in Austin."

"Oh, I've got an address for Carol Jenkins for you." He looked at a legal pad that had doodles and numbers scribbled all over it. "She lives at 2202 Pack Saddle." He wrote it down on a Post-It note and handed it to Shannon. "I also talked with Kim Clark in Dallas. She couldn't positively identify the picture of Gary Harrison as the man who attacked her in the club parking lot that night, but she said it's more possible than not. If I were a bettin' man-- which I am, by the way-- I'd wager that Harrison was the man who assaulted her, or tried to assault her."

Shannon felt drained. She sat there, holding the Post-It note, staring off into space.

Her mother enjoyed rough sex??

"Heard from your sister?" Stan asked.

"No. That's another thing that's put me in such a cheery mood."

Stan waved her away. "Don't worry about it. I understand. Listen, if there's anything I can do..."

"I know. I'm sure she'll get in touch when she can. I've got her son, and I know she loves him."

"Can I use your phone for a second?" he asked.

"Sure." He got up and dialed a number.

"Pete? Stan here. Yeah, I'm about through with this appointment, so I'll be at your office in, say, twenty minutes? Fine. Is the autopsy report in yet? Oh. Right, well, we can discuss that when I get there. Yeah. Bye."

He hung up and moved to gather up his things. "I should get me one of them cellular phones. Well, I better get going. This counterfeiting thing cracked wide open last night. There was a shooting in the south side of town, not far from where the Flats used to be. The Dixie Mafia had an operation goin' on there in an old building. It looks like someone double-crossed someone else and one of the kingpins got his brains blown out. The shooter's on the run with a whole lot of counterfeit dough. I happen to know a lot about this guy, because he's been in and out of Limite all his life. He's a habitual criminal with close ties to some of the head Dixie Mafia people in other states. I also have reason to believe he may have been the person who shot me back in 1975."

"Really?"

"Yep. He was just a kid then, about twenty, but he was hangin' around the Flats a lot then, and he even knew Gary Harrison."

"That's kinda creepy, isn't it?"

"He's an ugly son of a bitch, too. Pardon my French." Stan reached into one of his folders and brought out a mug shot. "This is him."

Shannon's stomach turned over again and she thought her heart actually skipped a beat.

The man in the photo was Travis Huffman.

LEADS

"You look like you've seen a ghost," Stan said.

"This is my sister's boyfriend," she said in a whisper. *"The one she ran away with last night."*

Stan whistled long and hard, then sat down. Shannon stared at the photo.

"Well, we knew he had a girlfriend but we didn't know who she was," he said. "We found out he was the guy we were lookin' for just a few days ago."

"And you say he killed someone?"

He nodded. "Last night. And that wasn't the first time. This guy's got a rap sheet a mile long. He's a suspect in several murders all over Texas and in other southern states."

"Oh my God," she said, suddenly feeling the panic return.

"Now hold on," he said. "Take it easy. We'll get the word out that his girlfriend is your sister. The problem is that she's gonna be arrested, too, when they find him."

"Why?"

"According to witnesses, she was present at the shooting."

"Oh my God."

"And we think she was helping with the counterfeiting stuff. We ain't sure but we suspect that she was in cahoots with him by distributing the bad cash."

She suddenly remembered the ten one-hundred dollar bills. Now it made sense.

"I want to show you something," she said. She got up and found her purse, then dug out the cash. "She gave me this."

Stan took the money and looked at it closely. He held a bill up to the light. "We have a machine back at the office that shines a special light on the bills. It tells us if it's counterfeit or not. Usually."

"You can't tell from looking at it now?"

"Not really, but it looks like the stuff the FBI found last night. It's crisp and new, just like what we found. It was over $100,000 in counterfeit money, by the way. We think this guy Huffman is carrying even more. He's probably on his way to distribute it. Do you have *any* idea where they might have gone?"

"No."

"Do you know any of her friends that might know? Any of *his* friends?"

"No, but I-- wait, yeah I do. The bar where Jackie works. Travis hangs out there and he has some buddies there that he shoots pool with. We could ask them, I guess. I doubt if they'd tell us."

Stan held up a finger. "They'll tell me, I can bet money on it. Where is this place?"

"It's the Blue Mirage."

"I know it. Yeah, some rough characters hang out there. Your sister works there?"

"She did until last night."

"Not a very nice place," Stan said. "Fights break out there all the time. I think the police have stacked the joint there a couple of times."

Shannon was really concerned now. She was on the verge of tears. "Oh, Stan, what do we do?"

"Sit tight. I'm gonna make another call to my FBI pals and let 'em know who she is. Her name's Jackie, right? What's her last name?"

"Parker."

"Right. Hold on."

Stan got on the phone once again. "Hey, Pete, I've got some news for you. The woman with Huffman is named Jackie Parker. She's-- how old is she, Shannon?"

"Uhm, she's twenty-seven."

"She's a twenty-seven-year-old divorcee. Listen, you gotta be careful with her. She's got family here in Limite. In fact, her sister is one of my clients on an unrelated case. Well, come to think of it, it *is* related, in a way. Never mind, I'll explain later. Anyway, this gives us a lead or two to follow. I'll be in touch."

He hung up the phone. "What say you and me go visit the Blue Mirage tonight and see what kind of information we can rustle up?"

"I'll have to see if it's okay with Carl, but I'm sure it will be. This is about Jackie now."

"What time do you think we should go?"

"I've always gone after ten o'clock. That's when she worked and that's when his friends usually shoot pool."

"I'll pick you up at ten, then. All right?"

"Why don't I meet you there?"

"Okay. Don't worry, Shannon. We'll find your sister. As for her legal problems, I don't know what to tell you..."

He was right. Jackie was in a lot of trouble, especially if she was an accomplice in last night's murder.

"Maybe she's really innocent and Travis was just making her do stuff she really didn't want to do," Shannon ventured.

Stan said, "It's been known to happen that way before. Let's hope that's the case."

He gathered up his folders and locked them in the briefcase.

"I gotta run. Ten o'clock, then?"

"Right."

She saw him out the door, then went to the kitchen and poured herself a glass of white wine.

Oh Jackie, she thought. You're wanted for murder. What have you gotten yourself into?

She looked up at the clock on the wall. Carl would be home soon. She had to get dinner ready. At least the activity would divert her attention for a little while.

The Post-It note with Carol Jenkins' address was stuck on the table. Shannon picked it up and looked at it.

After dinner, she was going to pay Carol Jenkins a surprise visit.

* * *

Shannon didn't remember much about Carol Jenkins. She must have seen her around when Shannon's mother was alive, but those years were vague flashes of memories that might or might not be real. She knew that Carol had been her mom's best friend at the time of the murder. She had worked at Donny's Cafeteria with her and they often went bar-hopping together. Carol was maybe three or four years older than her mother had been.

Shannon talked to her when she was digging into the case as a teenager. Carol was friendly enough but told Shannon that she didn't know anything except what was in the papers. "She was killed by one of them sex perverts," Carol told her. "That's all there was to it."

At that time, Carol worked as a secretary somewhere. Shannon couldn't remember if she had married or not.

Jackie still hadn't called; after dinner Shannon took the opportunity to ask Carl if he'd mind watching the kids for a little while. It was all right with him, so Shannon went out at 7:30. She drove west, close to the area where the cafeteria used to be. She found Pack Saddle Street easily and pulled into the driveway in front of the house. It was built of wood and painted white with brown trimming. Uneven hedges surrounded the front and sides, and several screens on the windows were torn. It was not a pretty sight.

Shannon got out of the car and went to the door. She could hear a television or radio inside.

She suddenly felt afraid and almost turned around to leave. The sound of a glass breaking inside stopped her. She heard a muffled voice say, "God damn it." For some reason, this encouraged Shannon to proceed with her mission. She rang the doorbell and waited.

The door opened abruptly. A woman dressed in a stained, dirty sweatsuit said, "Yeah? What is it?"

Shannon recognized her as Carol but she looked a lot older than Shannon remembered. The woman should have been in her late forties or early fifties, but she looked sixty-five. She had gotten fat, there were dark circles and bags under her eyes, and her grey hair was a fright wig. Carol was once an attractive woman with auburn hair. It was obvious that she had let herself go.

Before Shannon could say anything, Carol's eyes widened and her mouth dropped open. She gasped and stepped back slightly.

"Carol Jenkins?" Shannon asked.

"Yes?"

"I'm Shannon Parker Reece. Mary Parker's daughter."

A wave of relief passed over Carol. "Oh, my *God*, for a second I thought you *were* Mary Parker! You scared the *shit* out of me! I thought she'd come back to haunt me."

"I'm sorry, I--"

"No, no, don't be sorry, it's just that you look *just* like her, dear." Carol opened the screen door and gestured. "Come in, please."

Shannon stepped inside. The smell of booze and cigarettes was nauseating. The carpet looked as if it hadn't been vacuumed in years. The furniture was dusty and the wallpaper was terribly out of date.

"I hope I'm not disturbing you," Shannon said.

"No, no, I just dropped a glass and I have to clean it up."

Shannon followed Carol into the den, where two cigarettes were smoldering in an ash tray on a TV table. One of those "trash-TV" talk shows was on the television. A cowboy was trying to explain to the studio audience why he thought it was all right to marry his cousin.

Carol stepped into the tile-floored kitchen, which was marred by a pile of broken glass and a spreading brown liquid that appeared to be whisky or bourbon.

"Sit down," Carol said. "I'll clean this real quick. You want something to drink?"

The woman was drunk. She was wavering a little and her speech was slurred.

"No, thank you. Here, let me help you," Shannon said.

Together they cleaned up the broken glass and wiped up the mess. Shannon made sure the sharp pieces were properly disposed of and then they sat in the den in front of the television. Carol flicked it off with the remote, then turned to Shannon.

"So! Shannon Parker, you're all grown up," she said. She shook her head. "It's unbelievable how much you look like your mother."

"People say that all the time," Shannon said.

"Well, it's true. What brings you over to see an old girl like me?"

"Carol, you were good friends with my mom, right?"

"Best of friends," she said, proudly.

"Do you remember about twelve years ago or so, I was in high school? I came to see you to ask you what you knew about my mom's murder."

"Hmmm, I don't remember that. I was just going to say I hadn't seen you since you were a child."

"Well, we did talk, and you said you didn't know anything."

"I guess that's true if you say so."

"Well," Shannon said, not knowing quite how to express herself. "I'm looking into the case again and this time I need some answers. I know that you know more than you let on last time. I'm asking you as the daughter of your friend, my mother, to please tell me what you know about my mom and dad, and about Gary Harrison and his wife Janice."

The smile on Carol's face faded quickly. She looked down at the carpet and sat there a few seconds before saying, "I don't think I can help you, honey. There's really not a lot I know."

Shannon couldn't help herself. She suddenly felt rage and said, through her teeth, "Oh, yes there is. I know that you and mom knew Gary Harrison and his wife before the murder. I'd like to know how she knew him, and I want to know what she did at the Washington Hotel in those days, and I want to know about the wife-swapping clubs, and sex orgies, and all those things I know you did with her."

The woman stared at Shannon as if she were a beast. "How dare you! You come over here out of the blue, out of nowhere on a weeknight, and accuse *me* of that kind of crap? Who do you think you are?"

"I'm Mary Parker's daughter!" Shannon said forcefully. "I have a right to know."

"I don't have to tell you nothin'."

"No, you don't." Shannon attempted to pull back, calm down, and speak carefully. "You don't have to tell me a thing. But I'm asking you, Carol, please. I'll never tell anyone else. I won't go to the police or anything. It'll be between you and me."

Carol didn't say anything. She took a pack of cigarettes from the TV tray, removed one, and lit it. She offered the pack to Shannon, but Shannon shook her head.

The woman sat there and smoked a third of the cigarette, lost in thought. Shannon waited patiently for a response. She didn't want to rush her.

"All right," Carol finally said. "But I'm gonna get me a drink first. You want one?"

"No, thanks."

Carol got up and went into the kitchen. She came back with another glass of bourbon. She took a big swig, then started to talk.

"How do you know about the Washington Hotel?" the woman asked.

"Carol, I'm an adult now. I've learned a lot. I know all about the prostitution and gambling that was going on there. I know you were involved and that maybe my mother was involved. Was she?"

"Your mother was never a prostitute," Carol said. "She wouldn't do that. But she was a pretty wild party girl. She went out with a lot of men, even after she was married to your father. What does he say about all this, anyway?"

"My dad doesn't talk about it."

Carol nodded. "It's not surprising. He was involved in it, too. He knew Gary Harrison before the murder."

It was what Shannon had been afraid of hearing.

"Please tell me what you know," Shannon said.

"Let's see... I met your mother in 1970, I think? Maybe it was 1969. We worked together at the cafeteria. You remember Donny's Cafeteria? That's where we worked. Anyway, we got to be good friends. She had a wild streak that was a lot like mine."

"Did she do drugs or just drink?"

Carol took a drag on the cigarette and blew out a cloud of smoke. "Mostly drink, but she liked speed. Uppers. I did too. We'd get high together sometimes. We smoked pot a few times. I guess I was what you'd call a bad girl. Your mom was someone who was a good girl with a bad girl just itchin' to break out. We had the most fun when it was just me and her, driving around in her old car or mine, cruisin' the drag and lookin' for men."

"So she cheated on my dad?"

"Hell, yes. Lots of times. But he cheated on her, too. You knew that, didn't you?"

"I suspected as much."

"Hell, you're a big girl, I can tell you this-- I even slept with your dad." Carol said it as if it had been some kind of great sacrifice on her part. "Your mom put us up to it. Mary had been foolin' around and your dad caught wind of it. He was jealous. She thought that if he slept with someone else, then that gave her permission to sleep around. So she got us together one night."

"So there was wife-swapping going on?"

She nodded. "It was a small crowd that hung out at some of the bars. There were some policemen doin' it, too, I think. Yeah, that's right. Sometimes the groups would book rooms at the Washington Hotel. There was already prostitution going on there, so what was a little hanky panky between couples who weren't married to each other? No one was going to tell. It was a perfectly safe place to do that sort of thing. However, a lot of times we met in people's homes, too."

"How did it work?"

"Well, it wasn't like it was a club you signed up for or paid dues to be in. It wasn't an official 'club.' It was really just people who knew each other. It was no different from you gettin' together with your friends for a dinner and a game of bridge, except we'd all have sex together instead of playin' bridge. I honestly can't remember how it started."

"Was my mom already in it when you met her?"

"No. I guess I kinda helped introduce your mom and dad to the crowd. It must have been 1970 or so when they did it together for the first time."

"So what happened?"

Carol coughed loudly and didn't catch her breath for a few seconds.

"Sorry. Larry, your dad, he didn't like it much, I don't think. Maybe he did, I don't know. I remember him being pretty jealous of your mom. It was like-- it was okay for him to do it, but it bugged him that your mom did it and *liked* it so much. I just remember that your mom was always eager for those parties and went out actively searching for sex partners. I think she wanted to sleep with every man in Limite. She came to the parties alone more often than with your dad. She was obsessed with sex. I mean, I had a pretty healthy interest in it, but your mom was out of control."

"What about Gary Harrison and his wife?"

"I knew Janice from the Washington Hotel. I worked there off and on, and so did she."

"You were prostitutes?"

Carol was quiet a moment, then said, "I'd rather not say. I knew Janice from working there and I guess that's how I met Gary. He worked there as a bouncer or bartender or something. They came to a couple of those parties. Janice was more of a sex fiend than your mom was. Sometimes, though, I got the feeling that Gary made her do the things she did. It was hard to tell. Janice was a strange lady. She could be very sweet and friendly, then suddenly turn into a harpy. She lived a hard, rough life, and Gary didn't make it any easier on her."

"Did you know he was a killer?"

"No. All that came out afterwards. I always kinda thought the guy was sick. He was into bondage and S&M and that kind of thing. Janice was, too, but like I said, I think she did it only 'cause he liked her to do it, or made her do it."

"Did you sleep with Gary Harrison?"

"My, we're really gettin' personal, aren't we?" Carol said. "Yeah, I did. And it gives me nightmares when I think about it. He could have killed me."

"Do you think Janice helped him kill my mom?"

"I don't know. If I had to guess, I'd say not. But then again, I think she had it in her to do something like that. I think if the right buttons were pushed on her, she'd be capable of killing someone. But not in the way your mother died. No way."

"Why do you say that?"

"What happened to your mom, and to Grace Daniel, and Kelly White, and to all the others-- was sexual! Gary Harrison kidnapped them, did his thing with them, killed them, and left them out in the oil fields! No woman would do that! Come on!"

It made sense. The crimes were very demeaning assaults against women. The recklessness of the abductions and the subsequent indiscriminate dumping of the bodies in plain view felt very "male." They had to have been committed by a man who had little regard for the opposite sex.

"Have you ever heard of the Dixie Mafia?" Shannon asked.

Carol screwed up her forehead. "No."

"Did you know Guy Simms or Lucky Farrow?"

"Yeah, they were always down at the hotel."

"What about Sheriff Barton?"

"I saw him down there a few times, too. They say he had a controlling interest in the hotel and what we did there. He was real sweet on your mom."

"Sheriff Barton?"

Carol nodded. "I don't know if they, you know, *did* anything, but he liked talkin' to her when they were both there."

"Did Sheriff Barton know Gary Harrison before the murders?"

"I'm pretty sure he did," Carol said. "Barton was there at least once every two weeks or so. He would have had to run into Gary at some point."

"Do you think he knew Gary was killing women before he was arrested?"

"I don't know. I doubt it. He was still sheriff, wasn't he? He would have arrested Gary if he'd known!"

"Unless Barton was protecting him for some reason," Shannon said.

"What do you mean?"

"Never mind. What do you think happened to my mother?"

Carol put out her cigarette and promptly lit another one. "Gary went nuts and kidnapped her from that nightclub. He had the hots for her. She probably resisted him, so he raped her and killed her."

"And that's it?"

"What else could it be?"

"Well, in his first confession, he said Janice was in on it, too."

"I don't think so. Like I said, I don't think a woman would do that to another woman. I guess you could always go find her and knock on *her* door and ask her."

Carol suddenly started to cry but Shannon didn't feel much sympathy for her.

"It my fault," Carol sobbed after blowing her nose on a used tissue. "If I hadn't introduced your mother to Gary Harrison, she'd probably still be alive."

Shannon didn't know what to say, so she remained silent.

"It's haunted me ever since it happened," Carol continued. "That's why I was so shocked to see you at the door. I thought you were *her* comin' back to get me!"

Carol put her head down on the TV tray and sobbed loudly. Shannon finally patted her head and said, "Don't, it's all right. It wasn't your fault."

The woman raised her head. Mascara had run down her face and she looked even more hideous.

Shannon asked her another question in an attempt to get Carol to stop crying. "My mother was supposed to meet someone at the Fever club the night of her murder. Do you know who that was supposed to be?"

"Well, I think she was goin' to meet *me*, but I was late. I told the police that we had talked about meeting there, or maybe it was the Moonlight club, I can't remember. But now that you mention it, I think she was also supposed to meet some guy from the cafeteria there. No, wait, it was someone from the hotel. Maybe both. There were a couple of other employees-- men-- at the cafeteria who hung out at the hotel. Frank. That was his name. She was gonna meet Frank there."

"What's Frank's last name?"

"I don't remember. Besides, he's dead."

"He is?"

"Yeah, he was killed in a car wreck in the late seventies."

"Was this a meeting for sex?"

"Somehow, I don't think it was. It was about drugs, I think. He sold drugs, and I think she got speed from him, I can't remember."

"Are you *sure* you've never heard of the Dixie Mafia?"

"I'm sure." Carol wiped her face with a tissue.

"Maybe you don't know it by that name. What I mean is 'organized crime' in Limite."

"Well, there was plenty of that goin' on. The Washington Hotel lived off of organized crime in those days."

"That's what I'm talkin' about."

"Oh, I guess I've never heard it called that before. Yeah, there was certainly organized crime goin' on. We were all a part of it, too."

"My mom?"

Carol shrugged. "She wasn't a hooker but she was always hangin' around that crowd. She might have been involved in something crooked."

"Do you know a guy named Travis Huffman?"

Carol frowned. "No, I don't think so. Wait, there was this kid at the hotel. His name was Travis. Is that who you mean?"

"Possibly. Have you seen him in the past few years?"

"Honey, I haven't seen *anyone* in the past few years. I just go to work and come home now. I'm too old to be gettin' into any trouble."

She took a drag and went into another coughing fit. It was several seconds before the spasm subsided.

She put out her cigarette and got up. "I suppose I oughta give up smoking. I'm gonna have another drink. That's really all I know, honey." She went into the kitchen and dropped her glass on the floor again. It shattered with a loud crash.

"Oh god *damn* it! Look what you made me do!" Carol screamed. "That's the second glass in ten minutes. If you hadn't got me so upset...!"

"I'm sorry," Shannon said. "Maybe I'd better go, now."

Carol started crying again. "Yeah, maybe you'd better. Go on. I'm sorry about your mom and all."

"Me too," Shannon said. She got up and went to the door. Before she could leave, Carol stopped her.

"Wait," she said.

"What?"

"I'm sorry, I know you didn't make me do that. Your mother wasn't a bad person," she said. "She-- she was the kindest person I ever knew."

Shannon forced a smile. "Thanks."

She went out into the cold air, leaving behind a lonely, broken woman beset with the worst of all inner demons-- that ugly beast known as Guilt.

* * *

Shannon pulled into the parking lot of the Blue Mirage at 9:55 p.m. She got out of her Ford, looked around for Stan's Ranger, and found it parked on the side of the building.

She went inside and was once again assaulted by the obligatory loud music, smoke, and smell of booze. Stan was slumped at the bar, sipping a beer. She sat down on the stool next to him.

"Hey there," he said. "Buy you a beer?"

"No thanks, let's just get this over with."

"All right." He chugged the rest of his drink in one motion and slammed his chest with his fist. "Ahhhh. Nothing goes down better than a good dose of brew. Come on, you see the guy?"

Shannon peered back through the haze to the back of the room. Chaz was there, all right, playing pool with his rough-looking buddies.

"That's him. The ugly guy with the crew cut."

"Let's do it, then," Stan said, then started to walk back.

The man known as Chaz was with the young blonde girl that had been wrapped around Travis Huffman the last time Shannon was in the bar. He was aiming the cue stick for a difficult shot when Stan leaned against the table, obstructing the line of fire.

"Your name Chaz?" Stan asked.

The thug raised up and looked at the newcomer. "Yeah, who the fuck are you?"

Stan flashed an I.D. with a badge on it. "Inspector Stan McHam. FBI." That got Chaz's attention. The other guys around the table backed up a little, not knowing whether they should run or stand their ground. Shannon was surprised that Stan claimed to be an FBI agent. She knew the badge was fake.

Chaz gazed past McHam and saw her standing behind him. He squinted at her, trying to place where he'd seen her before.

"I'd like to ask you a couple of questions," Stan said.

"What about?"

"About your pal Travis Huffman."

"I haven't seen him. Now if you don't mind..." Chaz made a move as if to continue his game.

In a maneuver that surprised everyone, particularly Shannon, Stan McHam slid off the pool table, whipped out his .38 Special, grabbed Chaz's neck with his other hand, and slammed the brute's head down onto the pool table. He then stuck the barrel of the gun into Chaz's temple. For a man with a disability, Stan was quick and strong.

"Now, look, you asshole," Stan said with clenched teeth. "You have three seconds to tell me where Huffman is. I know he left town last night with his girlfriend. Now where did he go?"

Everyone in the bar stopped what they were doing. The music continued, but all eyes were on Stan McHam and the big guy they knew as Chaz.

One of Chaz's playmates made a move toward Stan. McHam swung the gun around and pointed it at the guy.

"Back off, butthead," he said. "Or you'll have three tits on your chest."

The man retreated. The gun went back to Chaz's head.

"One..."

"I don't know where he is, honest!" Chaz pleaded.

"Two...!"

"Please, wait, I think he might have gone to some other city."

"What city?"

"Uhm, well, I think he might have said something about San Antonio."

"Do you know where in San Antonio? That's a big place."

"I don't have a clue," Chaz said. He was sweating like a pig.

"Two and a half...."

"Wait!" Chaz said. "I think you might find him if you look up a guy named Forbes. Alan Forbes. He owns a strip club there called Legs. That's all I know, honest!"

McHam put away his gun. "Thank you, sir. You've been very helpful." He turned to Shannon. "Let's go."

Everyone in the club parted to make an aisle for them as Stan escorted her out. Without looking back, they got to the parking lot, then started to run for their vehicles.

"That was incredible, Stan," she said. "You scared the hell out of me."

"Scared the hell out of me, too," he said. "There's no telling what one of those guys might have done. Anyone could have been carrying a piece. We were lucky. Come on, we gotta get out of here."

"Come back to my house, all right?" she suggested.

"Fine."

They got into their respective automobiles and tore out of the parking lot, just as Chaz and his boys poured out of the building. They shouted at the Ranger but were too late to stop it.

* * *

"I need a drink," said Carl Reece.

They were in their kitchen. Shannon and Stan had sat Carl down and related the latest developments.

He got up and took a beer from the refrigerator. Carl looked up at Stan.

"Sure, I'll take one," Stan said. Carl looked at his wife.

"Okay, me too," she said.

Carl brought back three cold bottles of Corona and sat down. They drank in silence for a few minutes.

Finally, Shannon said, "Well, what do you think? Should I go, or shouldn't I?"

Carl said, "Honey, I'm just afraid it might be dangerous and that you're gettin' into something that's over your head."

"Stan'll protect me," she said.

"And how much is Stan charging you? No offense, Stan."

"None taken," Stan said. "As of tonight, I'm not charging you a cent. I'm on this case for personal reasons now. I want to track down that son of a bitch that shot me. Pardon my French. I'd be doing it regardless if you guys had an interest in the case or not."

"Well, I've gotta make sure my sister is safe," Shannon said. "That's my main concern. It's so *weird* that both Jackie and Janice Harrison are in the same city!"

"Maybe it's not a coincidence," Stan said.

Shannon looked at him sideways. "Maybe Janice is still involved in your Dixie Mafia?"

Stan shrugged. "Who knows." He gestured toward the phone. "You know I just talked with Pete. They knew all about that strip joint in San Antonio. They think that counterfeit job was masterminded out of it. It's a Dixie Mafia nerve center, one that controls a large part of the state. Huffman's bound to go there."

"Jackie's gonna get arrested," Shannon said. "It'll be terrible."

"Let's hope that *does* happen," Stan said. "'Cause other than her escaping, the alternative is far worse."

"So, Carl," Shannon said. "Will you be able to watch the kids? Stan and I want to leave in the morning and drive down."

Carl nodded. "I guess so. I have some vacation time I can take. I just don't want you to get hurt, Shannon. Maybe I should go too."

"I won't get hurt," she said. "And you need to stay here with the kids."

"She won't get hurt," Stan said. "You have my word."

"Well, I understand why you want to go, honey. I'd do the same thing if she were my sister," Carl said. "All right, go ahead, but you call me every hour on the hour!"

She laughed. "Don't be silly. I'm gonna call Jeff now."

She picked up the phone. The men began to discuss high school football and the Limite Lynx's admirable season last fall.

Her brother answered on the third ring. "Hello?"

"Jeff, it's Shannon."

"Hi! What's up?"

"Listen, Jackie's in a lot of trouble."

"What?"

"Just listen, okay? Jackie has a boyfriend who's a murderer-- he just killed someone in Limite and he's probably killed a lot of other people. He's wanted by the FBI and everything. Well, he's on the run and Jackie's with him!"

"My God!"

"We think they're in San Antonio. This detective I hired and I are driving down tomorrow. I want to know if you'd like us to come through Austin first and pick you up. It's on the way. Sorta."

"You want me to come to San Antonio with you?"

"Yeah, I may need help with Jackie, Jeff," Shannon said. "She's on drugs or something, and this guy has some kind of Svengali hold on her. Can you? Will you?"

"Well, sure, Shannon," he said. "What time do you think you'll be here?"

"It takes what, seven or eight hours to drive to Austin from here?" she asked.

"Yeah."

Stan heard her question and said, "Not the way I drive. Count on five or six."

"Look, we'll leave here around nine o'clock," she said. "Expect us sometime around two. All right?"

"Okay. What are we going to do in San Antonio?"

"Well, we're gonna try and locate Jackie. If we can, we're gonna talk to her and see if she'll give herself up and get away from that guy."

"And if we can't?"

"I don't know. We'll cross that bridge when we come to it."

"Where will we stay?" Jeff asked.

"I guess a hotel," she answered. "There's one other errand I have to do in San Antonio, Jeff."

"What's that?"

"Janice Harrison is there and I wanna talk to her."

"Oh, Christ, Shannon, really?" He sounded annoyed.

"Yeah, I've learned a lot about mom that we didn't know about. I'll tell you all about it tomorrow, okay?"

"Fine."

"You can get off work and all that?"

"Sure. I think this falls under the 'family crisis' excuse," Jeff said.

"Don't be funny."

"I'm not."

They hung up and Shannon sat back down with the men. "Okay, we're picking up Jeff in Austin. You'll like him, he's the brains of the family."

"Well, his sister's pretty damn smart, too," Stan said.

"One of them, anyway," Carl added.

Shannon took a swig from the Corona. Then she asked, "So, Stan, if you're not working for me anymore, then what's your agenda in San Antonio? Revenge?"

Stan drummed his fingers on the table top and replied, "I honestly don't know. I just figger I gotta go. I gotta know if Travis Huffman was the guy who shot me or not."

She thought about that and said, "That's a good enough reason for me."

Normally, an excursion like she was about to undertake would have made her nervous and anxious. If Jackie's life wasn't at stake, she probably wouldn't do it. Instead, Shannon found that she was calm, clear, and resolved. Like Stan, she was more determined than ever to find all the answers.

JACKIE

Jackie Parker had lost all track of time. She didn't know what day it was and she didn't know how long she had been gone from Limite. For all she knew, she'd been away for a month. It only *seemed* like three or four days.

She was sitting in the little room in back of the club-- where she and Travis had slept since they got to San Antonio. Travis had said it would be best if they weren't seen much. It was possible that the cops were watching the place. Travis spent most of his time with his buddy Alan, the guy that ran the Legs club. They were either in the bar itself, drinking beer and watching the strippers, or they were in Alan's office, laughing and cussing.

He kept promising they'd be rich soon. He kept promising that pretty soon they'd have enough money to go back to Limite, pick up Tyler, and go wherever they wanted.

So far it wasn't happening. For four days or a month, she didn't know which, all they had done was sit in the lousy strip joint and wait. Travis was very jumpy and nervous. She considered herself lucky that he had hit her only twice. As long as she stayed good, he'd give her the daily dose of candy.

Jackie examined her arms and felt the bruises and tread marks. She knew they were disgusting and that she was doing a terrible thing, but she was too far gone to be upset about it. She didn't care. As long as she got that daily dose.

In fact... wasn't it time now? She looked at the clock. It was after supper time. Wasn't it time for her candy now? Where was Travis?

Jackie got up and started pacing around the small room, which consisted of a sofa bed and a cot, a sink, a table and chairs, and an adjacent bathroom. There was no bath or shower. She might have noticed that the room smelled of body odor and urine, but she just didn't care. There was only one thing on her mind.

She opened the door-- something Travis had told her a number of times not to do-- and looked into the corridor. She could see Alan's office door, wide open with no one inside. They were probably inside the club. That's where the action was, right? She could hear the pounding beat of the bass speakers filtering down the corridor.

141

Slowly, she wandered down the hall until she came to a backstage area. Off to the side was a large dressing room occupied by two buxom dancers. Jackie ignored them and went on past the dressing room, found the "Stage" sign, then went through the door and into the side of the club.

The music was loud techno-pop. A topless girl writhed in a G-string onstage, smiling at a group of businessmen sitting at the edge of the walkway. The decor in the room was far too red and it was definitely too dark.

Jackie looked around and spotted Travis and Alan sitting on barstools at the back. Her vision was so blurry it was difficult to tell. She staggered toward them. Travis saw her and frowned. He pointed at her and mouthed the words, "Get back in there!"

She just kept going. She wanted her candy.

Travis hopped off the stool and casually walked around the room to meet her halfway.

"What the hell are you doing out here?" he asked when he got up to her.

"I want my stuff," she said.

"I already *gave* it to you, you stupid cow!"

"No you didn't, and stop calling me names." She couldn't understand why she was talking so slow.

"You're out of your head, Jackie! It's why you're so stoned right now! I gave it to you two hours ago! You're wasted! Go back to our room."

"No, I want to have some fun, too. It's boring here, Travis. You promised we'd get out of here."

Jackie started to lose her balance but Travis caught her.

"Aww, honey, come on." He sat her down at a table before she swaggered and fell over him. He knelt beside her chair. "Now listen to me. This deal we got going is probably gonna go down tonight. We'll be able to leave tomorrow. Now just be patient, be a good girl, and get the fuck out of here."

"Why do you get to come out here with the people and I don't?"

"'Cause I'm the one doing the business. Besides, they'll be lookin' for both of us, and it's best if we're not seen together."

"But I didn't do nothin'!"

"You were there when I shot him, Jackie. You ran with me. That makes you part of it. Now come on, let me take you back to the room."

"No. Just let me sit here for a little while. You don't have to sit here with me. Just leave me alone. Let me breathe some fresh air." Her words were slurring and she was staring at the flashing lights on the stage.

"You don't want to watch the dancers!" he said.

"Yeah, I do. Leave me alone. It beats watchin' the clock in that room."

"Fine." He got up and walked back across the floor to where Alan was waiting.

Jackie sat there, feeling a surge of pride and accomplishment. She had told him off and gotten her way. Now she could sit, enjoy herself, and... watch naked women. Oh, yuck, she thought. Not her idea of a perfect evening but it would have to do. She laughed at the irony of it.

A waitress came over and asked, "You want somethin' to drink, sugar?"

"Yeah," Jackie said.

The waitress waited, but Jackie didn't say anything else.

"What do you want?"

"Huh?"

"What kind of drink do you want?"

"Oh. Uhm, a Coke. Yeah, a Coke."

"Okay," said the waitress. She shook her head and walked on.

Jackie found that she was transfixed by the movement on stage. She enjoyed the dancer's limber body. It wasn't a sexual thing, of course, she told herself. But she had to admit that the girl was a pretzel. She wondered if she could do those moves herself. Could she put her ankles behind her head like that?

Without thinking, Jackie started pulling her right leg up and trying to get it over her head. There was a tearing pain in her thigh and she yelped. Travis looked over at her with a look of disbelief. Jackie put her leg down and rubbed it.

"Jackie?"

The voice would have startled her if things hadn't been moving in slow motion to begin with.

She turned and saw a man standing by her table. He looked vaguely familiar.

"Jackie?" he said again.

"Huh?"

"It's me, Jeff."

"What?"

"Jeff, your brother."

Jackie screwed up her eyes until the figure came into focus. He *did* look like Jeff.

"Jeff's my older brother," she said.

"I know," he said, laughing slightly.

"He lives in Austin."

"That's right. But I'm here now." He moved around her and sat down at the table. "Can I sit here?"

"Sure." Jackie furrowed her brow and stared at him. This couldn't possibly be happening for real. "Jeff? What the hell are you doing here?"

"I came to see you," he said.

"How did you know I was here?"

"Jackie, you need to get out of here. Come with me. Right now. Let's walk out the door. You'll be safe," he said.

Suddenly she became frightened.

"You're not my brother," she said. "You're one of *them*."

"Jackie, don't you recognize me?" he pleaded. "Look, Shannon's here, too. She's outside, in the car. And a friend of ours who helped us find you. You're in a lot of trouble, do you realize that?"

"Go away," she said. "Leave, before Travis sees you."

"I don't care if he does. Jackie, you're wanted for murder! You gotta come with me, please. We're at the Ramada Inn just down the street."

Travis' voice surprised both of them. "What's going on here?"

They looked up and saw him standing over them. The waitress was behind him with Jackie's Coke. Travis turned to her, snapped, "Beat it," and she disappeared.

"Travis, this is my big brother, Jeff," Jackie said. "Jeff Parker, this is Travis Huffman." She started to laugh at how funny that sounded.

Travis looked at him in astonishment. Then he held out his hand and said with disinterest, "Well, glad to meet you. You live here?"

"In Austin."

"How, uh... how did you know she was here?"

"I just tracked her down. She's in trouble. I'm here to help."

"Well, gee, pal, we really appreciate you thinking of us, but we don't need or want your help, so you'd better go now."

"Travis!" Jackie said. "No, wait, Jeff, he doesn't mean--"

"Yes, I do mean!" Travis grabbed Jeff by his jacket lapels and pulled him out of the seat. "Leave."

"You can't keep her here if she wants to go," Jeff said, swallowing.

"Let him go, Travis!" Jackie screamed.

Alan came running up and pulled off Travis. "Are you nuts, man?" Then he turned to Jeff and said, "You'd best go, mister."

Jeff backed up from the table. "I'll be back, Jackie. Remember what I said." He moved cautiously around Travis and toward the exit.

"There goes my brother," Jackie said in a sing song voice.

As soon as Jeff was out the front door, Travis grabbed Jackie by the hair and pulled her out of her seat. Jackie grimaced in pain but didn't make a sound.

"You're going back to the room, right now," he seethed.

* * *

The bed was spinning and she felt like vomiting.

Jackie opened her eyes and tried to fix on the bright naked bulb in the middle of the ceiling but it seemed to be moving in a circle. She felt horrible.

She tried to raise herself off the bed but ended up rolling over and landing on the floor with a slam. She didn't feel it, though. Her body had gone beyond feeling much of anything.

What had Travis been so pissed off about? Why did he have to hit her? She had only wanted to sit out front and watch the dancers.

Had she dreamed about her brother? She thought she had. There was an image of his face implanted in the front of her mind and she could still see him and hear him. He wanted her to come with him somewhere. She would have liked to talk to him some more but Travis had interrupted. And then she woke up. She thought. It had seemed real, anyway.

Jackie slowly got to her knees. The room was beginning to settle down, so she attempted to stand. One leg, then two legs... and she was up.

"Success!" she said aloud.

She looked around. She was alone in the same old room. God, she thought. She had to get out of here. What hotel did Jeff say he was at?

She opened the door and looked out into the corridor. Maybe she could just make a break for it and leave. Go back to Limite. But how would she get there? She didn't have any money on her. Travis had all the money. Unless... unless she took some of that money Travis had. He had a big bagful of money. Maybe she could take some of that and buy a bus ticket. Or even a plane ticket.

Even though her mind was far from clear, she knew she had to get away. If she didn't get out of that place, she was going to die.

The money... where was it? In Alan's office?

She peeked down the hall. The office door was closed. She could hear voices in there. Was Travis' deal going down now? Maybe she should go see. If she was lucky, she might be able to cause a diversion and pick up a stack of hundreds. She had done it before easily enough. She had been particularly proud of herself for snatching a thousand dollars worth of the cash to give to Shannon.

Jackie walked slowly toward the door. The muffled voices grew louder and she could hear a man saying, "I don't care what you've been through. You weren't supposed to kill him."

"The guy pulled a gun on me first! He was trying to rip us off!" That was Travis' voice. "I'm tellin' you, Hank, I didn't take anything!"

Jackie wanted to see what was going on. Travis probably wouldn't like it but she didn't care anymore what he thought. She was going to take some of the money and get the hell out of Dodge. She was going to walk right in and say that the cops were outside.

She reached for the door knob.

"I don't like it, Travis," the man named Hank said. "I smell a rat."

"I think he's tellin' the truth, Hank," came another voice. It was Alan.

"Bullshit," Hank said. "Travis has never told the truth in his life."

Jackie turned the knob.

"What the fuck are you saying?" Travis said. "You callin' me a liar?"

"I'm callin' you a rat, Huffman," Hank said. "You fucked up our operation. You gotta pay for it."

"It was Jimmy's fault, god damn it! He pulled a gun on me and tried to take all the cash! I tried to salvage what I could before the cops came and I had to get the hell out of there. All I've got is what's here, do you want it or not?"

"Oh, I want it, all right," Hank said. "And I'm gonna take it from you."

"Not without paying me what's coming to me," Travis said. "You owe me a hundred and fifty grand. It ain't my fault if your man in Limite fucked up. I still get full payment and you can't have any of this shit until I get it."

"You talk big, Travis," Hank said. "You think you're untouchable, eh?"

"I've been around a lot longer than you, punk," Travis said.

There was a scraping sound as chairs slid across the floor.

At that instant, Jackie pushed open the door and saw four men at a table. A suitcase full of money was on top of it.

It all occurred in about two seconds but to Jackie it felt like two minutes of a ballet in slow motion. Travis pushed his chair back from the table and pulled a gun out of a pocket. Alan, his friend, was in the process of drawing a gun, too.

The other men, the one called Hank, and another goon, had already drawn their weapons and were each falling down to one knee.

"Hey," Jackie said, but the word came out three octaves lower than her normal voice.

All four men turned to her, very slowly, with looks of surprise on their faces. Even though movement was at a snail's pace, she still didn't have time to react. All four guns fired in her direction.

She felt burning fire slam into her stomach and chest, knocking her backwards into the hall. As she slumped against the door frame and held on to the molding to keep from slipping, the dance in front of her erupted in a shower of blood and noise.

Hank and the goon turned back to Alan and Travis and fired again. The slugs hit both men, hurling them to the floor. Travis' gun fired as he fell. A lucky shot hit Hank in the middle of the face. The goon fired again and hit Travis in the chest. Alan's gun exploded another time and the goon was thrown back onto Jackie. Blood was pouring out of the man's throat and onto her blouse.

She was able to let out a scream before she slipped to the floor like a sack of potatoes. Her body was on fire. She could see the ceiling in the hallway and thought she might be able to count the water stains on it before it was time to go to sleep. One... two... oh, where was Jeff now? Had she really seen him? Three... four... Tyler? Where was Tyler? Five... there sure were a lot of stains in the ceiling... God, she felt terrible. Everything was getting even slower and the sound was dropping out of the picture. Was it her, or was the theater getting darker? Was the show about to begin? Would there be coming attractions? She usually liked to go pee before the movie started, and she hadn't done that. She hated having to go pee in the middle of the movie. It was definitely getting darker. Now let's see, what was it she was doing? Oh, yes, counting the stains. How many had she counted already? She couldn't remember.

What was that warm liquid in her mouth?

She coughed, spit, and saw that it was red. What had happened to her? Where was she?

Jeff? Shannon?

Someone?

It was very dark now. Why were they so late starting the movie?

JANICE

Shannon sat in the hospital waiting room, nervously chewing on her index finger. Jeff was in another chair a few feet away. His eyes were closed and his head had drooped down, chin to chest. She wished that she could fall asleep anywhere at anytime, which is something Jeff had always been able to do.

They had been there practically all night. Jackie was still in surgery. She had been hit by four bullets-- two in the chest and two in the stomach. Her condition was critical, and the first report the doctors gave them at 2:00 in the morning was not promising. It was now 5:30 a.m.

Stan was out with his FBI friends collecting data on the case. He promised he would return to the hospital as soon as he could.

Two days earlier, Shannon and Stan had picked up Jeff in Austin, then drove south on I-35 to San Antonio. Shannon hadn't traveled much. She had been to Limite's neighboring towns, to Austin, and to Dallas. She once got to go to Colorado on a church trip when she was a teenager. She had never been to San Antonio and she found its vastness overwhelming. It seemed to be nothing but a series of freeways.

They found the Legs club easily enough and luckily there had been a Ramada Inn a few blocks away. They checked in and began a surveillance on the place, hoping to spot Jackie at some point.

The FBI had been watching the club as well. Stan made contact with the agents in charge, explained who he was, and was helpful in providing them some information about Travis Huffman. The agents knew that Huffman and Jackie were in the club but the suspects hadn't emerged in two days. The FBI men were content to wait and see-- for another day-- but after that, they planned to raid the joint.

Jeff and Stan made three separate trips into the strip club. Shannon didn't want to go in, electing to stay outside in the car or at the hotel. Their mission was to locate Jackie and see what condition she was in. If she was lucid, Jeff was going to attempt to get her to leave. The FBI knew all about what they were doing, reluctantly sanctioning the plan. However, if Jackie refused to leave by 10:00 p.m. on the night of the planned raid, it would commence anyway.

After Jeff's unsuccessful bid at getting Jackie out of the club, the go-ahead was given for the raid. Eight agents in protective gear-- bulletproof vests, helmets, gas masks, and automatic weapons-- were set to go into the club shortly before the designated time. When the suspect known as "Hank" drove up in a limousine at 9:30, they knew something was going down. The team assumed their positions when, at 9:50, they heard gunshots. The officer in charge gave the order to move in early.

The agents found several shaken club employees, a few frightened naked dancers, three dead men, one seriously wounded man, and Jackie. Travis Huffman, Alan Forbes, and the man known as Hank had been killed. The fourth man, Hank's bodyguard, had been hit in the throat and would probably survive. Jackie's chances were slim, at best. Ambulances arrived at the scene moments later and she was rushed to the nearest hospital.

All of the counterfeit money was confiscated by the authorities.

Shannon looked at her watch and wondered if she should call her dad. It was still pretty early but he'd be getting up soon. She stood and went to the bank of pay phones along the wall. She used her calling card and soon got her father on the other end.

"Dad?"

"Shannon?"

"Yeah. Listen, I don't have very good news. Are you sitting down?"

"What's wrong?"

"I'm in San Antonio. Jackie's been shot."

"*What?*"

"She got in the crossfire of a shoot-out. I think that's what happened, we're not exactly sure, yet. Anyway, she was hit pretty bad. We got her into the hospital in the middle of the night and they've been operating ever since. Dad..." Her voice choked a little. "She might not make it."

"Oh, Jesus," he said. "Do I need to get down there?"

"Why don't you wait and see? Hopefully the doctors will come out pretty soon and tell me what's going on. Jeff is here with me. You go on to work and I'll let you know as soon as I hear something."

"Screw work, I'm staying right here by the phone," he said.

"All right. I'll call you soon."

"All right."

She hung up the phone and went back to her seat. Jeff was stirring. "Any news?" he asked. She shook her head.

Five minutes later, Stan McHam limped into the waiting room. "Any word on Jackie?" he asked.

"Not yet," she replied.

"Geez, she's been in there a long time."

"Yeah."

Stan sat down by Shannon and put his arm around her. "She'll make it. Don't worry."

Tears filled her eyes. She hated to say it, but something inside her didn't give her much hope. When she had seen Jackie being wheeled into the operating room, it looked as if her sister had been in a war.

"What did the FBI say?" she asked.

"Well, it's pretty much how we figured. The counterfeiting operation was being run out of that strip club. Travis was what you might call a 'regional manager'. He traveled to different towns and set up distribution centers. The one for the western part of the state and New Mexico was in Limite. Apparently, the guy runnin' the center in Limite tried to double-cross the mob and steal some of the fake cash. Travis killed him and took what he could salvage. But it looks like Travis embezzled a little on his own. Kinda weird, isn't it? Embezzling money that's not even real? Anyway, Travis had a price on his head. He had pissed off some of the Dixie Mafia leaders by makin' some unauthorized hits, shootin' his mouth off, that kind of thing. And, they caught him stealing from them. That's where that guy Hank comes in. He was a hit man from Biloxi. Poor Jackie just happened to be in the wrong place at the wrong time."

"He was a lot like Gary Harrison, wasn't he?"

"Practically what you could call a second-generation Gary Harrison," Stan admitted. "It makes sense. Harrison probably trained Travis back in the early seventies when Gary was the *numero uno* hit man in West Texas. The FBI told me that there were at least ten warrants out for Travis' arrest. He was a suspect in several murders-- four in Texas, two in Louisiana, and four in Mississippi. I'm pretty sure he was the one who shot me in 1975. I'll never be able to prove it now, but at least I can say I *think* I know who did it."

"God, how did Jackie get mixed up in this?"

"Shannon," Stan said. "Sometimes we don't have control over what happens to us. She allowed herself to fall into a dark hole. It happens all the time to people. Most of the time, a strong person can climb out. It's a pit that every one of us is capable of fallin' into."

"I guess that's what happened to my mother, too," Shannon said.

"Probably so. It don't mean that Jackie or your mother were bad people. They just... tripped and fell into a bad hole."

The doors to Surgery swung open and a doctor appeared. He removed his surgical mask and wiped his forehead with a handkerchief. He spotted Shannon and her party and walked toward them.

Shannon stood.

"I'm Doctor Winters. Are you Mrs. Reece?" he asked.

"Yes."

"Jackie Parker's your sister?"

"Yes. How is she?"

"Well, we got three of the bullets out. There's one dangerously close to her heart that we were unable to get."

Shannon's spirits fell sharply.

"We're bringing in a heart specialist today and we're going to go in again later this afternoon. In the meantime, she's still classified as critical. I'm sorry I don't have better news."

"Can I see her?"

"I'm afraid not. She's still unconscious and we've got her on a respirator. Your sister lost a lot of blood, there's some serious damage to one lung, and there may be parts of the heart that are badly injured. She's also in a coma and there's no telling how much the drug addiction is effecting her will to survive."

"So," Shannon said. "It really doesn't look very good, does it?"

"I don't want to give you false hope," the doctor said. "She might make it if we can get that fourth bullet. We still don't know how much damage it's done. All I can say is prepare yourself for the worst and hope for the best. We're doing everything we can, Mrs. Reece. You're welcome to stay, of course, but if you want to get away from the hospital for a few hours, it may be less of a strain on you. The next operation won't be until later, probably around 5:00 or so. I'm sorry I don't have better news."

"Thanks, doctor." He walked away, and Shannon fell into Jeff's arms and started to cry.

* * *

It would be a few hours before the surgery began. Shannon had called her father and told him what news there was. He was on his way to San Antonio and would arrive some time that night. Not having a thing to do at the hospital, she and Jeff waited at the hotel.

Stan had gone to find the Caribbean club, where Janice Harrison supposedly worked. He said that he'd be back before long, and sure enough, he knocked on the door at 2:30.

"Any news?" he asked.

"Not yet."

"I imagine you're not gonna know anything until tonight, Shannon."

"I know. So did you find Janice Harrison?"

"I did indeed. She's at the club now. I think she's some kind of manager or assistant manager. Still got that eyepatch, which makes her look wicked, but she seemed nice enough."

"You talked to her?" Shannon asked.

"Sorta. We didn't have a conversation, but she said 'hello' to me like she would any customer. Actually she said, 'How are we doin' today?' and I said, 'I don't know about you, but I'm fine,' and then she said, 'That's good and I'm fine, too.' Then she walked away and spoke to someone else."

"You think I should bother talking to her?"

"That's up to you, Shannon," he said. "I get the feeling that she wouldn't throw you out if you tried to."

151

She paced the room a couple of times without saying anything.

"So-- wanna go for a drive or not?" Stan asked.

Shannon didn't bother to answer. She simply gestured with her head and started moving toward the door.

It took them twenty-five minutes to get to the Caribbean, which was downtown. They passed by the Alamo, which Shannon had always wanted to see, but somehow the circumstances put a damper on the novelty.

Shannon expected the Caribbean to be a dive, but in reality it was a rather classy place. The clientele didn't consist of roughnecks, bikers, or cowboys but rather businessmen and women dressed in suits and casually-dressed folk. The music was reggae. The "tropical" setting was a bit too chic with its bamboo chairs and tables, colorful flowers, and a running fountain that formed a pool of water in the center of the room, but it evoked a pleasant atmosphere nonetheless. The place served snack food, too, making it almost suitable for all ages.

The three of them sat down at a table away from the water and placed an order for drinks.

"Do you see Janice?" Shannon asked.

Stan was looking around. "Not yet. She was just here, though. I hope she hasn't left."

Jeff said, "That's the entertainment? A fountain that trickles all day long? Won't it make everyone have to pee a lot?"

Shannon allowed herself to laugh. Stan said, "Who says bars have to have entertainment? Most bars don't have any at all except your obligatory pool tables, dart boards, electronic poker machines, and juke boxes. And the occasional gang fight."

Jeff shrugged. "The entertainment at Legs wasn't bad."

"There she is," Stan said, gesturing with his forehead.

Shannon and Jeff turned to look.

A smartly-dressed woman wearing a black eyepatch was behind the counter, checking something on the cash register. They saw her smile at a customer, a man in a business suit. He leaned over the bar to kiss her cheek, which she demurely offered to him.

Janice Harrison wasn't at all what Shannon expected. The woman was in her late fifties, but she didn't look a day over forty. Somehow she had preserved a smooth skin tone, a shapely figure, and a youthful energy. Shannon chalked it up to the fact that she had always been something of a "glamour" girl. Even back then, she had a reputation of being gorgeous and sexy. Men couldn't resist her. She still had that quality. Had she been an actress, she might have been a Hollywood star.

The most striking thing about Janice Harrison was her attitude. She carried herself like a rich woman, a woman with power and confidence. She wore jewelry that sparkled even from this distance. She was gracious and accommodating to customers, especially the men. Regulars seemed to know her name.

"Go say hello," Stan suggested.

"I don't think I can," Shannon said. She was petrified.

"You want me to go?" Jeff asked. "I don't much want to talk to her either."

"This would be easier if I knew for a fact that she was innocent in killing my mom," Shannon said.

Stan reminded her, "In the eyes of the law, she *is* innocent. Janice Harrison was not charged or convicted of any crimes."

"All right." Shannon got up. "Here I go. This will be as good a time as any to see if she recognizes my mother in me."

She walked the twenty feet across the floor to the cash register. Janice Harrison looked up with her one green eye. It widened, and Shannon could tell that for a slight second the woman froze.

"Mrs. Lopez?"

"Yes?"

"Weren't you Janice Harrison once?"

Janice paused before asking, "Why do you want to know?"

"My name is Shannon Reece. Mary Parker was my mother."

The woman flinched ever so slightly. Then she said, "Well, you certainly look like her. You actually gave me a fright just then."

"I'm here with my brother and a friend. They're over there." Shannon pointed to the table where they were sitting.

"Oh, I remember that man, he was in here earlier," Janice said. "So, what, you were lookin' for me or something? You had to send him in here, first?"

"Something like that. It's not what you think. I just want to talk to you."

"Talk to *me*? Whatever for?"

"Because you know... so much," Shannon said. "And I know so very little."

Janice looked away from Shannon, then gazed back at her. "What do you think I know?"

"Mrs. Lopez, you knew my mother. I didn't. You were married to the man who killed her. I would like to hear your side of things. Please, it's something I must know."

"Honey, even if there *were* something to tell you, I'm not sure I would. This makes me very uncomfortable. Why don't you run along and sit back down with your friends and I'll have a round of drinks brought out to the three of you."

"Oh, please, Mrs. Lopez... you don't understand. I've been struggling with this for a lifetime. So have my brother and sister. My sister... she's in the hospital here in town, a victim of the same people you and Gary Harrison were involved with in Limite back in the early seventies."

"What do you mean?"

"The mob. The Dixie Mafia. Organized crime. You know what I mean."

"No, I don't."

"Please, Mrs. Lopez, I'm not stupid."

"Neither am I."

"What happened in Cortez, when Sheriff Buck Barton spent several nights in that hospital talking to you and Gary Harrison? What kind of deal did y'all make?"

"I don't have to listen to this," Janice said. She started to walk away, but Shannon followed her.

"I don't *care* what you did in your past, Mrs. Lopez," Shannon said. "We're not the police. I just need to know the truth. I'll *pay* you to answer some questions. Were you there when my mother was killed?"

The woman stopped and faced her. "No, I was not! Listen, you little fool, you have *no right* to come into my place of business and start askin' me questions about that, something that happened twenty-five years ago! Don't you see I've tried to forget all of that, too? My years with Gary Harrison left me with so many scars-- physical *and* emotional-- that I've only just begun to heal. He took out my eye, the bastard! I was *never* a part of his murders. He was a sick son of a bitch."

A bouncer, a big brute of a guy, walked up to them. "Everything all right, here, Janice?"

"Yes, Juan, thanks," Janice said. He walked away and she continued in a lower, more controlled voice. "You can't imagine what I've gone through and what I've felt. Gary Harrison *fathered* my children! A sick, woman-hating, sex pervert killer. How does anyone get over that kind of shame? My children have all gone away, changed their names, turned their backs on me. I'm sure it was terrible to be the child of a victim, but I can tell you it's just as bad, if not worse, to be the child of a killer."

With that, Janice turned away and walked through an "Employees Only" door, leaving Shannon standing in front of the bar. Shannon sighed heavily, then walked back to her table.

"I take it that it didn't go too well," Stan said.

"She was very defensive," Shannon said.

"Should we leave?" Jeff asked.

"No, let's wait a minute," Shannon said. "I'm shaking. I want to finish this drink, I need it." She started guzzling the glass of wine she had ordered.

Then, to their surprise, Janice Lopez came out from the back and walked to their table. She pulled up a chair and sat down.

"I'm sorry," she said to Shannon. "You took me by surprise."

"It's understandable. I'm sorry, too."

"Do you have cash?" Janice asked.

"What?"

"You said you'd pay me if I answered your questions. For a thousand dollars, I'll tell you anything you want to know."

A thousand dollars! "I don't know..." Shannon said.

"One-time-only offer," Janice said. She wasn't the customer-friendly manager any more. She had changed to the calculating, hardened woman that Shannon had expected all along.

Then something extraordinary happened to Shannon. It was as if her surroundings suddenly disappeared and she thought a vision of Jackie stood in front of her. Jackie silently mouthed something, telling Shannon what to do. Then Jackie's apparition blurred and faded away.

"Well?" Janice asked, bringing Shannon back to reality.

She hesitated, then felt a surge of emotion. She wasn't quite sure where it came from, but it was something that Shannon had never felt before. Had she imagined what "Jackie" had told her? Whether she had or not, her sister's suggestion seemed perfectly reasonable. It was the only thing to do.

"All right." Shannon reached into her purse and pulled out the ten counterfeit one hundred dollar bills that Jackie had given her. She counted it out on the table and gave it to Janice. Stan didn't say a word.

"Well, you certainly came prepared. What do you want to know?" Janice asked, taking the bills and putting them in her jacket pocket.

"All right," Shannon said, adjusting her seat. "Is it true you were both involved in that Dixie Mafia I was talking about?"

"We didn't call it that," she answered. "We didn't call it anything. It was just a 'network,' I guess. There were connections in every town. Limite happened to be the biggest connection for West Texas. It's how we made our money, Gary and I. I... well, I worked for them in a number of ways... and Gary, he... did some jobs for them..."

"I know that you were a prostitute," Shannon boldly said.

"Hmm, well, then, you know a lot," Janice said. "That was a big part of their business back then."

"Was Sheriff Barton a part of it?"

Janice nodded. "You'd better believe it. As sheriff, he had the authority to close down the brothel and gambling parlors in the Washington Hotel. So why didn't he do it? Of *course* he was part of it! He was best pals with Guy Simms and Lucky Farrow. Lucky Farrow owned the hotel!"

"And how would you describe their part in all of it?" This came from Stan. Janice just looked at him and answered, "They were the bosses in Limite. Everything went through them. Lucky Farrow ran things at the hotel and did other jobs, I don't know what. Guy Simms was sort of a recruiter. If a job needed to be done, Guy Simms would find someone to do it."

"What kind of job?" Stan asked.

"You name it."

"Murder?" Shannon asked. "Was my mother murdered for a reason that was mob-related?"

Janice shook her head. "No. We all knew your mother. She was mixed up in drugs or something, I'm not sure what. She partied with us a few times. You know about the parties?"

"Yes."

"The Dixie Mafia, as you call it, didn't kill her. Gary killed her because he liked to commit sex crimes."

"Did Sheriff Barton know he killed her?"

She nodded again. "Let me explain something. Gary Harrison was the number one hit man for the network in all of West Texas. He killed two or three people in Limite under orders. The others-- the women he abducted-- they just happened to be part of his sick obsession. He was a sexual predator and that's how he got off."

"Do you mean to say that Sheriff Barton was turning his back on the sex crimes because Harrison had committed murder under orders, too? His orders?"

"That's about the size of it," Janice said. "I can't say they were *his* orders, because that kind of stuff came through Guy Simms. Yeah, he knew about them and didn't do anything. That is, until the last one, Kelly White. There was so much public outcry and state-wide interest that Gary had to be stopped then. And that's when Sheriff Barton made us a deal in Cortez, Texas."

JANUARY 1974
CORTEZ

The hospital room was private, seeing that Gary Harrison was a prisoner of the county. Three Cortez deputies took turns guarding the small room outside in the hallway.

He was in a pretty good mood, considering that he had been shot, arrested, and was probably going to have to face prison on some of the murders he had committed in Limite. Sheriff Barton would be arriving any minute.

Well, Harrison thought, if this was the end of the line, then he was going to make sure it was finished with the best possible outcome. He had several aces in the hole and Sheriff Barton knew it.

Damn Janice, he thought. Why did she have to go run off and leave him? She was the root of all his problems, yet he couldn't live without her. He couldn't believe that she was living with some Mexican deputy. Their kids were confused as hell. He didn't see how he was ever going to get his family back together, so he might as well make sure they were going to be safe and taken care of.

He planned to squeeze that old sheriff until he got what he wanted.

The transistor radio in the room was broadcasting the local radio station. Barbra Streisand was plaintively singing *The Way We Were*. Gary was a sucker for music, although sometimes tunes would get into his head and they'd stay there forever. They often drove him crazy. Streisand's song was particularly annoying, because it invoked painful memories of his life with Janice. When the song finished, he said aloud, "Thank you Jesus for small fucking favors!"

The next song was Steve Miller's *The Joker*, which Gary liked a lot. It was on the radio a lot these days. When he had first heard it, he thought Miller was singing about him.

Sheriff Bill Dunham knocked, then walked in and strolled over to Harrison's bed.

"Gary, you got a visitor, all the way from Limite," he said.

Sheriff Buck Barton, as big as the state he represented, walked into the room.

"Hello, Gary," Barton said.

"Howdy, sheriff," Harrison said with a grin.

157

"Sheriff, do you mind leavin' Gary and me alone?" Barton asked Dunham.

"Not at all. Holler if you need me," Dunham said, then left the room.

Barton pulled up a chair and sat next to the bed.

"Whatcha doin' here, sheriff?" Harrison asked. "Didja hear I was in the hospital and you come to visit?"

"I heard you got shot and then arrested," Barton said.

"Yeah, can you believe that Selling Mortgaged Property charge is still haunting me? Won't those bastards in Posse leave me alone?"

"You jumped bail, Gary."

"Aww, sheriff Barton, come on, I was lookin' for my wife and kids. Any man woulda done it."

"Who shot you, Gary?" Barton asked.

"Come on, sheriff," Gary spat, his good humor disappearing. "You should know the answer to that. It was your buddies that gave the order, right?"

"I don't know nothin' about it."

"Sure. Right."

Barton sat forward in the chair. "Gary, I'm here because of Kelly White."

"Again? Sheriff, I thought we went over all that last summer. You know I don't know anything about it," Harrison said, defensively.

"Now, Gary," Barton said just as calmly as he could. "You know, and I know, that that ain't true. You know, and I know, that you killed Kelly White and dumped her body somewhere. Gary, I ain't leavin' Cortez until you tell me where the body is."

Harrison brought his voice down to a whisper. "You know I can't do that, Buck! Everything else will come out, then!"

"Not if we're careful. Listen, Gary, just think about something, all right? I've talked to Guy Simms and he wanted me to tell you something."

"What's that?"

"He said you'd better listen to me."

Harrison snorted. "Fine. I'm listening."

"Gary, you were hired to perform three jobs. You did 'em and you did 'em well. But you've got a serious problem. A personal problem. You know what I'm talkin' about, Gary. You know you do."

"You tell me, sheriff."

"It's a sex problem. You like to abduct and rape women."

"That ain't true."

"Gary, we both know it's true."

"Are we off the record? You ain't given me my rights or nothing," Harrison said.

"Forget that I'm sheriff for the moment, Gary, if that makes you feel better," Barton replied. He was handling it as coolly as he could. "This is just two businessmen talkin' here."

Harrison was still wary. He didn't know if he should reveal anything or not.

"Now, Gary," Barton said. "The people of Limite are mighty upset about that last abduction. The whole state is interested in it. The FBI is sniffing around, Gary, and we don't want that. If the FBI gets in there, they're going to find out the truth not only about Kelly White, but about the others, too. Gary, listen to me. You *have* to take the fall for Kelly White. If you agree to do that, then I'll see what we can do about the other murders. Maybe we can make them go away."

"I'm gonna want more than that, sheriff. Don't forget what all I've done for your pals."

"We know that, Gary. You were hired because you came recommended. They needed someone who wasn't afraid of killing someone. You certainly fit the bill. But what they didn't count on was that you would turn out to be a sex pervert with a habit of committin' homicide! Gary, they ain't gonna tolerate it no more. The more of these things you do, the quicker someone else is gonna come along and figure out that you did 'em. And once that starts to happen, then they're gonna uncover the three you did for the network. And you *know* you can't let that happen. You *know* what happens to people who incriminate the powers that be. That little gunshot wound you got should convince you that they mean business."

Those words alone scared Harrison. He didn't know what to say.

"Now, you think about it a while, Gary," Barton said. He stood up. "I'll be back in a few hours."

* * *

Gary thought about it for nearly a week. In the meantime, Barton visited the hospital room every night and they talked about anything and everything. They discussed the Limite Lynxes' football record, fresh water fishing, and even childhood reminiscences. But the murders were never discussed.

When Harrison made the request to see Janice alone in the room, Buck Barton wasn't surprised. He had been anticipating it, so he had already got in touch with her. She was prepared to see him, if that's what he wanted. She wouldn't mind at all, especially if it would help speed up the process of getting him to jail.

"I'm not scared of him, sheriff," Janice had told him. "I just don't want to live with the son of a bitch anymore."

When she got to the hospital, Sheriff Barton asked her if she was carrying any weapons, and she said that she wasn't. She was wearing a short, low-cut black dress and had put a good deal of make-up on. The eyepatch, still relatively new, made her look like a *femme fatale* from a spy movie.

"Ernie and I will be right outside," Barton told them. "I'll make sure you have privacy."

When they were alone, Gary asked his wife to sit on the bed.

"How are you feeling?" she asked.

"Pretty good," he said. "I can probably leave soon."

"Is Sheriff Barton takin' you back to Limite?"

"I reckon so."

"What have you told him?"

"Nothin'. Yet."

"Just what are you gonna tell him?"

"Where Kelly White's body is."

"Wouldn't that be like confessin' to rapin' and murderin' her?" she asked.

"Technically, no. I'd have to make a separate confession, you know, officially. But it would be strong evidence against me without a confession."

"So, you're gonna get charged with murder..."

"I have to take the fall for Kelly White, Janice. It's orders. I have no other choice. But we can demand some things in exchange. I already know I'm going to ask for complete immunity from the other murders."

"Are you talking about Barbara Lewis, Tina Peters, and the Saldañas?" she asked.

"All of them. Those, plus the... uhm, women."

Janice turned away and sighed. "Oh, Gary. Our entire life stories are gonna be made public. Everything I did at the Washington Hotel will come out. What about our children? They're gonna find out their mother was a whore and their father was a murderer." Despite her words, she didn't appear to be too worried. Janice Harrison was always calm and collected. It was her demeanor of nonchalance and sensuality that made her so attractive.

"That's not gonna happen," Gary said.

"How do you know?"

"Just do what I say and nobody will find out anything. But if you insist on living with that damn Mexican and taking my kids away, I just might tell the world everything."

"You wouldn't do that."

"Just try me," he threatened.

"Then your children would have two parents in jail."

"I could get the death penalty," he said. "By talking, that would make sure that I don't."

"What do you want me to do, Gary? Why'd you want to see me?"

"Spend a few nights here with me. We had it pretty good for a few years. If you can sell your body to strangers, you can be my wife again for a few nights."

"What about your wound?"

"Aww, it don't bother me."

Janice thought about it. "I'm gonna want some things in return, too. I see this as a give-and-take situation."

"Hasn't it always been that way with us, Janice?" he asked with a sly grin. "Now, what is it you want? I'll probably go to jail for a long time. I want to make sure you and the kids are taken care of."

Janice thought about that a minute. "Cash is always helpful."

"All right."

"And a new car. Mine's always breakin' down and costin' money gettin' it fixed..."

"I'll ask him."

"And one more thing..."

"What?"

She paused and looked back at him. "I want immunity, too."

* * *

She spent all night with him. She let him do whatever he wanted. It was something she was accustomed to. It was something she enjoyed. They played their little games, the ones they had always played together in bed. The fact that they were in a hospital room with a sheriff and his deputy right outside made it that much more exciting.

She hated Gary but she loved him, too. It was impossible to forget fifteen years of marriage. True, it was an unusual union, something most people might call "abnormal." Nevertheless, Gary and Janice understood each other sexually. She was sensitive to his needs and he was perceptive of hers.

When his hands were around her throat, she briefly thought of what those hands had done and what they could do to her. What was to prevent him from going too far? What if he killed her right there in the hospital room? What if she became the next in a long line of strangled victims, the necessary nourishment for a predator who was unstoppable. He was like a vampire who needed his regular fix of blood.

The moment of doubt quickly passed, and Janice put her trust in Gary. He wouldn't kill her. She was his wife. The other women had been objects, the means to an end. They could not compare with her. They couldn't do, would never do, what she was able to do.

Sheriff Barton and Captain Jones waited patiently each night that Janice came to visit Gary in the room. Then, on January 12, Barton joined them in the room before they could get started.

"You two have had plenty of time to think about this," he told them. "We gotta start talkin' turkey."

"I think we're ready," Harrison said. "Isn't that right, Janice?"

She nodded.

"First of all, what are you prepared to offer off the top?" Harrison asked.

Sheriff Barton said, "Well, let's talk about these murders, one by one. All right?"

"Whatever."

Barton took out a notepad and referred to some notes he had made. "Barbara Lewis. Tina Lee Peters. Johnny and Laura Saldaña. It's very important that you're never charged for them. We can't have it."

"Fine by me."

"I'll make sure you won't ever get charged for them. They were hired jobs and we need to protect ourselves. Do you agree, Gary?"

"That's right, Buck."

"Barbara Lewis went behind Lucky's back and started runnin' whores out of that motel. She tried to play ball by herself without lettin' her teammates in the game, you know what I mean? Tina Lee Peters-- she was warned several times not to be hookin' out of her own apartment. That's what we had the hotel for, and the Flats. The Saldañas-- well, if you hadn't got to 'em, I'm sure somebody else would have. Richie had made a lot of enemies. He was stealing from us and we didn't like that. He deserved what he got. Since his wife was in on it, too, I guess she had it coming as well. But I don't understand why you had to take Mrs. Saldaña away from that motel and do to her what you did to those other women. That was really hard to cover up, you know? Anyone with half a brain could see that she was killed by the same person who had killed Grace Daniel."

"Luckily there aren't too many people in Limite with half a brain!" Harrison said, guffawing.

"Okay, those hits are gone. Off the record. That leaves us with Grace Daniel, Susan Powell, Mary Parker, and Kelly White. What are we gonna do about them, Gary?"

"What do we have to do, Buck?"

"You gotta go down for Kelly White. When we're done here, you're gonna tell me where she is."

"All right. But not the others."

Barton breathed deeply. "I don't know if I can promise that."

"Sheriff, unless I confess to 'em, you ain't got nothin'."

"Gary, you gotta understand that there is some circumstantial evidence against you in three of the cases. Grace Daniel, Mary Parker, and Kelly White-- especially Kelly White. A good D.A. like Rusty Franklin could successfully prosecute you on Kelly White. You'd probably get the chair. Franklin wants to prosecute you real bad on the others, too."

"Okay, I'll cop to Kelly White. That'll keep me from the death penalty, won't it?" Harrison asked.

"Probably. You know, you covered your tracks pretty good with Susan Powell. I think I can make that one completely disappear. The Mitchell sheriff's office did a terrible job investigating the crime scene where you left her body. There was no evidence at all. You almost blew it, though, when you left Tina Lee Peters' billfold in that vacant house you were hidin' in. I can't believe you didn't leave anything else there that could identify you."

"I can't believe I left the billfold there either! I meant to take it with me. That *was* a screw up," Harrison admitted.

"Well, that could have connected you to the Susan Powell case, but it didn't. Sometimes you are so stupid, Gary. Anyway, there's no case there, unless, of course, you confess to it."

"He won't confess to her," Janice said.

"Then it's gone. You don't have to worry about Susan Powell."

"So if I just keep quiet on Grace Daniel and Mary Parker, I should be okay?" Harrison asked.

"I can't promise that the Limite police department and the FBI aren't goin' to grill you pretty heavily on them. They might break you."

"They'll never break me."

"They'll never break him," Janice concurred. "I never could in fifteen years."

The three of them chuckled, providing a moment of levity in the conversation.

"That's everything I'm coming to the table with," Barton said.

Harrison moved over on his side and rubbed the bandage covering his wound. "The only problem is that it itches like hell, now."

Barton waited patiently until the prisoner was ready to make his demands.

"Janice and the kids need money," Harrison said. "They're livin' next to poverty as it is, and if I'm gonna be in jail then they're gonna need a little help."

"How much help are we talkin' about?" Barton asked.

Harrison paused for dramatic effect. "I was thinkin' about... five grand?" He licked his lips when he said it.

Barton laughed. "I couldn't do that much. Where's it gonna come from? Just take it out of the state's defense fund and tell 'em I paid off your wife in exchange for a confession? That'll look real good."

"Well, how much can we get away with?"

Barton thought a minute. "You know, there's a reward out for information leading to the whereabouts of Kelly White's body."

"How much?"

"Fifteen hundred dollars."

"That ain't enough," Harrison said. He grimaced and folded his arms in front of him. He reminded Barton of a spoiled child not getting his way.

"I could sweeten it a little, I guess," Barton said. "I can throw in two more grand of my own money."

"Why would you do that?" Janice asked.

"Because I *have* to close this case," Barton said. "I'm willing to do it for you, Janice. I always liked you."

"Oh ho, the truth comes out," Harrison said. "The sheriff has the hots for you, honey."

Barton glared at the prisoner. "I *meant* that she's always been a nice person."

"Right," said Harrison. "I know all about those nights at the Washington Hotel. You specifically asked for Janice at least a half dozen times. *And* Mary Parker..."

"Gary..." Barton warned.

"All right, I'll shut up," Harrison said. "So you're sayin' three thousand, five hundred dollars, am I hearin' that right?"

"Yep."

Gary looked at Janice for approval. She nodded.

"All right, thirty-five hundred dollars," Gary said.

"We're gonna have to say it's reward money, probably," Barton said. "I'm not sure how we'll explain it, but for now we'll just keep it quiet. This is between the three of us, and maybe no one will know."

"Fine."

"Anything else?"

"I need a car," Janice said. "Mine is really shitty. Can you give me a *loan* for a used car, sheriff?"

Barton rubbed his brow. This was going to be a long night. "All right. I can give you another three hundred dollars, but if it comes out I'll say it's a loan until you get on your feet. All right?"

"Sure," Janice said. She knew she would never have to repay the money.

There was a bit of silence, then Barton said, "Okay, then, where's Kelly's body, Gary?"

"One more thing," Harrison said.

"What's that?"

"Janice gets full immunity for anything and everything," Harrison said.

Barton expected that one, but he pretended to think about it hard. "I don't know, Gary..."

"Come on, Buck," Harrison said. "You know Janice didn't have anything to do with those killings."

"I do? How do I know that?"

"You'll just have to trust us."

Barton turned to Janice. "Janice, did you have anything to do with those crimes?"

Janice looked at the sheriff with her one lovely green eye and said, "Like Gary said, Buck. You're just gonna have to trust us."

"I take it that's a 'no.' But you *knew* about 'em all along," the sheriff grumbled. He rubbed his chin. "I don't know..."

He finally held out his hand and Harrison shook it. "Now there's a condition for all of this," Barton said. "You can never talk about what went on in this hospital room tonight. There was never a deal struck. If any word gets out that you were responsible for hitting Lewis, Peters, or the Saldañas, you know what will happen to you, whether you're in prison or not?"

"I suppose."

"Gary, don't take this lightly. You'd never know when someone might come up from behind and let you have it. If you fuck with the network, they'll fuck you back. When you least expect it. Don't think that bein' in prison will protect you."

"I hear ya, sheriff."

"So, should I ask Ernie to come in and take down directions to where Kelly's body is now?"

"Sure, Buck. Bring him in. I'm ready."

JANUARY 1999

Janice finished telling her story and then sat there, waiting for a reaction from her stunned audience.

"There," she said. "I went and told it. I figger that it's ancient history now and no one can come after me. Everyone's dead, ain't they?"

"Buck Barton's still alive," Stan said.

"Barely," Shannon added.

"Well, I doubt he can do anything to me," Janice added.

"Did Buck Barton and my mother... you know?" Shannon asked.

Janice screwed up her mouth, then said, "Buck Barton was crazy about your mother. She was the only one at the hotel that turned him on. He never paid for her services but I'm almost positive they partied together a couple of times. That was something he almost *never* did. But your mom got to him. He couldn't resist her. And I guess she got off to the power he had back then. He wasn't a bad-looking man."

"God..." Shannon muttered. Everything was falling into place. "So, the Dixie Mafia hired Gary Harrison to be a hit man but it turned out they screwed up and hired a sex killer by mistake," Shannon said.

"That's about the size of it," Janice replied.

"Did you know that he was a sex killer before all this happened?" Jeff asked.

"No," Janice said. "I mean, he had his kinky little hobbies. He got me involved in wife swappin' parties and sex orgies and dirty movies. And he liked doin' the bondage thing. He got off to hurtin' women during sex, I knew *that* much about him. Lord knows he hurt *me* enough times."

"Why didn't you leave him sooner?" Jeff asked.

She looked at him and replied, "Maybe 'cause I kinda liked it, too."

Shannon couldn't believe that a woman could really enjoy being a masochist but apparently it happens. She had simply lived too sheltered a life.

"Why did Gary confess to Barbara Lewis and Tina Peters later?" she asked.

"It was a stupid thing to do," Janice said. "It's what got him killed. He thought he could scare the network into helping him get out of prison somehow. He ratted on them and they didn't like it. I was amazed that the Limite Grand Jury refused to indict him on those murders. They

166

didn't believe him! I suppose that's understandable. The story, true or not, was far-fetched. He was *hired* to kill these women? No one was gonna believe him, especially since he already had a reputation of lyin', changin' confessions, and all that."

"And he confessed to Grace Daniel and Mary Parker after that, too," Stan said.

"That was just another of his ploys to manipulate me," Janice answered. "He thought if he implicated me, then I wouldn't divorce him. He was wrong. Once he was sentenced to life in prison, he figured he didn't have anything else to lose. He didn't believe that the network could kill him in prison. He started mouthing off on all kinds of things. There was all that about the confessions being coerced and then gettin' burned on the arms by the police detective. Total bullshit. I think he just wanted to screw the network."

"And it backfired," Jeff said.

"It sure did. He wasn't in Huntsville two weeks when they got him. They tried to shoot him in Cortez before he was arrested, but that failed. It's too bad-- it would have saved everyone a lot of grief."

There was another moment of awkward silence.

"So, are you happy now? You heard what you came to hear?" Janice asked Shannon.

Shannon nodded. "I have one more question."

"What?"

"Gary Harrison implicated you in the first confession he made about my mother. Did you, or did you not have anything to do with it?"

Janice thought about that one for a few moments, then said, "I'm gonna say this once: I didn't kill her. Gary did. I wasn't there. And that's the truth."

"But you knew the murders were going on, didn't you?"

Janice looked at her hard, and for a moment a cloud passed over the single green eye. "Yeah, I knew. I'm sorry."

Somehow, that wasn't very satisfactory, but Shannon figured it would have to do.

"Thank you," she said.

"You're welcome. Now I gotta get back to work. Thanks for the money. Have a nice life." As she got up from the table and sauntered back to her office in the club, Shannon thought that Janice Harrison might be the most unusual and mysterious woman she had ever met.

"You gave her the fake money," Stan said.

"Yeah, I know," Shannon said.

"She's gonna get in a heap of trouble when she tries to spend some of it."

"Yeah, I know. But I doubt she's gonna tell anyone where she got it and how. Let's get out of here."

They got up and left the Caribbean. On the way back to the hospital, Shannon thought about what she had done. She had paid off Janice with counterfeit money! She had committed a crime! It was a felony! What had come over her? It had been an impulse act, but one that seemed perfectly natural to do. Had Jackie really "spoken" to her? Or had she received some kind of spiritual message from her mother? Whatever it was, it had felt right. It was as if Shannon was paying back Janice Harrison for whatever role the woman had played in her mother's corruption and ultimately grisly death. Perhaps Janice hadn't participated in the actual slaying, but she wasn't totally innocent, either. Shannon felt that in her gut. It served the woman right.

So did she feel good about what she had done? Damn right, she thought. The score had been evened out a little.

Perhaps there was more of her mother in her than she wanted to admit.

A half hour later, they arrived at the hospital and went inside. It was nearly 5:00. Shannon hoped they weren't too late to talk with the doctor before Jackie's next surgery began.

She stepped up to the nurse behind the counter on Jackie's floor and said, "Uhm, I just wanted to ask about Jackie Parker. Has she gone in for surgery yet?"

The nurse looked down at something and frowned. "Oh, uhm, Doctor Winters wanted to speak to you. Are you her sister?"

"Yes."

"Just a second." She picked up the phone and dialed a number. "Doctor Winters? Jackie Parker's sister is here. All right."

She hung up and pointed down the hall. "There's an office marked H2 just down the hall. Doctor Winters would like to speak to you."

Shannon suddenly felt apprehension. The old panic and anxiety swelled up inside her. Had something gone wrong?

She knocked on the door and heard a voice say, "Come in." Dr. Winters was sitting at a desk, looking at papers.

"Mrs. Reece, sit down," he gestured. He got up and closed the door behind her, then sat on the edge of his desk, facing her.

"I'm afraid I have some bad news. A little over an hour ago your sister went into cardiac arrest. She was being prepped for surgery. We did everything we could to resuscitate her heart, but all our attempts failed. I'm sorry."

Shannon didn't quite hear him right. "What?" she asked. "So you can't operate?"

He tried to tell her again, this time a bit more bluntly. "Mrs. Reece, your sister is dead. She died an hour and a half ago. There was nothing we could do to save her. I'm sorry."

Shannon felt her cheeks flush as her heart started pounding. She couldn't have heard this right. Jackie, her little sister? Dead? Impossible!

"That can't be right... I... " Shannon started to say. It was approximately an hour and a half ago that she had experienced the "vision" of Jackie and her mother-- the one that told her to give Janice Harrison a thousand dollars in counterfeit money.

The doctor put a hand on her shoulder in an attempt to reassure her. "I'm sorry. I'll be happy to give you something to calm you down if you need it."

Then it hit her full force. "Oh my God," she muttered. She gasped, shuddered, and was overcome with a flood of tears.

FAMILY

The funeral was held on the last day of January. The weather was cold and bitter in Limite. There was a rare light snow on the ground. The sharp West Texas wind penetrated heavy coats and chilled one to the bone.

There wasn't much of a turn-out, just as Shannon had expected. There was the immediate family-- Shannon and Carl, Jeff, their father Larry and his wife Caroline, Larry's three children from his third marriage, and Uncle Fred, who flew in from Colorado. Shannon got a sitter for Cathy and Billy, since Billy had a cold and she didn't want him standing outside in the wind. Besides, she thought they were too young to attend a funeral. Little Tyler, however, sat with Shannon in the church and would accompany everyone to the cemetery. She thought it was important that he be at the funeral, whether he understood it or not. She wanted him to remember as much about his mother as he possibly could. Tyler's father, Zach Thompson, didn't make it. He gave some excuse about having to work, which Shannon chalked up to his displeasure at Tyler's last name being changed back to Parker.

A few friends had also shown their respects by attending. Stan McHam came, which Shannon appreciated. There were two or three couples from the church there, but Shannon thought they might be the type of people she had heard about who went to a lot of funerals-- for people they didn't know-- as a form of entertainment.

She didn't know why anyone would want to go to a funeral if they didn't have to. She hated funerals.

Her mother's funeral was but a hazy memory for Shannon. She had been the only one of the children there, as Jeff and Jackie had been much too young. She recalled being very upset by it all, not understanding why her mother was dead and wondering why everyone looked at her with such pitiful expressions. As a result, she had despised the mere concept of funerals from that moment on. She had attended only one other-- that of her grandmother's on her father's side-- when she was ten. That was an unpleasant experience too. It was the only time she'd seen her dad cry, which disturbed her a great deal. He hadn't cried at his wife's funeral, which was something she never fathomed. After that, Shannon resolved never to attend another one.

Until now.

Reverend Wyatt spoke softly and gently to the small crowd that had gathered at the Forest Grove Christian Church that morning.

"Jackie Parker was a child of God, just as everyone who walks on this earth is a child of God. As children of God, we are all given choices. We are given Right on the one hand and Wrong on the other, and God allows us to choose for ourselves which path we ultimately take. Sometimes, we have to make these choices on a daily basis. When Eve was alone in the Garden that fateful day that Satan came to visit in the form of a serpent, she was forced to make a choice during that time we call the Evil Hour. It happens to all of us at one time or another. Each of us experiences an Evil Hour in which we are presented with a difficult choice-- it might transpire only once in a lifetime, or it could happen several times a month. For some of us, Evil Hours are daily occurrences. We must be prepared to make the right choices during these vulnerable moments. Jesus himself was tempted by the Devil several times before he accepted his destiny as the Son of God and Savior of Mankind. He had to face his own personal Evil Hour and make his own fateful choices. When we have to make choices during our Evil Hours, it is quite easy-- and I submit to you that it is quite *human*-- to almost always make the wrong ones.

"This is why God is a forgiving god. This is why Jesus allowed himself to be nailed to the cross. Each and everyone of us, all children of God, are human. We all make mistakes. Jackie Parker was not a bad person. She was not an evil person. What happened to her was that she got caught up in a series of wrong choices during her own personal Evil Hours. She was, after all, only human.

"When we lay Jackie Parker to rest today, don't blame her for the mistakes she might have made. It is not for us to judge a person in that manner. We leave that responsibility to God and Jesus, for they are the ones who know best. They are the ones who will look at Jackie Parker and say, 'This was a good person. She did no wrong. Let us embrace her and welcome her to the Kingdom of Heaven, where she will join other family members who have passed on.' They will look at Jackie Parker and say, 'This is a child of God, and we love her.'"

After the service, the entourage of six cars and a hearse drove west to the only cemetery in Limite. There were hundreds of graves there, some dating back to the early 1800s. It seemed much larger than it really was, mainly due to the flatness of the land and the illusion of endlessness that the distant horizon created.

A small plot had been dug next to Mary Parker's grave. The family gathered around it for the reverend's final words, the blessing, and the interment. Shannon held Tyler's hand with her right and leaned into Carl on her left. Tyler was silent and solemn during the entire proceedings. He never cried, never asked questions, and never complained. Shannon

171

knew he would be a good boy, and she looked forward to welcoming him into her family.

The cold wind turned to sleet just as the dark brown, mahogany coffin was lowered into the ground. Shannon said, "Goodbye, Jackie," softly to herself, then turned away. She stepped up to the adjacent gravestone that read: "Mary Jo Barnes Parker, Beloved Wife and Mother, 1945 - 1973." She gazed at it for several minutes, reflecting on all that had happened during the past month. She now knew practically everything there was to know about her mother's death and the Evil Hours that forced Gary Harrison to commit the horrible crime that put her into the ground. In a way, the evil that had led her mother into Gary Harrison's web had also seduced Jackie. It was so powerful that it had managed to transcend and poison a second generation.

She said a brief silent prayer, then walked back to the cars with Tyler and Carl at her side.

Shannon was nearly ready to finally bury the memory of her mother along with her sister, but there was still some unfinished business to take care of.

* * *

The mourners moved to Shannon's house for a reception. That was another thing Shannon always found strange about funerals. After burying the dead, everyone congregated at someone's house for food and socializing. It might not be a "happy" occasion, but there was still a party atmosphere to it that seemed out of place.

Stan McHam brought an inedible casserole his mother had made out of chicken breasts and canned cream of mushroom soup. Two couples from the church both brought identical salads. Caroline Parker brought a lopsided chocolate cake that she probably bought at the grocery store. It was a skimpy spread but it would have to do. Shannon wasn't about to prepare anything. Not only was she in mourning, she was physically exhausted.

She sat on the couch and didn't get up, pausing only to say "Thank you" when people paid their respects. She noticed that her father sat glumly in the corner, immersed in thought and nursing a glass of vodka. Jeff was deep in conversation with Reverend Wyatt and seemed to be handling the loss pretty well.

After Uncle Fred left, Stan plopped down beside her. "How ya holdin' out, kid?" he asked.

"All right for now," she said. "I'll probably fall to pieces after everyone leaves."

He nodded. "I ever tell you I was married?"

"No, you didn't."

"Yep. She died of breast cancer in 1986."

"I'm sorry."

"It's okay. But I just wanted you to know that I understand how you feel."

"Thanks."

They sat there a minute before she asked, "So what's next for you? Now that Travis Huffman is dead, are you gonna be able to put it behind you?"

"I was gonna ask you the same thing."

"I asked you first," she said.

He shrugged. "I'll never be able to prove the guy shot me, but I'm ninety-eight percent sure. Yeah, I can forget it. I'll still have work to do on the case, finishing up with the FBI. They're good guys to work with. And I have all my unfaithful spouse cases that are always so exciting. It's great fun tailin' some guy to a motel and takin' pictures of him. Every day is a new adventure. What about you?"

She shrugged, imitating him. "There are still some loose ends I want to chase down but I think I'll be able to give it a rest soon. I want to thank you for all you've done."

"Forget it."

"No, really. I couldn't have done it without you."

"Well, it was a pleasure. Keep in touch, okay?"

"Sure."

He got up and groaned as he put a hand on his bad hip. "It's always gettin' up and gettin' down that hurts the worst. I'm gonna take off. Take care, Shannon."

"You too, Stan."

He was the last to leave. Now only the immediate family were left-- Jeff, Carl, the kids, and her father, his wife, and her half-siblings.

Larry Parker hadn't said a word since the funeral ended. Shannon thought he looked much older than he really was. He had become terribly thin-- his suit practically swallowed him up. The bags under his eyes betrayed the pain and sadness he obviously felt.

When he finished the glass of vodka, he stood to go to the bathroom. Caroline was busy in the kitchen cleaning up. This was her chance. Shannon got up and followed him, then waited outside the door while he did his business. When he opened the door, she ambushed him.

"Dad, we need to talk," she said.

"What about?"

"In here." She motioned to the bedroom, then led him in. He sat down on the edge of the bed as Shannon pulled up a stool.

"Dad, all of this is gonna end here. Today," she said.

"What is?"

"Your keeping secrets."

"What do you mean?"

"You know damn well what I mean." She felt her blood begin to rise. She had to be careful and try to control herself or he would remain the speechless statue he had always been.

"I don't have any secrets," he said, softly. He looked down at the carpet.

"Dad, look at me." He raised his head and she could see tears welling up in them.

"Dad, I know about you and mom. I know that you both knew Gary Harrison and his wife before her murder. I know that you were both involved in stuff going on at the Washington Hotel. You were both in wife-swapping clubs and sex parties and all that. Look, dad. I don't care about that. I'm not gonna judge you. I'm not gonna blame you. I just want to know the truth. From *you*. I know you've got a story to tell, and you've kept it inside all these years. You *need* to tell it, dad. And I need to hear it. We're not going to ever get over this until you do."

"Shannon..." he began, ready to protest.

"No, dad. We just laid my sister-- your daughter-- in the ground next to her mother today. I can't help but believe that what happened to Jackie was some sort of indirect fallout from what happened to mom."

Then, for the second time in her life, Shannon saw her father break down and cry. He put his head in his hands and sobbed. She got off the stool and sat beside him on the bed. She put her arm around him and held him close to her.

"I'm sorry," he choked. "It's all my fault..."

"Shhh," she said. "Just tell me the story, dad. I promise you'll feel a lot better after you do."

He got hold of himself after a few minutes. He removed a handkerchief from his pocket, blew his nose, and wiped his face.

"Your mother was the one who got us into the sex clubs," he began. "She... she was just so wild. If I hadn't agreed, she would have gone off and done it on her own, and I couldn't have handled that. I was just too jealous. As a bail bondsmen, I knew a lot of the Limite policemen. There were three or four guys in the police department that were into a wife-swapping thing. Your mom was friends with their wives and she got to know the husbands. We were invited to one of their parties."

"When was that?"

"Oh, late sixties. Nineteen-sixty-eight, I want to say? I dunno."

"How did you get involved in the stuff at the Washington Hotel?"

"That was through her friend Carol Jenkins. She was moonlighting as a hooker down there. She got your mom to go to some parties there."

"When was that?"

"I don't remember. It was before any of the murders happened."

"Is it true you and Carol Jenkins slept together?"

He looked surprised. "How the hell did you know that?"

"She told me."

"Carol?"

"Yeah. Listen, I've been workin' on this case! I know just about everything," Shannon said. "It's okay. Just keep talking."

"Well, anyway, she met the Harrisons at the hotel. I think--"

Shannon interrupted him. "Wait. Did mom do any... you know, was she a prostitute?"

"No," he said, emphatically. "I made sure of that. I told her that if she really wanted to do all this swingin', then it would be just for fun and nothin' else. I don't think she wanted to *sell* her body-- she just wanted to have fun with it."

"All right, go on."

"Anyway, she knew the Harrisons from the hotel. The Harrisons had their own sex party thing going, and of course, Janice Harrison was a hooker there."

"Did you sleep with her?"

He hesitated, then nodded.

"Did mom sleep with Gary Harrison?"

"I don't think so. I think that's one reason why he targeted her. He always felt that he was entitled to have sex with her because I had had sex with his wife."

"How many times were the four of you together?"

"Well, we were at the hotel a few times just in a social setting. We were only in a bedroom together once."

"The four of you?"

He nodded.

"But I thought you said that mom and Gary Harrison didn't...?"

"They didn't. What happened was..." His voice started to shake and tears rolled down his cheeks again. "Your mom and Janice. They did it while Gary and I watched. Gary had this thing about watching his wife with other people. After she was finished with your mom, then I got in bed with her."

Shannon took a deep breath after hearing that one. Apparently part of Gary Harrison's first confession involving Janice and her mother was true. "So what did mom and Gary do while you were with Janice?"

"They watched."

"Did Gary *try* to go to bed with mom?"

"Yeah," he said. "But she wasn't interested, for some reason. I don't know why. She went to bed with just about everyone else, including the goddamn sheriff! I guess I was just never good enough for her." He broke down again and cried on her shoulder. "Oh, Shannon, I'm sorry..."

"Dad, it's not your fault."

"But I let her do it. I shoulda stopped her. I coulda stopped her and I didn't!"

"Well, why didn't you?"

"Because I wanted to make her happy," he said, wiping his tears with his sleeve. "I loved her so much. I was afraid I'd lose her if I didn't let her do what she wanted. She had a will of her own that was a helluva lot stronger than mine."

Shannon let him compose himself, then she asked, "Did you know any of Gary's other victims?"

He nodded. "Mary knew at least a couple of 'em. Grace Daniel worked at the hotel sometimes. Kelly White had been to a couple of the parties. Her employer at the mobile homes was into a rent scam that was controlled by Guy Simms. That's how she got to know some of the people. I'm not sure about the others."

It was all starting to make sense now. Gary Harrison wasn't the type of serial killer who picked strangers as victims. He picked women that he knew and wanted but couldn't have. They probably all knew each other at some point. The connection running through it all was the Dixie Mafia. They operated the brothel at the hotel and they allowed the sex clubs to flourish there as well.

"What can you tell me about mom's murder?" she asked. "Do you know anything at all?"

"I have a pretty good idea of what happened," her father said. "I've never really tried to lay it all out before, but here goes. We'd been out partying on New Year's Eve. Nothing bad, we were just out at the Moonlight club. We both got pretty smashed. We came home and tried to have sex but we were both too out of it. We had hangovers pretty bad the next day. I got a call around noon from my boss. There was a client in jail near Ft. Worth. I had to go get on a plane that day so I could be there the next morning. So I was gone that night and all day January second. I didn't get back until the morning of the third, which was too damn late. Mary had to work on the second, and Fred was over watching the kids. He slept over there a lot in those days. Anyway, I'm pretty sure Mary went out that night after work to go score some drugs."

JANUARY 1973
MARY

It had been an unusually busy night at Donny's cafeteria. The doors were locked at 9:00 p.m. but there were several customers left inside eating. It meant that she would be late meeting Frank at the Fever club.

Mary Parker looked at her watch as she finished closing up the cash register. 9:43. She was usually out of there by 9:30. It looked like she'd be delayed another ten minutes or so. There were still three tables with customers. Despite the unsubtle, continuous noise the busboys made as they cleaned off adjacent tables, the people kept eating. Some had decided to sit back and relax with a cup of coffee.

Mary despised Limite. She couldn't stand the people-- they were all *so* dumb, she thought. Those men over there in the baseball caps-- they just sat at the table chewing their cud and talking about "this rig" or "that rig." Then there was the table with two middle-aged couples. The men did all the talking and the women sat there quietly like lumps of coal.

She thought just about everybody except the crowd she hung out with was dumb. She may have dropped out of high school but she was confident that she was a lot smarter than any of these people. Sometimes her own husband was dumb. She hated dumb people.

Damn! She didn't want to miss Frank. He had told her that he'd be at the Fever between ten and eleven. She had no way to call him and say she might be late. She knew where he lived, though, but he didn't like dealing drugs out of his house. He insisted on a rendezvous like the Fever club or the Moonlight club. The exchange always took place in the parking lot. Mary had just popped her last upper at 9:30 and she needed to pick up a new supply-- one for her and one for Carol. Carol also wanted some pot. It was a good thing that Frank still charged ten dollars per ounce of marijuana. Carol had told her that some O-Zs were going for $15 now. Inflation had even hit the drug market.

The last group of dumb Limiteans left at 9:51. Mary tore off her apron and cap, signed off on the "Closing Checklist" that was tacked onto a bulletin board in the back, and left the building. She got into her 1968 Chevrolet Impala and drove home a little too fast. She was already starting to feel the effects of the speed.

177

She wondered what the night might have in store. Fred said he'd stay there all night since Larry was out of town. That meant that the kids had their favorite babysitter, Uncle Fred, until morning. Depending on who else she ran into at Fever, she might end up having a good time that night. Hell, she thought, she wouldn't mind checking under Frank's hood. He was hung like a horse.

It took five minutes for Mary to get home. She wanted to change out of her uniform and spruce herself up just a bit. She rushed inside, working on the buttons down the front of the brown dress that was standard uniform issue for the cafeteria employees. She passed Fred, who sat in the living room watching the news.

"The kids went to bed on time, more or less," he said.

"Thanks," she said, breathlessly, rushing into the bedroom.

Fred, a perceptive person, called out, "You must be going somewhere."

"Yeah, I gotta go out for a bit. I need to run to the grocery store."

"I could do it," he offered.

"No, thanks. I need to go. I have an errand or two to run. Don't worry about me, just go to bed."

"Well I was gonna stay up and watch TV for a while."

"Fine." She emerged from the bedroom wearing tight brown pants, a cream-colored blouse, and a beige winter coat. She had taken her long black hair down, which made her look younger than her twenty-eight years. She was stunning and she knew it.

"Gee, Mary, is there something happenin' at the grocery store I don't know about?" Fred asked facetiously.

"Yeah, *I'm* happenin'," she replied, gathering her purse. "Don't wait up."

She ran outside and got into the car. It was just a few minutes after 10:00.

Mary never went to the grocery store.

* * *

She pulled into the parking lot of the Fever club at around 10:25. It was crowded, and she had trouble finding a spot. She was forced to park a little further away from the front door than she liked, but it would have to do. She was in a hurry.

Mary stepped into the Fever, which was not one of her favorite nightclubs in town. She preferred the Moonlight, simply because they had taken the time to actually decorate it. It was also a lot more civilized. The Fever was sometimes downright depressing, boring, and way too male-oriented. Not that having a lot of males to choose from was particularly a bad thing, it's just that she thought most of the men at the Fever were usually like everyone else in Limite. Dumb.

"Hiya, Mary," the doorman said. She didn't know his name, but she knew his face. She wasn't sure how he knew her name.

"Howdy," she said. "You seen my friend Carol tonight?"

"Carol? No, no, I don't think so."

"Thanks." She left him and went inside what might have been the quintessential honky tonk in Limite. There was the intense smell of smoke and beer. It was full of roughnecks, cowboys, and bikers, each group keeping to themselves. There were as many women in the club as men. The place was darkly illuminated except for the bright lamps hanging over pool tables. The "entertainment" was simply playing Limite's most popular radio station over loud speakers at a very high volume. Stevie Wonder was singing his newest song, *Superstition*.

She looked around for Frank and didn't see him. Damn, could she have the time wrong? Or maybe he was there earlier, figured she wasn't going to show up, and left early?

Not sure what to do, Mary sat at the bar. The bartender, a cowboy with long hair, a sleeveless vest, no shirt, and a tattoo of a naked woman on each bicep, asked, "What'll it be?"

"Uhm, I'm waitin' for someone. I don't want anything right now, thanks," she said. Mary had a sweet, very friendly voice. She had the capacity to charm anyone, man or woman. There was a Snow White quality to her looks, yet her manner was flirtatious and carefree. There probably wasn't a man alive who could say "No" to Mary Parker. Even smart men. And she knew it.

"That's okay," the bartender said.

"Hey, have you seen my friend Carol?"

The bartender wrinkled his brow.

"You know, she's a redhead, I've been in here with her before."

"Oh yeah, I know who you mean. No, I haven't seen her tonight."

"Thanks."

Well, she wouldn't wait long, she thought. If Frank, or Carol, for that matter, showed up in the next ten minutes, fine. If not, she'd go check out the Moonlight.

Did Frank say he'd meet her at the Fever or the Moonlight? Come to think of it, Mary wasn't sure. She lit a cigarette, something she did only when she was out at bars. It was a nervous habit, but she was also once told by her dad's business partner, Chuck, that she used it "as a prop" quite well.

Right on cue, the music segued into Carly Simon's *You're So Vain*. She chuckled to herself as she recalled the night that Chuck Davenport first saw her at the Washington Hotel. He was embarrassed and acted foolishly. It was as if she had caught him doing something nasty.

He probably *had* been, she thought.

After a few months, Chuck treated her like any of the other women at the club. Although it was left unsaid, Mary knew it was "their little secret" and that it had to be kept from her father.

She decided she'd finish the cigarette and go to the Moonlight. There would be more people there she might know.

Then, someone walked in that she *did* know. More surprisingly, it was a woman by herself. Mary didn't know her well, but she had seen her at the cafeteria with her two twin daughters. They were cute and their mom was very pretty-- blonde and blue-eyed. She was astonished when she first saw the same woman at a couple of parties at the Washington Hotel. That's where she actually got to know her name.

"Hi, Kelly," she said to the newcomer.

"Mary! How are you?" Kelly White was dressed in blue jeans, a t-shirt, and a black winter jacket.

"Okay. I was waitin' on Carol, but she hadn't shown up. You actually caught me on the way out. I was just about to get up and go to the Moonlight."

"I came to meet Stuart here when he gets off work at eleven. Brrr, it's cold outside."

"Is that your boyfriend?"

"Just someone I'm seein'," she said. "You going to that party for Washington's Birthday or whatever it is?"

"Probably," Mary said. Kelly was referring to what Lucky Farrow called an "excuse to throw a party." He tended to do that on odd holidays-- Veteran's Day, Labor Day, Memorial Day-- rather than one of the more traditional ones like Christmas. Washington's Birthday was especially significant, given the hotel's namesake. Mary didn't know that Kelly was already in the inner circle. Only the inner circle knew about the parties.

Was Kelly White a swinger?

"How did you get to know about the hotel?" Mary asked her.

"Oh, my boss goes there. He takes me. He's the manager of the trailer park where I live. I work there, too, as assistant manager. He's kinda sweet on me and takes me to some of the nice parties there. He likes to be seen with me, I guess."

On second thought, Mary convinced herself, maybe Kelly *wasn't* the partying type.

"Well, I gotta go," Mary said, standing up. "I promised Carol I'd meet her, and I think I got the places mixed up."

"Well, have fun," Kelly said.

"You, too."

Mary waved to the bartender, said goodbye to Nameless the Doorman, and went out of the club into the cold night air.

It was 10:40.

* * *

She drove the six blocks north to the Moonlight Club, a joint that was quite a bit larger and classier than the Fever. It was owned by the same people, so Mary wondered why they didn't fix up the Fever and make it more attractive.

Her car radio was playing Santana's *Evil Ways*. She found herself singing along with the chorus in a phony, exaggerated Hispanic accent: "You got to change your evil ways, *bab-ee*, before I start lovin' you...!" Despite her irritation at not finding Frank or Carol, the speed she had taken had put her in a pretty good mood. She would definitely have a drink inside the Moonlight while she waited for someone to show up.

The parking lot was completely full. Not surprisingly, the night crowd was out in force. Like any city, Limite had its share of day people and night people. She was definitely a night person. The fact that New Year's Eve had been two days earlier didn't stop the lonely and the bored from going out on a cold night to drink beer, dance, and meet strangers. Mary had made more sexual contacts at the Moonlight than she had anywhere else in Limite.

She circled the parking lot a number of times and made up her mind to park illegally, when someone in a pickup pulled out of a space not ten feet from the front door. What luck! She swerved around behind the truck, let him out, then pulled into the space.

Mary turned off the ignition and looked in the rear view mirror to take stock of her appearance. She thought a little touch up was needed. She reached into her purse, found the lipstick, and evened the shade on her ruby red lips. She blew a kiss to herself in the mirror, then put the lipstick back into her purse.

That's when the car door opened.

It startled her and she gasped. She relaxed a little when she saw Gary Harrison standing there by the car.

"Hi there, good lookin'," he said.

"Hi, Gary," she said. "Jesus, you scared the shit out of me."

"Come with me, all right?"

"What?"

"Come over to my car. I want to show you something. Hurry."

She didn't like the urgency in his voice. He seemed nervous; but then, Gary Harrison always seemed nervous. It was one reason she really didn't find him attractive, although Carol and other women she knew did. Mary knew that Gary had always wanted to get into her pants and she wouldn't let him. He didn't turn her on at all. She thought he was obnoxious. He also sometimes went a little overboard with the bondage stuff. It was too bad he wasn't more like his wife, Janice. Mary liked Janice, although she found her to be a little strange. She certainly was attractive. Janice's glamour girl persona wasn't just an act-- Mary believed she was truly a sexpot. She flashed briefly on the night when she and Larry met up with the Harrisons. That had been an incredible evening! A few weeks later, she had gone over to their house on Chestnut Street without Larry. That had been an even more interesting night. She and Janice had put on a show for Gary but he wasn't able to perform for some reason. So he just watched.

"I gotta see if my friend Frank is inside," she said, starting to get out of the car.

"Oh, well, if you're looking for *Frank*, then I've got what you want. Real good stuff, too," Gary said. He kept looking around the parking lot and at the front door of the club as if he was afraid to be seen.

"Really?" There was something about Gary's demeanor that set off warning bells in Mary's mind; but before she could do anything about it, he made his move.

Out of nowhere, the knife appeared in his hand. He pressed the blade flat against her neck as he grabbed the back of her hair with his other hand.

"Don't make a sound," he whispered threateningly. "Walk to my car. Now."

Her heart jumped into her throat. "Gary, what are you do--"

"Shut up and walk!"

She felt the sharp edge of the knife press into her neck. All he had to do was slide it across her skin and she would be cut.

He closed her car door and took her by the arm. He removed the blade from her neck and held it low, at her side. She couldn't do anything but walk with him.

It was about twenty feet to his car, a red 1964 Chevy. He opened the driver's side and pushed her inside, then got in beside her. Before she could protest, he started the car and pulled out of the parking spot. It was 11:00 sharp.

"Where are we going?" she asked, nervously.

"Come on, Mary," he said, "You and I are gonna do what we shoulda done a long time ago." He pulled out onto the highway and drove north. Mary looked back at the parking lot and didn't spot a soul. No one had seen what had happened.

He drove intently, glancing at her every few seconds. He had a sly grin on his face, as if he knew something that she didn't. The silence got to him, so he put on the radio. Roberta Flack's *Killing Me Softly With His Song* filled the car.

After a few miles, Gary put away the knife and said, "Relax, Mary, I ain't gonna hurt you. I like you. I think you're the most gorgeous girl on the planet. Come on, relax, don't be scared. We'll get high and have a little fun."

A thousand things were going through Mary's head. She had always thought Gary Harrison had a violent streak in him but she had never seen him *be* violent. The couple of times she had been at sex parties with him, he had done some... well, *unusual* things. The night she was alone with him and Janice, he kept urging Janice to tie her up with nylon stockings. Mary went along with it and soon found herself bound to the bed. Janice had done just about every conceivable thing to her-- and all Gary did was watch and pull his own pud. He kept asking Janice to "choke" her, but Janice refused to do that.

Maybe if she complied with what he wanted, he'd let her go and everything would be all right.

"I... I've never been taken by force before," she said, trying to keep the fright out of her voice.

Gary chuckled. "Oooh, I like that. Playing the innocent virgin, are you? I like that... I tell you what. Why don't you take off that top and let me see those lovely tits of yours."

It was then that Mary remembered the abductions of women that had occurred in Limite over the last couple of years. Grace Daniel's body had been found out in the oil fields. There was another woman missing who hadn't been found yet. Could Gary be the one responsible?

Doing her best to keep calm, she told herself that she would get through this. Just do what he wanted and she'd get out of this alive.

"All right," she said. She removed her coat, then slowly unbuttoned her blouse. She was wearing a white bra underneath.

Gary pulled off onto a gravel road. The car crossed a cattle guard, then drove into the darkness away from the security of the highway.

Mary thought he was going to take her out there and rape her, then bring her back into town. She could get through this, she could get through this...

"Take off your shirt and bra," he commanded, driving with one arm and running his right hand along her leg.

She obeyed him, feeling terribly exposed. Once she was topless, he slowed the car to a stop and turned it off. He doused the lights and sat there in the dark with her for a moment.

"Let's get in the back seat," he said. She nodded and reached for the door handle. He grabbed her other arm and said, "Don't try runnin' away. You're out in the middle of fuckin' nowhere."

"I won't," she said. He let her open the door and get out. She opened the back door and got in. Gary climbed over the seat and got on top of her. Before she knew it, her pants had been pulled down to her ankles.

Mary closed her eyes and let him do what he wanted, which turned out to be not too much. He seemed to be having trouble getting an erection. He tried several times to penetrate her, but due to his lack of stiffness and her lack of lubrication, he was unsuccessful. So instead, he got up on his knees and stroked himself like she had seen him do at parties. He finished over her breasts, making grotesque grunting noises that sounded more like a wounded animal than a man having an orgasm.

She felt humiliated and violated. She wanted to scream and cry and claw his eyes out. But she didn't dare. He still had a knife somewhere.

He got off of her, reached over to the front seat and found her blouse and bra. He threw them at her and said, "Get dressed."

Thank God, she thought. It was over. She didn't bother trying to wipe off his mess, she just quickly put on her bra. While she dressed, he opened the glove compartment and began to search for something. After she had her blouse back on, she got out to return to the front seat. He got out, too, holding her coat.

"We're going for a walk," he said.

Oh my God, she thought. She was going to die. Oh my God, oh my God... please don't let this happen, please don't let this happen...

He forced her to walk away from the car, out into the brush. There were prickly mesquite bushes and tumbleweeds all around, but not a tree in sight. The half-moon above cast a pale glow over the desert. It was just enough illumination to enable them to walk around obstacles.

After a few minutes, Gary stopped and spread her coat on the ground. "Lie down," he said. Her knees weak, she got down on the cold ground.

Before she knew it, he had wrapped something around her neck. It was a cloth of some kind... a nylon stocking...? He pulled it tighter and tighter.

He held the knot with one hand while he ripped open her blouse with the other. She thought she heard music coming from somewhere. He pulled hard on her bra, tearing it off of her. What was that music?

Then she realized that it was the song they had heard in the car, *Killing Me Softly*. He was humming it! He was singing it to himself!

She tried to fight him, tried to kick him, but he was too strong. There was some kind of stick or something in the nylon stocking that he was twisting. He'd tighten it, then loosen it, tighten it, then loosen it...

After a few minutes of this torment, Mary Parker started to drift in and out of consciousness. She was trying to remember the Lord's Prayer, but images of her children zipped through her head and confused her. She thought of something funny that her little girl Shannon had once said. Mary had tried to teach her the Lord's Prayer, and Shannon asked, "Is God's name really Harold?"

Mary had looked at her and said, "What??"

Shannon repeated what she thought she had heard. "'Our Father, who art in Heaven, Harold be thy name...!'"

Mary had laughed out loud and hugged her first born. "That's right. God's name is Harold," she said.

The last thing Mary remembered was the litany of terms of endearment that she had made up especially for Shannon. "I love you, Shannon-girl. I love you, Shanna-banana. I love you, Shannon-wannon. I love..."

Then there was nothing but the cruel, cold wind, the rustle of tumbleweeds, one hundred and eighty degrees of a star-filled night sky, and a killer with his corpse.

FEBRUARY 1999
SHANNON

The cold weather had intensified on the first morning of February. Now there was ice on the streets and schools were closed. People had forgotten how to drive. Cars were skidding all over the place and keeping the police busy with fender benders.

Shannon was supposed to have gone in to work, but her employer let her have some time off for mourning. She actually wouldn't have minded going-- she needed the money-- but it was a disaster area outside. Carl had to go to work, so he left the house bright and early to avoid the little bit of traffic that Limite claimed as a rush hour.

So, instead of typing drilling reports, Shannon sat in the kitchen drinking a cup of coffee. Cathy, Billy, and Tyler were home, playing together nicely. So far, the loss of his mother and the experience of the funeral hadn't had any noticeable negative effects on Tyler. A pediatrician who was with the city's Social Services Department told her that it would probably hit the boy in two or three days.

The talk with her father had certainly taken its toll on her. Last evening, after he had told his version of the story (which Shannon believed was as close to the way it actually happened as anything she had heard), they had embraced and cried together. She reassured him that it wasn't his fault. What she didn't say was that from now on she would have a completely different image of her parents than what she had grown up with.

Larry Parker promised to be more open and honest in the future. He said he didn't spend enough time with his grandchildren, so he wanted to do that. Shannon said that would be a good thing.

He had left with Caroline and his kids around 9:00. Jeff was the last one to depart. Shannon gave him a big, long hug and admonished him to keep in touch.

"I will," he had said. "But you should think about getting out of Limite. It would probably do you a lot of good."

It had taken another hour to get all three kids in bed. Shannon was exhausted when she finally crawled between the covers around 10:30 p.m. She had slept like a stone.

Now, today, she felt like she had been asleep for a week. Everything-- the investigation, her sister's death, the funeral-- had all seemed like a strange dream. Any other day she would have considered giving Jackie a call to see if she'd like to have lunch, but she knew no one would answer the phone. Instead, she picked up the receiver and called her husband. When she got through to him, she said, "Hi, it's me."

"Hi, honey," Carl said. Stan McHam's voice cheered her up when she heard it but nothing compared to what her husband did for her. He really *was* Mr. Perfect, she thought. "You all right?" he asked.

"Yeah," she sighed. "Hey."

"What?"

"Let's move."

She heard him chuckle to himself. "I was wondering how long it would take you," he said.

"You're great at what you do, Carl, you can get a job anywhere. Let's get out of Limite. I don't think I can stay my whole life here."

"Well, believe it or not, I was thinkin' the same thing."

"Oh, Carl..."

"Where would you like to go?"

"Oh, I don't know... Austin's pretty nice..."

"I know," he said. "In fact, I've been researching some firms in the area. I know some guys at an independent firm down there, and it just might suit me."

"Really?" She was very pleased.

"Really. Let's talk about it when I get home, all right?"

"Yes, let's," she said, then giggled. "Oh, Carl, all of a sudden I feel like there's hope again."

"There's always that," he said. "See you tonight. Love you!"

"Love you too."

She hung up and hugged herself. That had made her day. It was going to give her a whole new outlook and she couldn't wait to get started shifting her energy in that direction. It would give her something to concentrate on, which is something else the social workers had advised that she try to obtain.

The manila folder full of her mother's case notes still sat on the kitchen table, along with a pile of unopened mail. Shannon gingerly opened the folder and gazed upon that first clipping, the one with the picture of lawmen finding her mother's body. It had taken over a month, and a secret deal between the killer and the sheriff's office, to finally locate the remains.

To think that it all could have been prevented...

Shannon still had one last bit of business left to do.

That night, once Carl was home to watch the kids, Shannon changed out of her sweatshirt and put on a cotton blouse. She took the photo of her mother from the dresser and studied the hairstyle. Shannon did her best to brush her own black hair in the same manner. A hair clip on the left side did the trick. She put on a little too much make-up, which was the norm back in the early seventies. She was ready.

Carl stared at her hard as she walked through the living room to the door.

"Where are you going?" he asked.

"Have to run an errand," she said.

He watched her leave, shaking his head. He knew exactly where she was going.

* * *

Shannon wore sunglasses and a floppy hat into the hospital, hoping that no one would get a good look at her. She made her way to the third floor and peered out of the elevator lobby into the hallway. One nurse was at the station and the rest of the corridor was clear. She turned to the left and sat down in the waiting area, but positioned herself so that she could see room 335. The door was slightly ajar.

She picked up a magazine and pretended to look at it, every now and then glancing up at the door.

Fifteen minutes passed. Twenty... Then just as she was about to give up, the door swung open. Naomi Barton left the room and said something to the nurse at the station. Shannon caught the words "about an hour." Mrs. Barton then walked toward the waiting area. Shannon bent her head down so that her hat and the magazine covered her face. Mrs. Barton passed her and went to the elevator bank to wait for the next one.

Buck Barton was alone in the room. Shannon waited another five minutes until the nurse at the station finally rose and walked to the opposite end of the hall. Shannon put down the magazine and stood. With her mind made up to continue her plan, she quickly stepped past the vacant nurse's station and into room 335.

Buck Barton was lying in the same position he was in the last time Shannon had been there. There seemed to be even more tubes and drip-bags, and a little machine on a table next to the bed was beeping steadily. The beeps were obviously the man's heartbeat.

Shannon removed her hat and sunglasses, then stepped to the bed. She was scared to death and trembling but she was resolved to go through with it.

"Mr. Barton?" she whispered.

Buck Barton opened his eyes. Unable to move his head, the eyes darted to one side and focused on her. They were blank for a second, then they registered surprise.

"Yes, it's me," Shannon said. "I'm Mary Parker. Remember me?"

Barton's eyes widened. He was attempting to speak, but a guttural noise was all he could manage.

"It's been a long time, sheriff," she said. "I hear you're under the weather."

More throaty sounds.

"Don't try to talk, Buck. I'll do the talkin'."

Barton was straining to do something-- scream, yell, cry-- but he was helpless.

"We had some fine nights at the Washington Hotel, didn't we? You and I? Those were the good ol' days, weren't they? Let's see, there was you and me, and there was Lucky and Guy... Oh, and let's not forget Chuck. That was quite a set up you all had goin', wasn't it? Profiting off the bodies of women like Janice Harrison and Grace Daniel. Remember them? Remember Janice? I saw her the other day. She said to tell you hello. I'll bet you remember her husband. Remember Gary Harrison, sheriff?"

The beeping began to increase in tempo. Shannon noticed droplets of sweat appear on Barton's forehead.

"So you're the big hero around these parts, is that right, sheriff?" she asked. "Everyone loves you. The best sheriff Limite ever had. Well, what I want to know is, how come you were involved in a network of criminals? You know, the Dixie Mafia? How come you protected the prostitution and gambling rackets in Limite? How come you allowed a murderer like Gary Harrison to roam around free, when you *knew* he had killed a lot of people."

More guttural sounds. The beeps were getting faster.

"Let's see, you knew that he was following orders to kill Barbara Lewis. Poor woman. She was just trying to make a buck. He had orders to kill Tina Lee Peters because she had crossed your pals. A single woman trying to make ends meet. Then there were the Saldañas, Richie and Laura-- your buddies had them killed, too. And you knew all about it, but you let their killer run around free. Didn't you?"

She moved in closer, about a foot away from his pale, frightened face. There was true terror in his eyes now.

"You *knew* that Gary Harrison was a serial killer, didn't you? They didn't call 'em that back then, but that's what he was. He was a sexual predator, wasn't he? You knew it. You knew he'd killed Grace Daniel. Then he abducted and murdered Susan Powell. And then... there was me. Kelly White was the last of his victims. And they're just the ones *I* know about. There must have been more, all over the state, all over the south... weren't there? Why didn't you stop him, Buck? You were the *sheriff*, for God's sake! You *could have prevented my murder* if only you had stopped him sooner!"

Tears ran down the side of Barton's face. He was terrified. His breathing was fast and shallow.

"Don't worry, Buck," she said. "You'll be judged accordingly. The people of Limite may be too dumb to realize what a liar and a crook you are... but the angels know. They're waiting for you."

Then, something happened. There was a sharp intake of breath as Barton's eyes widened even more. The awful sounds he was making turned into a loud, unearthly wail. The machine by the bed went crazy. Some kind of alarm went off.

Shannon turned around, put on the hat and sunglasses, and walked quickly out of the room. The nurse was running toward her. Shannon pointed to the door and said, "Something's going wrong in there," then kept on walking to the elevator. No one paid any attention to her as she left the building.

* * *

The next morning, the *Limite Observer*'s front headline bore the legend: "FORMER SHERIFF BUCK BARTON DEAD." The obituary related how the beloved lawman had been in the hospital for over a week following a stroke. He had died suddenly of heart failure, and was survived by his wife, six children, and five grandchildren. It went on to list the many achievements in his career and his record for holding the office the longest in Lucas County's history. A few of the more well-known cases he had solved were mentioned, including the apprehension of the infamous "Oil Field Killer," Gary Harrison.

Shannon Parker cut out the article with a pair of scissors, then added it to her mother's case file. It had grown considerably since she had pulled it out of the filing cabinet in the garage. Now, perhaps, it was complete. She could finally put away the folder and not look at it again for a long, long time.

The kids were busy with a game of Junior Monopoly. Carl was at work and he had come home the night before with promising news about job leads in Austin. After the incident at the hospital, she had spoken to her father on the phone. He was back at work and seemed to be doing fine. When he heard that Shannon and her family were thinking of moving away from Limite, he said that he hoped it would work out for them.

Everything was supposed to be better now, but Shannon was wise not to deceive herself. She knew she had a long road of recovery ahead of her, especially after what she did at the hospital. Someday she would be judged for it, her own Evil Hour, but Shannon strongly believed that she had made the right choice. The challenge was having to live with it.

She sat at the kitchen table and looked through the glass doors that faced the back yard. The weathermen had predicted that the winter storm was going to last the rest of the day. The West Texas wind blew cold sleet against the house, creating a ghostly whistle effect that the kids liked to imitate. All kinds of debris from the surrounding fields blew through the unfenced yard.

Shannon saw an icy tumbleweed blow in from the left side of the yard. She watched it intently as it rolled and hit the one tree in the back-- an apricot tree that never produced any fruit. The tumbleweed lodged there for a few seconds, then the wind carried it up and around to the portable swing set. She wanted to see where it went next, so she got up, unlocked the glass doors, and slid them open. The cold, wet wind struck her in the face, but she didn't mind.

Shannon stepped out onto the back porch just as the tumbleweed was once again picked up by the wind current and carried off into the fields. She stood in the sleet and watched it bounce away until it was just another speck in the grey, endless horizon.

EPILOGUE
SEPTEMBER 1970

The eight-track tape deck was playing James Taylor's *Fire and Rain*. The music filled the lounge on the seventh floor of the Washington Hotel with a mellow ambience that was unusual for a Limite nightspot. Most places were rowdy and noisy. Here, it was quiet and subdued. It was the perfect atmosphere for serious gamblers, wealthy gentlemen with mistresses, and attractive hookers.

The lounge occupied the central area of the floor. A bartender was on duty beginning at six o'clock every night. The decor was tasteful and the lighting was dark. It was conducive for couples, as there were little nooks and crannies all over the lounge where the prostitutes could sit with customers and get to know them before making the hard sell.

Down the hallway to the right of the elevators were hotel rooms that had been converted into gambling parlors. Each room specialized in a particular game, much like a casino. Poker was the hands-down favorite and there were games going on in four of the seven rooms on that end of the floor. Craps was popular in two rooms and the seventh room was used for whatever game the occupants wanted on a particular night.

The other end of the floor had traditional hotel rooms. The hookers used these rooms for business purposes, or they were rented out to VIPs who came to the hotel when they wished to be discreet. The swingers crowd would congregate at the hotel on weekends and take up half the rooms.

A person needed a password before being allowed onto the seventh floor. The password changed once a month to keep out undesirables. This didn't mean that the place wasn't filled with them. The Washington Hotel seventh floor attracted low-life from under every rock and tumbleweed in Limite. They just happened to have money or connections. It was where middle to upper class white trash went for a good time. The lower class and the colored folks had to go to the Flats to get their kicks.

Grace Daniel sat in the lounge, hoping that some more men would come in. It was still fairly early on a Wednesday night. Tina Peters was busy with a lawyer that came to see her every week. They were down in room 703. Janice Harrison was over in a dark corner with a man who claimed to be in insurance. He was a friend of Lucky Farrow's, so they had been told to "treat him good."

192

Janice's husband, Gary, was working as bouncer that night. He had come in at 8:00, and had only been working an hour when he started drinking steadily. Now that it was 10:15, he had transformed from a rather quiet man to the extroverted, overly-confident hustler that Grace knew him to be.

Grace didn't know what to think of Gary. He was nice enough, but there was something about him that was menacing. She liked Janice, although she was awfully moody. Janice could be sweet and friendly one minute, then turn into a witch the next. Grace hadn't known the Harrisons long. Tina was pretty nice. She was certainly the best-looking of the girls that worked at the hotel. She was always getting customers. Janice told Tina the other night that she could probably go into business for herself and make a lot more money. The cut they had to give to the hotel was pretty steep.

"I wouldn't do that," Gary warned Tina. "They don't like it when a girl goes into business for herself."

At 10:40, three people from the swingers club came in. Two of them were regulars-- Richie and Laura Saldaña. Richie was a Limite policeman. The third was a man whose wife was out of town on business, so they were looking for a lady to join them in some fun. Grace was the only one available, so they agreed to take her along. They paid Gary the fee for use of the hotel room, then disappeared down the hall with Grace.

A fifteen year old boy, tall and lanky, came into the lounge from the kitchen. He had slicked-back black hair and a cigarette dangling out of his mouth.

"This garbage needs to be taken out," Gary told him.

"Okay," the kid said. The boy started to gather up the two cans behind the bar and haul them back where he could dump the contents into an incinerator. "Hey, Gary," he said.

"What?"

"Can I ask you something?"

"Sure, kid."

"I heard that... well, I heard that you've killed people. Is that true?"

Half-amused, Gary looked at the kid with a feigned look of anger. "Where the hell did you hear shit like that?"

"I don't know, I just heard it. It's why you're hangin' around the hotel now. You hopin' to get to do some dirty work?"

"I don't know what you're talkin' about, kid," Gary said. "They just want me to be a bouncer here some nights."

"What's it like to kill someone?"

"Forget it, kid. I never killed anybody."

"Right," the kid said, smiling. "I understand. But listen, if you ever want to tell about it, I'm willing to learn, you know? I already got me a gun. It's a--"

"I don't want to hear about it, all right?" Gary pretended to lose his temper.

"Sorry." The kid moved to take the trash away, but Gary stopped him.

"Hey, kid. What's your name, anyway?"

"Travis. Travis Huffman."

"Glad to meet you. I'm Gary." They shook hands.

"I know." Travis took the garbage into the back. Gary Harrison chuckled to himself. He got a kick out of giving shit to the kid. Gary glanced over at his wife in the corner. Her male companion was groping her like there was no tomorrow. A streak of jealousy flashed inside of him, but he concentrated on the 150 dollars she would make, minus the house take. They would be able to feed the kids and themselves for another two or three days.

Down the hall, in one of the smoky poker rooms, four men sat around a table with piles of chips in front of them.

"I call," Chuck Davenport said, lighting another cigar.

"I raise you ten," Lucky Farrow challenged.

"I fold," Guy Simms said.

The three men looked at the fourth man to see what he was going to do.

"Well?" asked Guy. "What are you doin', Buck?"

Sheriff Buck Barton spit tobacco juice into a coffee cup, then counted out six chips and said, "I'll raise you a hundred."

"Aww shit," Lucky said. He counted out the chips and threw them in the center of the table.

"I fold," said Davenport.

With him and Simms out, it was just between Barton and Farrow.

"Well, let's see what y'all have!" Simms said.

"Two pair," said Lucky, showing his hand.

"Full house," Barton countered, revealing the three sixes and two jacks.

"You son-of-a bitch," Lucky grumbled. His fat quivered like gelatin when he was pissed off.

The other men shook their heads as the sheriff shoveled the chips to his side of the table.

"How's ol' Ed Barnes doin'?" Simms asked Chuck.

"He's fine, I guess," Chuck answered.

"He doesn't know about the little scam you pulled, does he?"

"Hell, no! If he did, he wouldn't be my most trusted friend and business partner!" Chuck said. Everyone but Barton laughed at that.

"Have you ever seen his daughter?" Chuck asked.

"Whose daughter?" Lucky replied.

"Ed Barnes'."

"No. Why?"

"She is one good-looking girl," Chuck said. "If she wasn't Ed's daughter, I'd go after her myself. She hangs out with Carol Jenkins."

Lucky snorted. "I'm sure Carol'll be a good influence on little Miss Barnes."

"Mary's her name," Chuck said. "She's married to a guy named Parker."

"Then I'm sure Carol'll be a good influence on little Mrs. Parker. Sheesh."

"By the way," Simms said, "we gotta do something about Barbara Lewis. She was warned about operating out of her motel, and I think it's time we show her that we mean business." His large Adam's Apple bobbed up and down when he spoke, which sometimes distracted his audience.

"We decided on a course of action last week, didn't we?" Davenport asked.

"Well, yeah, but we didn't have anyone to do it. I think we do, now."

"Who is it?" Farrow asked.

"You know Janice? The blonde girl that's really sexy?"

"You bet!" Farrow chuckled. "She's one helluva lay! I could spend all night with her. Buck, have you been with her yet? She is fucking *amazing*!"

"Shut up, Lucky," Barton said. "I'm a married man."

"As if that stopped you before!" Davenport laughed.

"Shut up, Chuck," Barton repeated.

"Anyway," Simms continued, "her husband came highly recommended by our boys in San Antonio. His name is Gary, Gary Harrison. He's here tonight, in the lounge. You may have noticed him working as a bouncer the last few weeks."

"Well, I certainly have," Lucky said. "You *made* me hire him!"

"I've seen him," Davenport said. "He's real skinny. Don't look too tough to me."

"From what I hear, he's plenty tough," Simms said. "He did two hits in Biloxi, a couple in Atlanta, several in the Dallas area... the guy's a professional killer and he's never been caught."

"So, give him the job if you're so sure," Lucky said.

"I was goin' to. I just wanted everyone to know about it. Especially Buck."

Sheriff Barton took the cards and shuffled them. "I don't want to know a fuckin' thing about it, Guy. You know that. It's better if I don't."

"Well, you need to meet him anyway," Simms said. "Hold on, let me get him." He got up and stuck his head out the door. "Harrison! Come here a minute, will ya?" he called.

Gary entered the room, eager to please and ready to work. "Uhm, Gary, could you bring us all a round of beers?" Simms asked.

This wasn't what Gary had expected, but he figured that he had to pay some dues. "Sure," he said, then left the room.

"He don't look so tough," Davenport repeated.

"Believe me," Simms said. "The guy's a mean son of a bitch."

"Does his wife get a lot of work?" Barton asked.

"She sure does. She's sexy as hell," Lucky said. "I'm tellin' ya, Buck, you really ought to try her out."

"What about Tina Peters?" Simms asked.

"What about her?"

"How's she doing?"

Lucky shrugged. "She's the most popular girl here. She's always busy."

Simms said, "We'll have to keep an eye on her. Willie Bennett told me that he saw her hustlin' somebody at Freddie's Paradise the other night. She might get tempted to work solo. We can't have that."

"Awww, Willie Bennett, that nigger? We give him way too much power in the Flats, y'know?"

"The Bennetts do a fine fuckin' job, Lucky, and don't you forget it," Simms said. "If Willie says he saw her at Freddie's Paradise, then I believe him."

"Okay, you're right," Lucky conceded. "I'll watch her."

"That reminds me," Simms said. "Buck, what's gonna happen with that assault charge on Willie's brother Abe?"

Barton cleared his throat, then spit tobacco into his cup. "I'll make sure it disappears."

Gary Harrison brought back the beers and set them on the table.

"Gary, you know everyone here?" Simms asked.

"Uhhm, I haven't met the sheriff," Harrison said.

"Buck Barton, Gary Harrison," Simms said.

Harrison held out his hand. Buck Barton frowned, then reluctantly shook the new man's hand. "Pleasure," he said unconvincingly.

"Likewise," Gary said. "Well, I'll get back to the lounge now. If you need anything..."

"We'll hollar," Simms said.

After he was gone, Davenport said, "I still don't think he looks very tough."

"Well, we'll see how he handles the Lewis job," Simms said.

"Shut up about all that," Barton said. "I don't want to hear it. Just deal the goddamn cards."

Back in the lounge, several couples and a few men had come in. Gary found himself helping out the bartender filling drink orders. The man who was with Janice had decided to leave, so she sat on a barstool near her husband.

"What happened?" he asked.

"I dunno, he got cold feet or something," Janice said. She looked great sitting on the stool with her blonde hair, black cocktail dress, and high heels. She was quite aware of the visual effect she achieved when she crossed her legs.

"Then the guy's an idiot," he said.

The elevator dinged again and two women entered the lounge. One of them was Carol Jenkins, a regular. The other girl was someone Gary hadn't seen before. She had long black hair and was terribly attractive. She looked like she was in her mid-twenties. Needless to say, she got his attention.

"Hi y'all," Carol said, joining them. "What's going on?"

"It's pretty slow tonight," Janice said. "No parties to speak of."

"Shoot," Carol said. "I was hoping there would be a party. I brought my friend here to show her what a fun place this was."

Both Janice and Gary looked at the newcomer, undressing her with their eyes.

"Janice, Gary, meet Mary Parker," said Carol. "Mary, this is Gary and Janice Harrison."

"Glad to meet you," Mary said, shaking their hands.

"What would you like to drink?" Gary asked her.

"Gin and tonic?"

"Coming up."

"So, you're looking for a good time?" Janice asked.

"Mary's always lookin' for a good time," Carol explained. "She usually does this stuff with her husband, but he's off doing something else. So us girls decided to go out on the town together, right, Mary?"

"Right." She seemed shy, but both Gary and Janice thought that she would get over that quickly. They instinctually spotted a quality in Mary that they both liked. The hungry look in her eyes appealed to them. This was a girl who might suit both of their needs.

Gary set the glass on the bar. "Here you go."

"Thank you," Mary said.

"You're welcome." When she reached for the glass, he took her hand in his. He held it tightly, stroking the back with his thumb. Her skin was soft and smooth. She was a jewel, a rare gem of a girl. He looked deeply into her blue eyes and said, "I think you're one of the most beautiful women I've ever seen."

Mary blushed and said, "Why, thank you."

"I hope we can get to know each other better real soon," he said. Then, in a gesture that would seal her destiny, he brought her hand to his lips and kissed it.

Janice patted the barstool next to her. "Well, now, sit down, honey, and tell us all about yourself."

ABOUT THE AUTHOR

Raymond Benson is the author of the James Bond novels *The Man With the Red Tattoo, Never Dream of Dying, DoubleShot, High Time to Kill, The Facts of Death,* and *Zero Minus Ten,* as well as the novelizations of the films *Die Another Day, The World is Not Enough,* and *Tomorrow Never Dies.* His Bond short stories have been published in *Playboy* and *TV Guide* magazines. He is also the author of the suspense novel, *Face Blind,* and the non-fiction books *The Pocket Essentials Guide to Jethro Tull* and *The James Bond Bedside Companion* (the latter was nominated for an Edgar Allan Poe Award for Best Biographical/Critical Work in 1984). Raymond also has extensive experience directing stage plays, composing music, and designing and writing adventure computer games. He is married, has one son, and is based in the Chicago area.

Please visit out website, to hear about forthcoming puplications by Raymond Benson and other authors. We welcome your feedback, if you wish to visit the website and contact us by email.

www.twentyfirstcenturypublishers.com

OTHER BOOKS AVAILABLE FROM
TWENTY FIRST CENTURY PUBLISHERS

RAMONA

How did a little girl come to be abandoned in the orange scented square of the Andalusian City of Seville? Find out, when the course of her life is resumed at age seventeen.

Ramona catches the mood of Europe in transition, as Ramona, brought up in a quiet village in southern Spain, moves into the cosmopolitan world. Her strange background holds a mystery, revealed as the novel develops, but then events take on a different hue as a new perspective emerges. But that is not all, and reality seems to bend further, but does it?

From a novel within a novel, we move on to ... well, let's not say. Read it, and the author challenges you to predict each step of the unfolding plot, and just when it defies belief, read on – you will believe.

Ramona by Johnny John Heinz
ISBN: 1-904433-01-4

MEANS TO AN END

Enter the world of money laundering, financial manipulation and greed, where a shadowy Middle Eastern organisation takes on a major corporation in the US. As the action shifts through exotic locations, who wins out in the end? Certainly, the author's first hand experience of international finance lends a chilling credibility to the plot.

As well as being a compelling work of fiction this book offers, in a style accessible to the layman, a financial insider's insight into the financial and moral crisis, which broke in the early millennium, in the top echelons of corporate America.

Means to an End by Johnny John Heinz
ISBN: 1-84375-008-2

THE SIGNATURE OF A VOICE

The Signature of a Voice is a cat-and-mouse-game between a violent trio, led by a psychopathic killer, and a police officer on suspension. Move and countermove in this chess game is planned and enacted. The reader, in the position of god, knows who is guilty and who plans what, but just as in chess, the opponents' plans thwart one another. The outcomes twist and turn to the final curtain fall.

There is a sense of suspense but also anger as the system seems to be working against those who are fighting on the side of right, while the perpetrators of vicious crimes seem able to operate freely and choose to do what they wish. They choose the route of ultra-violence to stay ahead of the law in an otherwise tranquil community: they plan and execute, in all senses of the word. Is it possible to triumph over this ruthlessness?

The Signature of a Voice by Johnny John Heinz
ISBN: 1-904433-00-6

TARNISHED COPPER

Tarnished Copper takes us into the arcane world of commodity trading. Against this murky background, no deal is what it seems, no agreement what it appears to be. The characters cheat and deceive each other, all in the name of grabbing their own advantage. Hiro Yamagazi, from his base in Tokyo, is the biggest trader of them all. But does he run his own destiny, or is he just jumping when Phil Harris pulls the strings? Can Jamie Edwards keep his addictions under control? And what will be the outcome of the duel between the hedge fund manager Jason Serck, and brash, devious, high-spending Mack McKee? And then one of them goes too far: life and death enters the traders' world........

Geoff Sambrook is ideally placed to take the reader into this world. He's been at the heart of the world's copper trading for over twenty years, and has seen the games - and the traders - come and go. With his ability to draw characters, and his knack of making the reader understand this strange world, he's created an explosive best-selling financial thriller. Read it and learn how this part of the City really works.

Tarnished Copper by Geoffrey Sambrook
ISBN 1-904433-02-2

OVER A BARREL

From the moment you land at Heathrow on page one the plot grips you. Ed Burke, an American oil tycoon, jets through the world's financial centres and the Middle East to set up deals, but where does this lead him? Are his premonitions on the safety of his daughter Louise in Saudi Arabia well founded? Who are his hidden opponents? Is his corporate lawyer Nicole with him or against him?

As the plot unfolds his company is put into play in the tangle of events surrounding the 1990 invasion of Kuwait. Even his private life is drawn into the morass.

In this novel Peter depicts the grim machinations of political and commercial life, but the human spirit shines through. This is a thriller that will hold you to the last page.

Over a Barrel by Peter Driver
ISBN 1-904433-03-0

THE BLOWS OF FATE

It is a crisp clear day in Sofia and three young friends are starting out in life, buoyant with their hopes, aspirations, loves. But this is not to be, as post war Eastern Europe comes under the grip of its brutal communist regime. Driven from their homes and deprived of their basic rights, the three friends determine to escape ... but one of them cannot seize that moment. It may seem that life cannot become worse for the families who are ostracised and trapped in their own country, but the path of hopelessness descends to the concentration camps and unimaginable brutality.

For those who escape there is the struggle to survive, tempered by the kindness they encounter along their way. We see how talent and determination can win through. Yet, though they may have escaped those terrible years in Bulgaria, they can never escape their personal loss of family, homeland, friends and love that may have been.

While life is very difficult for the three friends, they do not forget each other. After forty years of separation, they meet. For each one fate has prepared a surprise....

Can beauty, art and love eclipse the manmade horrors of this world? You will think they can, as Antoinette Clair brings out the beautiful things in life, so that the poignancy of her novel reaches into the toughest of us, and moves to tears.

This is a tale of beauty, music and a grand love, but it is also expressive of the sad recurring tale of Europe's recent history.

The Blows of Fate by Antoinette Clair
ISBN 1-904433-04-9

THE GORE EXPERIMENT

William Gore is not a mad scientist: he is a dedicated medical researcher working on G.L.X.-14, an AIDS serum. He is on the brink of a major breakthrough and seeks to force the pace, spurred on by his knowledge of the suffering to be spared, if he is right, and the millions of lives of AIDS victims to be saved. But as things begin to go askew, how far dare he go? What level of risk is warranted? What, and who, is he prepared to sacrifice? The answers become worse than you can imagine as William Gore treads a path to horror.

The Gore Experiment may be fiction, but it addresses real issues in the world of experimental vaccines, disease-busting drugs and genetic engineering. Is science unknowingly exposing us to risk through overconfidence in ever narrowing fields of expertise, ignorant of ramifications? Or is the red tape of bureaucracy signing the death warrants of the terminally sick? Well, William Gore at least is confident. He is convinced of what he must do. Should he do it?

This is not a book for the faint-hearted. H.Jay Scheuermann adds a new high-tech dimension to the traditions of vampires, Jekylls and Hydes as William Gore paves his own road to hell. But there is a twist....

The Gore Experiment by H. Jay Scheuermann
ISBN 1-904433-05-7

CASEY'S REVENGE

Is this the best of all possible worlds? Well, almost, or so Casey Forbes thinks. She is a college professor with bbb successful career and good friends; boyfriend trouble in the past, perhaps, but who hasn't? And her prospects are excellent.

But no woman can expect to descend into the real life nightmare, that envelopes Casey ... out of nowhere.

Mary Charles's heroine is forced to confront the darkest side of human nature and the most bestial of acts committed by man. Yet it is the strength of will, the trauma inflicted on Casey's personality and the resourcefulness of the female psyche that Mary Charles explores in this novel. What does it take to survive overwhelming adversity and does Casey have it?

Many dream of revenge but wonder if they have within themselves the capacity to carry it out. Can Casey? And is the price going to be too high?

Read this thriller and one thing is certain: don't ever let this happen to you.

Casey's Revenge by Mary Charles
ISBN 1-90443-06-5

SABRA'S SOUL

From the heart of the California rock music scene comes this story of much more than just love and betrayal.

Does Sabra know who she is? She thinks she is a loving mother and a trusting wife, but her husband Logan, a powerful figure in rock music, seems consumed by commitments to his latest band, 23 Mystique. Sabra begins to feel that something is missing, to feel a yearning for something more. Is she too trusting and too slow to spot Logan's lapses in behaviour?

When Sabra meets the pop idol of her sub-teen daughters, things begin to change. She can't believe the attraction growing in her for this youthful figure, her junior by several years.

Lisa Reed paints a picture of virtue and vice in this tale of love, lust, betrayal and drug-induced psychosis, set amidst the glitter of the rock scene. It is not fate that leads these people on but their own actions. Can they help it and where does it lead?

Who better than Lisa Reed, with her access to the centre of rock, to weave this tense plot as it descends from the social whirl into the deadly serious. If you are a successful rock star, this is a book for you, and if not ... well, read on and dream.

Health warning: this book contains salacious sex scenes demanded by its setting.

Sabra's Soul by Lisa Reed
ISBN 1-90443307-3

FACE BLIND

From the pen of Raymond Benson, author of the acclaimed original James Bond continuation novels (Zero Minus Ten, The Facts of Death, High Time to Kill, DoubleShot, Never Dream of Dying, and The Man With the Red Tattoo) and the novel Evil Hours, comes a new and edgy noir thriller.

Imagine a world where you don't recognize the human face. That's Hannah's condition - prosopagnosia, or "face blindness" - when the brain center that recognizes faces is inoperable. The onset of the condition occurred when she was attacked and nearly raped by an unknown assailant in the inner lobby of her New York City apartment building. And now she thinks he's back, and not just in her dreams.

When she also attracts the attention of a psychopathic predator and becomes the unwitting target of a Mafia drug ring, the scene is set for a thrill ride of mistaken identity, cat-and-mouse pursuit, and murder.

Face Blind is a twisting, turning tale of suspense in which every character has a dark side. The novel will keep the reader surprised and intrigued until the final violent catharsis.

Face Blind by Raymond Benson

ISBN 1-904433-10-3

CUPID AND THE SILENT GODDESS

The painting Allegory with Venus and Cupid has long fascinated visitors to London's National Gallery, as well as the millions more who have seen it reproduced in books. It is one of the most beautiful paintings of the nude ever made.

In 1544, Duke Cosimo de' Medici of Florence commissioned the artist Bronzino to create the painting to be sent as a diplomatic gift to King François I of France.

As well as the academic mystery of what the strange figures in the painting represent, there is the human mystery: who were the models in the Florence of 1544 who posed for the gods and strange figures?

Alan Fisk's Cupid and the Silent Goddess imagines how the creation of this painting might have touched the lives of everyone who was involved with it: Bronzino's apprentice Giuseppe, the mute and mysterious Angelina who is forced to model for Venus, the brutal sculptor Baccio Bandinelli and his son, and the good-hearted nun Sister Benedicta and her friend the old English priest Father Fleccia, both secret practitioners of alchemy.

As the painting takes shape, it causes episodes of fear and cruelty, but the ending lies perhaps in the gift of Venus.

'A witty and entertaining romp set in the seedy world of Italian Renaissance artists.' Award-winning historical novelist Elizabeth Chadwick. (The Falcons of Montabard, The Winter Mantle).

'Alan Fisk, in his book Cupid and the Silent Goddess, captures the atmosphere of sixteenth-century Florence and the world of the artists excellently. This is a fascinating imaginative reconstruction of the events during the painting of Allegory with Venus and Cupid.' Marina Oliver, author of many historical novels and of Writing Historical Fiction.

Cupid and the Silent Goddess by Alan Fisk

ISBN 1-904433-08-4

TALES FROM THE LONG BAR

Nostalgia may not be what it used be, but do you ever get the feeling that the future's not worth holding your breath for either?

Do you remember the double-edged sword that was 'having a proper job' and struggling within the coils of the multiheaded monster that was 'the organisation'?

Are you fed up with forever having to hit the ground running, working dafter not smarter - and always being in a rush trying to dress down on Fridays?

Do you miss not having a career, a pension plan or even the occasional long lunch with colleagues and friends?

For anyone who knows what's what (but can't do much about it), Tales from the Long Bar should prove entebrtaining. If it doesn't, it will at least reassure you that you are not alone.

Londoner Saif Rahman spent half his life working in the City before going on to pursue opportunities elsewhere. A linguist by training, Saif is a historian by inclination.

Tale from the Long Bar by Saif Rahman
ISBN 1-904433-10-X

COUSINS OF COLOR

Luzon, Philippines, 1899.   Immersed in the chaos and brutality of America's first overseas war of conquest and occupation, Private David Fagen has a decision to make - forsake his country or surrender his soul. The result: A young black man in search of respect and inclusion turns his back on Old Glory - and is hailed a hero of the Filipino fight for independence.

Negro blood is just as good as a white man's when spilled in defense of the American Way, or so Fagen believed.   But this time his country seeks not justice but empire. Pandemonium rules Fagen's world, Anarchy the High Sheriff, and he knows every time he pulls the trigger, he helps enslave the people he came to liberate.

Not just an account of an extraordinary black solider caught in the grip of fate and circumstance, Cousins of Color tells the story of Fagen's love for the beautiful and mysterious guerilla fighter, Clarita Socorro, and his sympathy for her people's struggle for freedom. Cousins also chronicles Colonel Fredrick Funston's monomaniacal pursuit of victory at any cost and his daredevil mission to capture Emilio Aguinaldo, the leader of the Philippine revolution.   Other characters include the dangerously unstable, Captain Baston, particularly cruel in his treatment of prisoners, and Sergeant Warren Rivers, the father Fagen never had.

Himself a Vietnam combat veteran, author William Schroder hurtles us through the harsh realities of this tropical jungle war and provides powerful insight into the dreams and aspirations of human souls corrupted and debased by that violent clash of cultures and national wills. Based on actual events, David Fagen's pursuit of truth and moral purpose in the Philippine Campaign brings focus to America's continuing obsession with conquest and racism and provides insight into many of today's prevailing sentiments.

Cousins of Color by William Schroder
ISBN 1-904433-11-1

Please visit out website, to hear about forthcoming puplications by Raymond Benson and other authors. We welcome your feedback, if you wish to visit the website and contact us by email.

www.twentyfirstcenturypublishers.com

Printed in the United Kingdom
by Lightning Source UK Ltd.
117102UKS00001B/38

9 781904 433125